THE MORONI DECEPTION

A NOVEL

JACK L. BRODY

V

Visigoth Press

www.visigothpress.com

THE MORONI DECEPTION
Copyright © 2012
ISBN-13: 978-0615722269
ISBN-10: 0615722261

<u>Dedication</u>

For my parents, both of whom inspired me.

Moroni /mə-rō`-nī/

One of the most important figures in the theology of the Latter Day Saint (Mormon) movement, Moroni was an ancient prophet believed to have buried Gold Plates containing the sacred history of the Americas compiled by his father, Mormon, in the early Fifth century. Fourteen hundred years later in Palmyra, NY, Moroni was to have appeared to Joseph Smith as an angel and reportedly directed him to the burial site of the plates. Smith then reportedly went on to translate the ancient texts and record *The Book of Mormon.*

PROLOGUE

Utah territory. September 6, 1857

The Utah fields had just begun to change from green to gold, and as they shimmered in the fading afternoon sun, the last of the Fancher wagon train party made its way up to the pristine mountain clearing to camp for the night. As the wagon train came to a halt, restless children, bursting with energy after their long day's ride, leapt down from their families' wagons, as the pet dogs ran barking excitedly through the encampment. The weary westbound settlers then began to unpack whatever sundry items would be needed for that night's stay, while several of the younger men headed out on horseback to round up the trailing 800 head of cattle.

As a young mother knelt down to tend her small fire, a single shot rang out, hitting her in the left temple and sending her tumbling to the ground. A seemingly endless volley of shots coming from all directions soon followed, hitting several other members of the Fancher party and sending them on to an early rendezvous with their Maker.

But as they had trained, the remainder of the proud Arkansans circled their wagons and lay down return fire at their unseen assailants. Surely it was one of the tribes of murderous savages they had heard tales of, coming after their livestock and provisions, sensed Alexander Fancher, the leader of the besieged settlers. The gun battle raged on for four more days, consisting mostly of a few more members of the Fancher party and a number of their livestock being picked off one by one by the Indian snipers. Water and supplies began to run dangerously low, and the putrid stench of the dead, both human and livestock, begin to overcome the settlers.

But then, like a gift from God, he came forward-- a white man--a frontiersman who stated that he was an emissary from the nearby Latter Day Saint community. His name was John Lee, and he promised that he and his fellow Mormons could negotiate with the Paiute savages and escort the survivors to safety. There was, however, one condition--the surviving members of the Fancher party would first need to lay down their arms to show the Paiutes the sincerity of their intentions. Only then, Lee told them, would he be able to guarantee them safe passage.

The firing had indeed stopped at this point, and

the weary travelers were further persuaded by Lee and several of his companions that this was their last and best hope for survival. Sensing that they were honorable men of faith, Fancher took the Mormons at their word and directed the rest of his party to lay down their weapons. He then led the surviving 155 members in prayer, thanking God for delivering them into the hands of their Mormon guardian angels.

CHAPTER 1

Greenwich Village. November 5. Present day.

I gotta find that one missing piece was the last thing Michael Chenault remembered thinking before closing his eyes that night. The solving of a jigsaw puzzle was not a literal reference, but over the past thirteen years that was how he had come to think of his job as an investigative reporter. He would slowly but surely come across one seemingly unrelated tip or lead after another, some appearing to have absolutely no connection to the next, but after a while, after enough twisting and turning of the "pieces," the puzzle--his story--would begin to take shape.

As he lay in bed drifting somewhere in the land between sleep and awake, and running through the events of the past day, he at last began to feel the heavy, blissful wave of sleep he'd been waiting for start to roll over him. That's when the faraway, but piercing electronic buzzing began. The first thing that ran through his mind was the annoying sound was just part of a dream, but the persistent buzzing kept on, until Chenault finally realized he was indeed awake and that his late night visitor likely wouldn't stop pressing his door intercom until he answered.

Looking a second too long over at the digital glow of his alarm clock, the numbers "2:45" seared into his eyes so that even after he closed them and rolled back on to his pillow, he continued to see the numbers on the back of his eyelids. *Christ almighty*, he thought, as he rolled out of bed and heaved an exasperated sigh, *Doesn't anybody in this town ever sleep*? Despite the clanking radiators running full blast throughout his two bedroom apartment, the old oak floors still felt as cold against his bare feet as the frozen city sidewalks outside, as he trudged to the front door wearing only boxers and an old gray tee shirt with a faded "New York Mets" logo emblazoned across his chest.

As he approached the end of his short hallway and flicked on the light, Chenault caught a brief glimpse of himself in the mirror by the front door and half laughed over his disheveled appearance. Although he might have passed for an aging male model with his trim medium build and six foot height, Chenault's features were slightly askew with a visible break in his nose that he had never bothered to have corrected. Along with his five o'clock shadow, his mussed, dark hair in a longish, over-the-ear style was probably more befitting of someone in his early twenties than for a man a few years away from forty. People he met often would tell him that he kind of looked like a certain actor, but they could never quite remember the actor's name or which films he had been in, so Chenault never really knew whether to be flattered or not.

"Who is this?" Chenault muttered into the intercom by his door, making sure to convey a certain degree of irritation in his greeting, half expecting it to be one of his neighbors who'd partied a little too hard that night and misplaced their keys.

"Police. Buzz us in."

Other than a few New York state gambling statutes he'd probably violated earlier in the evening at his regular Friday night poker game, Chenault couldn't think of any other laws he'd broken lately, and at the moment he wasn't covering any stories that worthy of note. "I'm sorry, what is this concerning?"

CHAPTER 2

As his uninvited guests made their way up the building's three flights of stairs, Chenault threw on an old, plaid flannel robe and a pair of well-worn slippers before opening the door.

"I'm Detective Wheatly. This is Detective Garcia. We'd like to ask you a few questions."

Well obviously, Chenault mused to himself as he closed the door behind them. "At 3:00 in the morning?" he said through a yawn.

"Actually, it's only. . .2:48," the portly, middle-aged detective informed him after glancing at his watch.

By his pale complexion, the mustachioed Wheatly appeared to do most of his work at night. The wiry, and better-dressed Garcia appeared to be the junior partner of the duo, with his jet black hair gleaming with "product," and a stylishly trimmed goatee and sideburns framing the lower portion of his bronzed face. By his demeanor, he gave the impression he was indifferent to the proceedings as he casually glanced around the well-kept apartment, the décor of which could perhaps best be described as "New York City men's club." Mahogany paneled walls in the main living area, overstuffed, brass studded leather chairs, wall-to-wall bookshelves lined with Chenault's past, present, and future reading material, and a few tasteful oil paintings completed the ensemble. The only modern touches he noticed were a high-end stereo system accompanied by an extensive blues and jazz collection, most of which was still on vinyl, and a wall-mounted flat screen with a nearby library of mostly classic films.

"So how you afford a place like this?" Garcia asked in his accented English.

With a raised eyebrow, Chenault glanced over to Wheatly as if to pose the one word question, *Seriously?,* before looking back to Garcia.

". . .Rent control. So what is it that you have to ask me that's so important that you couldn't have waited until, say like 9 a.m. and over the phone?"

"Well, seeing as how you're our only possible suspect right now, we didn't want to take the chance you might not be here at 9 a.m." Wheatly answered.

"Suspected of what?" Chenault shot back as if he'd been insulted.

"First, we need to advise you that you don't have to speak to us if you don't want to, and if you need a lawyer and can't afford one, one can be provided for you. Also, anything you say. . ."

"Wait a minute!" Chenault interrupted. "You're reading me my rights?"

When Wheatly nodded in reply, Chenault first shook his head in exasperated disbelief. ". . .I'm really tired, fellas. I know you're just doing your job, but I've hardly slept in the last three days, and I really don't feel like going downtown with you to the pokey tonight. So just what's this all about?"

Wheatly, not used to having his slightly botched rendition of Miranda rights waived half way through, was at first put off until he realized that the sleep deprived Chenault might very possibly hang himself with a few careless answers. ". . .Do you know a Martin Koplanski?"

"No, I don't know a Martin Koplanski."

"Well then, would you know why records were found of a phone call placed from Mr. Koplanski to you, and why your work address was in Mr. Koplanski's possession?"

Chenault paused for a moment. ". . .That's what you got me out of bed for at three o'clock in the morning? Look, I can only guess this is someone I talked to one time about a story."

"What kind of story?" Wheatly asked.

"Do you not know who I work for?"

"Yeah, *The New York Times*. What, are we supposed to be impressed?"

"No, it's just I write stories for a living. I'm a journalist."

"Isn't that just a fancy word for 'reporter'?" Wheatly said with a somewhat derisive note in his voice.

"You got me."

"All I know is, this Koplanski didn't have much of anything to do with anybody--he didn't get out much if you get my drift. He places just four long distance calls in the last two weeks--one to his daughter, one to you, and one each out to L.A. and someplace out in Utah, and two days later after talking to you, he turns up dead."

"Murder?" Chenault said with half a laugh. "Well why not go wake up somebody out in L.A. or Utah?"

"Because Koplanski lived upstate and it just seemed like a little shorter drive for you to kill him."

"And I killed him because. . .he called me on the phone?"

"I don't know, why don't you tell us?"

"Fellas, I don't mean to be rude, but unless you've got anything else, or you're gonna take me downtown, I'm going back to bed."

"You don't seem to have a whole lot of remorse. We tell you someone you know got offed, and you want to go back to bed."

"Guys, if you haven't figured out yet, I don't even know who you're talking about. I probably talk to close to fifty people a day or more. Naturally, I feel bad some poor guy got murdered, but it's really got nothing to do with me."

"Yeah, that's an original defense--'You don't know nothin' about it.' You ever hear that one before, Julio?"

"No, never," the Hispanic detective deadpanned.

"You guys are a regular 'Laurel and Hardy.' Look, I tell you what," said Chenault. "Give me your card and I'll come downtown tomorrow and answer whatever questions you have. And I'm really not normally this cranky, but I've got to get some sleep. When I get to work, I'll look up and try to see what I have on this guy. Deal?"

CHAPTER 3

Cottonwood Heights (a Salt Lake City suburb)

Safe inside her stucco and stone suburban palace, and the anonymity of being tucked away in a gated community of 250 other sprawling homes, an attractive blond housewife in her late thirties finished up the last of her evening duties. The dishes had been washed and put away, and her four children had just finished watching a movie and were now in their rooms getting ready for bed. When the front doorbell rang, the only thing she had left to do before curling up under the covers with a good book was to let the cat back in and ready herself for bed. As she made her way down the stairs, she assumed at this hour her unexpected guest was one of her neighbors looking to borrow a cup of something.

On her front porch, two men waited. Both had similar features--narrow set, pale blue eyes, short cropped, straw colored hair parted in the middle, and fleshy, brutal faces. Similarly, they both wore white oxford shirts buttoned to the top, and well-worn overalls and leather work boots. The only thing that distinguished the two was the slightly smaller one wore an unbuttoned dark suit jacket. To those who knew them in the small isolated community from where they came, they were simply known as "The Brothers."

As she unlocked the door, the two strangers forced their way in and immediately filed their way past her with blank stares as they headed up the stairs.

"No!" she screamed, as she grabbed the arm of the larger man bringing up the rear. With little effort, he shrugged her off, slamming her back into the wall so hard, her head left a five inch indentation in the sheetrock. As she came to a few moments later, the other intruder made his way past her down the stairs with her sobbing thirteen-year-old daughter slung over his shoulder.

"Mommy, don't let them take me!" the girl pleaded as she tried to grab onto anything she could.

As he dragged the screaming girl out the front door, the man looked back to his brother and gave him a little nod. The remaining man, still

restraining the screaming mother, knew what he
was to do.

CHAPTER 4

"He told me that he'd found some kind of
treasure--an historical artifact that he couldn't
reveal to me yet, because he was possibly in
negotiations with an interested party and he didn't
know if they would want it publicized or not."

Chenault had called the detectives earlier that
morning to meet him for lunch at the Skylight, a
diner near their precinct generally populated by
local working folk on a budget and the occasional
stray yuppie. Since discovering the Skylight years
earlier, he'd always found a certain reassuring
familiarity in the aroma of bacon grease that
permeated every nook and cranny of the joint, along
with the Seventies hits that seemed to perpetually
play on the old Wurlitzer in the corner. He'd
always suspected his affection for the joint had to
do with the way it conjured up fond memories of his
favorite greasy spoon back in his hometown of New
Orleans, because it certainly wasn't the cuisine.

Wheatly and Garcia appeared to be clean-shaven
and refreshed, but looked to be wearing the exact

same jackets, ties and slacks that they'd had on the night before. Although no fashion plate himself-- Chenault's standard work uniform consisted of a blue or white oxford dress shirt, khakis, and his one apparent fashion affectation, a navy pea coat--he did have a keen eye for detail. Figuring, based on their limited wardrobe, the oft-reported poor-mouthing heard from New York's Finest was very likely justified, he decided to treat the two to lunch.

"What'd you think of his story?" Wheatly asked before putting a forkful of mashed potatoes in his mouth.

"I thought he was a crank. He was well spoken, but I get all kinds of leads from all sorts of peculiar folk who are 'motier foux.'"

"Come again?" said Wheatly with a quizzical expression, as he swiped at his mouth and mustache with a balled-up napkin.

Chenault, who had a way of occasionally working in his native New Orleans Cajun vernacular, saw he was going to have to translate.

"People who are 'half crazy.' They seem to funnel to me for some reason now."

Chenault, however, knew the reason quite well. Early in his career, while working for the occasionally scandalous *Gotham Post*, he had been a little too convincing on a back page, tongue-in-cheek story he had written as an April fools lark. A certain segment of his readership had taken his story a bit too literally about a half-man, half-insect, rumored to be living and breeding with several of the local women in rural southeastern Pennsylvania. Given that about a quarter of the calls he had to field on a daily basis were from this same fringe element who continued to try to provide him with all sorts of bizarre leads and story ideas, he'd regretted it ever since. While it was at times occasionally annoying and time consuming, Chenault did have a sense of humor about it, and would politely tell most of his unwanted callers that he was a serious investigative journalist now, more in the Bob Woodward vein. But he would then say with a wink if a colleague were listening in, "Of course that's the Robert Redford version of Bob Woodward." Yet despite his humble beginnings, Chenault had made a believer of most in the news industry with his numerous journalistic prizes and nominations.

"Last week I had a guy call up who swore to me that his wife had been replaced by some alien life form. The week before that, a woman in Tennessee who said she'd been living with a Sasquatch for the last ten years. I could go on. So when somebody calls me up and tells me he's found a 'buried treasure,' but that he can't tell me what it is, yeah, I tend to dismiss him as a crank. In fact, I remember now, I asked him, 'If you can't tell me, why are you calling me?'"

"And what did he say to that?" Wheatly asked.

"I think he said, 'insurance.'"

"Insurance?"

"Yeah, and I asked him, insurance from what?

And he said, 'Hopefully, I'll never have to find out.'"

"And you're just remembering all this stuff now after last night when you said you didn't even remember this guy?"

"I tape everything and then if I feel it's possibly worth anything I transcribe it. I reviewed my notes. That's what I had."

"Well, that does go along with what his wife says. The Mrs. says Koplanski claimed to have found some kind of treasure on their property. She never saw it and said that he just kept it locked away in an old box. She said one day when he wasn't looking that she tried to pick it up, but that she could just barely lift it. She's not too big, so I'm figuring this thing couldn't have been over fifty, sixty pounds, and that's probably a little high after looking at her. She also said when she asked him if it was so valuable, why didn't he just put it on the open market and try to sell it to the highest bidder, and he said, 'It wasn't that kind of treasure.'"

Chenault raised a skeptical eyebrow. "So a treasure that doesn't have any value? See fellas, I told you he maybe wasn't playing with a full deck."

"Well, she did go on to say that he said it was something that would only be valuable to a very few selected buyers."

By his reaction, Chenault expressed his first sign of mild interest. "Did it appear he'd been robbed?"

"Apparently. The place was turned over. But

we're not sure if that was done before or after his throat was slit from ear to ear. There were definitely a couple of other very strange things. This weird character, or symbol, was written across his forehead in blood."

Wheatly reached into a legal-sized manila envelope and handed Chenault a glossy police photo of just the top of Koplanski's head. The three inch symbol, which looked like a rounded backward figure three, was quite prominent across his forehead. "Mean anything to you?"

Chenault shook his head. "And what was the other weird thing?"

"The holes. All over Koplanski's little farm there were these holes he'd dug. I asked his wife about it, and she said he'd been digging them ever since they moved there seventeen years ago down from Minnesota to that exact spot when it became available on the market."

"And he never told her why?"

"Nope. She just says he went out just about every day with his metal detector and shovel and that he found all sorts of old musket balls and iron flintlock gun parts. I'm guessing probably stuff left over from early Indian and Revolutionary War battles."

Chenault furrowed his brow as he pondered these strange new facts. ". . .But what artifact from that period would he possibly consider to be so valuable, and it sounds like, make his life's work?"

"You got me. But back to that symbol, you

don't have any thoughts on it?"

"Just, I guess it looks a little like an Egyptian hieroglyph or maybe even a Cyrillic character. But obviously not English, or should I say a Latin character. . .This whole thing, though, just keeps getting weirder. You know, it almost kind of reminds me of those cult killings from a few years back."

"If you're talking about the so-called Long Island Satanists who left their bloody graffiti all over the place--turned out to be just a bunch of bored rich kids hopped up on acid and whatever else they could get their hands on, who killed a few of their own. Several prominent parents of the kids got strings pulled to not only keep it quiet, but got 'em just a year in rehab. And that's, of course, off the record. Oh yeah, I just got a copy of the autopsy report faxed over this morning."

"There's something I've always been curious about," Chenault said. "Why would they perform an autopsy on a man who's had his throat cut from ear to ear?"

"Funny you should mention that," Wheatly said, looking up from the report a bit smugly. "Because they found out two rather interesting things. First, that he very likely was drowned--he had water in his lungs."

"So they drowned him and cut his throat afterwards?"

"Why do you say 'they'?"

"I don't know, it just seems like if you're going

to drown someone that it might take more than one person to hold him down."

"Well see, that's the other thing--Koplanski, at the time of his death, was a very frail man. They also found that he probably had less than a month or two to live. He'd been suffering from pancreatic cancer and was in the final stages, which was confirmed by his wife."

"Speaking of which," Chenault said, "Where was she when all this happened?"

"He'd actually sent her away for the week to see their only daughter and her family back in Minnesota."

"Almost like he knew something bad was going to happen. . .or at least might." Chenault was beginning to get that old familiar feeling in his gut that somehow, somewhere, beyond just the murder of Martin Koplanski, there was a story that needed to be uncovered.

CHAPTER 5

When Chenault got up the next morning, he anticipated one of his typical leisurely Sundays. He would usually begin the day browsing through *The Times* for several hours as he sipped one of his three cups of coffee, which was then followed by the partaking of one his precious once-a-day smokes off his back fire escape. That morning ritual was usually then followed by catching up on any of his correspondences, a phone call to or from his mother after she had returned from morning Mass back in her 7th ward Parish, and occasionally catching one of his beloved adopted underdogs, the Mets or the Jets, in action if either happened to be in town that day.

After having gone through his email, deleting most of it along the way, Chenault arrived at the last one. Not recognizing the sender, he assumed it to be junk and was just about to hit "Delete" when he noticed his name in the Subject line--"CHENAULT

-- FOR YOUR EYES ONLY." Since spammers generally had little idea whom they were sending their various get-rich-quick schemes to, Chenault figured it might be worth a look. A second after opening the email he regretted it. Attached was a photo of a pretty blond woman from neck up, whose throat had been slit from ear to ear. Even more startling than the gruesome picture was the strange character emblazoned in blood across her forehead, identical to the one left on Koplanski.

Chenault recognized the woman instantly. She was Lauren Ratchford, the recently murdered wife of Senator Brockston Ratchford, the junior Senator from Utah. It had been the lead story the previous day, made even more poignant by the fact that the Senator's thirteen-year-old daughter had been kidnapped by the assailants and was still missing.

Senator Brockston Ratchford, "Brock" to his friends and family, had recently attained national prominence when by default, he had emerged as the only serious challenger to the sitting Vice President for the Republican Presidential nomination. Charismatic and fiery, where the Vice President was much more of a tepid, consensus building moderate, Ratchford had not been the only conservative candidate at the outset of the primary race.

Zeb McCall, only the third Republican to be elected governor from the state of Georgia since Reconstruction, had been gunned down a month and a half earlier while making his campaign kick-off speech in his adopted hometown of Atlanta. A slight young man with long dark hair, and wearing jeans and a black trench coat, had leapt from the crowd and shot McCall twice in the gut as he ran across the stage toward the rear of the high school auditorium. The assailant had then disappeared back into the school, where he had taken his own life by shooting himself in the right temple after holing up in a bathroom.

In the drama of receiving the email and opening the disturbing attached photo, Chenault had almost forgotten about the unmarked envelope he had picked up the day before at work and had neglected to open. Inside the envelope he found a very brief note from Martin Koplanski. Other than the date and his signature, "Read my book," was all that was written.

CHAPTER 6

For the most part, Brockston Ratchford had led a relatively charmed life, with only a few stumbling blocks along the way. Many years earlier, his first wife, reportedly suffering from chronic depression, had committed suicide, and several of his early businesses had gone belly up. But other than those early setbacks, everything else he touched seemed to turn to gold. From his successful chain of stock brokerages, to his even more successful financial advisory services, he was a millionaire many times over, and in his short political career, he'd won every election he had entered from state senate, to Congressman from Utah's Third district, to U.S. Senator. Even though he was a shoo-in to replace the outgoing governor, he and his supporters felt his skills could best be served in the Oval Office as the chief executive of the entire country. Few who were familiar with Ratchford's résumé doubted his executive and managerial skills, but there were still lingering doubts about him because of his little known religion. Some fundamentalist Christians had gone so far as to brand Latter Day Saints as heretical and even Satanic. Cooler heads tended merely to write the religion off as "Nineteenth Century Scientology." No matter what Ratchford did to try to remind voters that the founding fathers had declared that there should be no religious litmus test for anyone running for office, he was constantly reminded that there was an unwritten one. As the only tried-and-true conservative in the race, however, he had gradually started to make inroads and win over some previous detractors through perseverance and a massive out-of-pocket advertising campaign.

As the last of the homicide investigators filed out of his home, Ratchford stopped the two lead detectives on his doorstep. "I just wanted to thank you two personally for the sensitivity and compassion that you've shown to not only myself, but my entire family throughout this whole ordeal."

"Honestly, Senator, it's the least we can do after everything you've done for everybody in this state. I'm just sorry we don't have more to go on right now to catch these bastards," the detective said.

"Just please find my little girl. That's all I ask right now," Ratchford said, as he then slowly closed the door. He walked back from the entryway to his living room where his three children and their nanny waited, and crumpled onto the sofa. As Ratchford began to openly weep, the nanny sat down beside him and placed her hand over his in a touching gesture of support, as several of the younger children hugged their father around his chest and neck to comfort him.

CHAPTER 7

Chenault already knew his destination, but to go through proper channels, as well as get his expenses covered, he checked in first with Hal Sikorski, his assignment editor and best friend, the next day. Chenault had known Sikorski for almost twelve years, ever since Sikorski had first seen the promise that Chenault had exhibited in several riveting pieces on city hall contracts corruption and had lured him away from *The Post*.

Sikorski had grown up in a working class family from Queens and had brought that same no-nonsense, blue-collar attitude to his work at *The Times*. He at one time had dreams of becoming the next Woodward or Bernstein, but early in his career had come to the realization that his strengths lay more in identifying, or particularly in Chenault's case, approving the best story ideas, and then helping his "all star" talent sort out their stories and tell them in the best way possible. As the assignment editor, he often found his job to be more about running Chenault's story proposals by the "brain trust," as they referred to their superiors on the top floor, to see if he could get them to go along. With rare exception they would, since over the years Sikorski had built up a trust with his higher-ups that he would never just send one of his reporters out on a junket or wild goose chase and have them foot the bill. The occasional times that Sikorski would propose a possible story idea to investigate, Chenault, invariably, was already at work on another story that was almost always a bigger and better one than the one Sikorski had for him.

After Chenault had relayed a few of the stranger details from the murder in upstate New York, along with the cryptic connection between Koplanski's and Lauren Ratchford's deaths, he proposed flying out to Salt Lake City the next day.

"Sometimes I wonder why I don't just give you a stack of signed travel vouchers and just set you on your way," Sikorski said.

"Because then they wouldn't need you, Hal."

"Good point. Bad idea. Forget I ever said it."

"Done."

"So what's your angle on this?" Sikorski said.

"I thought probably it would be best if we concentrate on the Ratchford murder/kidnapping, and then maybe later try to see if there's an actual tie-in to Koplanski's murder," Chenault replied, even though Koplanski's murder and the motive behind it were still foremost in his mind.

"That's just the way I would have put it," said Sikorski with a wink, since he knew as well as Chenault if they made it just about Koplanski's murder, the "brain trust" never would have gone along. But by tying the story into the very high profile murder of Lauren Ratchford and her daughter's kidnapping, they both knew it was a shoo-in. "And good luck out there. I hear Utah's kind of like Las Vegas."

"Yeah, how so?" Chenault said with a puzzled look.

"You know how they say 'What happens in Vegas, stays in Vegas?' Well, from what I hear, what happens--or what Mormons do in Utah--pretty much stays in Utah."

Sikorski's dry wit was one of the things that had cemented their friendship over the years. And as odd a comparison as it was, Chenault had to admit he'd heard the same thing about this relatively isolated Western state, founded and mostly still run by members of the secretive homegrown religion that at one time had plans to form their own country spanning to the Pacific Ocean.

As he was packing the next morning, it occurred to Chenault that even though he was just going to Utah--technically, still one of the lower forty-eight, and a place he'd visited once before--he was feeling the same sense of trepidation he occasionally experienced before traveling abroad. That uneasiness, though, was usually when it was to a destination where he didn't know the language or the customs. *That's very odd*, Chenault mused to himself.

CHAPTER 8

After touching down at Salt Lake City International and checking into the Marriott, Chenault spent the next several hours wandering around the snow-dusted city and reacquainting himself with the downtown. As he'd remembered, the inhabitants were mostly blond and smiling, the streets immaculate, the buildings all gleamed, and the heady scent of commerce crackled in the air. If ever there was a safer, cleaner, and seemingly less exciting city, Chenault had yet to come across it. There was still, however, a certain odd duality to the city, an undercurrent that things were not quite the way they seemed that ran just below the surface of a place that from all outward appearances seemed to be extraordinarily normal. Somewhat paradoxically, in a city centered around the austere and authoritarian Church of Latter Day Saints, where the use of alcohol, nicotine, and caffeine was frowned upon in even some of the more free thinking circles, these very same pious teetotalers had a long, somewhat bizarre history. From widespread institutionalized polygamy, to a number of bloody confrontations and power struggles within the Mormon community, the religion and its adherents, until only fairly recently, had been less than a model of decorum.

As Chenault made his way up the near spotless sidewalk in search of the possibility of some coffee, even as he gazed out over the majestic, snow-capped peaks that towered over the Salt Lake City skyline, his thoughts drifted back to his own adopted city. As much as he still loved New York, he was no longer "in love" with it. As with most romances, the infatuation had eventually faded. But that first time he stepped out onto the street from Penn Station, the sense of awe and wonderment that had swept over him as he looked out over the amazing Gotham skyline was probably, he imagined later, much like how a small child would have felt if he were to have been whisked away overnight and been dropped off to wake up in the middle of Disney World. It was not only the sheer scale of everything--the immense buildings and the teeming masses of humanity that had assembled from every corner of the world--but the excitement in the air, part uncertainty, part unlimited opportunity, coupled with his own ambition, fresh out of college, to prove that he could make it in the greatest city in the world.

But times had changed. Yet despite the attacks on the Twin Towers, the Yuppification and

Disneyfication of large portions of the city, and two mayors who defied description, there wasn't any place he'd rather call home--especially when compared to this odd city, which appeared to have sprung up in the middle of a desert, seemingly in the middle of nowhere.

As Chenault finished reading *The Deseret News*, one of the two local papers he'd picked up, he downed the last of his Starbucks espresso and checked his watch. His 4:30 meeting was fast approaching. In return for his cooperation with the NYPD, Wheatly had called ahead to the FBI field office in Salt Lake City and requested a brief sit-down for Chenault with one of the investigators on the Ratchford case.

Chenault arrived a few minutes early, and while waiting for whoever had drawn the assignment of answering his questions, reached back and pulled his trusty fanny pack around from its concealed position beneath the back flaps of his navy pea coat. Inside the oversized, well-worn, and he realized rather unfashionable, blue nylon pack that he wore almost everywhere while on assignment, were pen and pencils, a small writing pad, glue, a palm-sized digital camera, flashlight, and micro recorder, along with several ziplock bags, and the Taser his mother had purchased for him several years earlier in response to his being mugged at knifepoint. Although he had repeatedly tried to convince her that being mugged was just part of a New Yorker's rite of passage, he had finally relented and kept his promise to carry the device at least occasionally.

After unzipping the pack, he removed the pad and pen along with the digital micro recorder, in anticipation that he might take something useful from the upcoming interview. After about fifteen minutes, the receptionist informed him that Special Agent Patterson would see him shortly. Fifteen minutes later, at about five minutes before five--or closing time Chenault realized--a muscular man with close-cropped brown hair and a scowl on his face, and whose ill-fitting dark suit looked a half size too small, made his way down the hall.

Chenault stood to greet him and held out his hand. "First, Agent Patterson, I just wanted to thank you for agreeing to meet with me."

Patterson ignored his outstretched hand and walked on by, giving a half-hearted gesture to follow. "You can save it. I'm only here because my superiors instructed me to meet with you," he said back over his shoulder.

Chenault came to a halt as Patterson continued down the hall. "I don't understand. I thought you had agreed to this interview, and if it's going to be adversarial on your part, it's probably not worth wasting any more of each other's time."

Patterson stopped in his tracks and turned around. "I couldn't agree with you more."

"But if I could just ask," Chenault said, "What is it exactly that I've done to apparently elicit your disdain?"

"Oh, don't get me wrong--it's nothing personal.

It's just the whole lot of you--like vultures--
swooping in from all over the country to latch on to
anything you can get your teeth into for the sole
purpose of being able to sell a few more papers or
up your ratings."

"So you were under the impression. . ."

Patterson cut him off. ". . .That you're here to
exploit Senator Ratchford's family tragedy to sell a
few more papers, or get a little more face time on
one of the networks as one of the so-called experts
on the Ratchford murder/kidnapping."

Chenault first let out a little exasperated laugh. ".
. .I'm afraid you've got me confused with some of
the tabloid journalists. I'm actually working on a
backstory that may very possibly help law
enforcement get to the bottom of this."

"Oh, so you're here to help us do our job? Well,
why didn't you say that in the first place? In fact,
I've got a whole filing cabinet full of unsolved
cases. Why don't I just run back into my office and
grab them for you."

Chenault checked his first instinct to roll his eyes
at Patterson's sarcasm, and seeing that trying to
counter the agent's doubts was fruitless, decided on
a new tack. "Did you know that two days before
Lauren Ratchford had her throat slashed, a 73-year-
old man in upstate New York was murdered in the
exact same way?"

"You mean to tell me that out of over three
hundred million people in this country, that
somebody else 2000 miles away was actually

murdered by having their throat. . ."

"Just let me finish. Not only was his throat slit from ear to ear, but just like her, he had the identical character scrawled in blood across his forehead."

Patterson's face took on a sudden glower, and upon reaching his office door, he turned back to Chenault. "Why don't you come in and have a seat?"

Chenault walked in past him and sat down in a wobbly, mostly plastic chair opposite Patterson's government-issue, gray metal desk.

"And just how is it that you came to be in possession of this information? As best as I can recall, that information about the character that was scrawled on her was never released to the public. In fact, we made a point of it to weed out any false confessions."

Chenault reached into a manila envelope he'd brought along, and pulled out a copy of the emailed photo and laid it on the desk in front of Patterson.

"And you got this how?" Patterson asked, more with a look of irritation than disbelief.

"Through an anonymous email."

"And why do you think this would have been sent to you?"

"Other than the fact that it seems more than a bit coincidental I would have been one of the few privy to seeing both photos, I don't know."

"And the man who was murdered in upstate New York, who was he? And where exactly in upstate New York? I may need to contact law enforcement there."

"His name was Martin Koplanski--a retired history professor--and he lived just outside a small town called something like Palmarra. . .Pilmarra. . ."

"Palmyra?" Patterson said.

"You've heard of it?"

"Yeah. It's pretty much the birthplace of the Mormon religion."

"Really? Palmyra, New York?"

"What, you thought it just started here in Salt Lake?"

"No, I think I recall that Brigham Young set out from, I believe it was someplace in Illinois or Missouri," Chenault said.

"Nauvoo, Illinois. That, of course, was just after Joseph Smith had been murdered by a mob, and his followers had been systematically harassed and persecuted and run out of at least three other states before that."

Chenault decided it was probably best not to get into a debate over historical points with someone who was clearly, if not a Latter Day Saint himself, at least sympathetic with the local religion. From past research, he had some faint recollection of Palmyra being historically significant, and that the chronology was generally correct as far as the Mormons' state-to-state migration during the mid to late 1800s. However, out of a habit he'd picked up from one of his early mentors, Chenault sometimes did what he referred to as his "Columbo act," and played a little dumb in the hopes of getting an interviewee to be more forthcoming with details to help educate him. It worked best he found if he could get them to open up early on and enlighten him about a few relatively unimportant things, so that by the time he got to the tough questions and the heart of the interview, the source generally couldn't seem to hold back.

Unfortunately for Chenault, he soon found that the tight-lipped Patterson was most likely playing him as well. During the next half hour, aside from the Mormon history lesson and several other off-topic points, the only details Patterson shared on the Ratchford case, Chenault could have just as easily picked up from that evening's news. And while he was clearly stonewalling, the FBI agent did, though, at least drop his hostile front, likely out of appreciation for the bona fide lead, and because he took Chenault at his word that he wasn't there to score some salacious cover story. Chenault, however, would have much preferred the earlier boorish behavior if it had at least been accompanied by anything useful.

CHAPTER 9

As the dinner hour approached, Chenault slipped into the City Bistro, a nearby restaurant that reminded him a bit of one of his favorite eateries back in New York, with its low lighting and wood paneled interior. It was also one of the few spots in town where he could actually get a glass or two of wine with dinner. After the waitress took his order and poured him a glass of Cabernet, Chenault's thoughts drifted back to his encounter with Patterson.

Despite getting very little in the way of any useful information from him, he had still come away feeling somewhat satisfied, because in the end, he had managed to "turn" Agent Patterson. It usually happened that way with those he met in law enforcement. Upon first meeting Chenault, they made the natural assumption that he was some long-haired "Lefty" out to make them look bad. What they eventually saw in him, though, was that he was a straight shooter with a generally neutral stance, a passion for seeking out the truth, and a more than decent respect for the law and seeing justice carried out. They would then eventually see that they really were on the same side, and whether or not it was a bonding of sorts, Chenault knew that he could frequently count on their help down the line.

Washing down the last of his ribeye with a second glass of wine as he finished a *Time* magazine article on the latest White House scandal, Chenault looked up to see an attractive young woman approaching. By her shy demeanor he sensed she was a bit nervous, which was further confirmed by her somewhat halting introduction.

"I know you. I mean, I don't know you, but I know who you are," she stammered endearingly.

"And who am I?" Chenault replied with a wry smile.

"You're Michael Chenault. You're one of the best investigative journalists there is--I believe, anyway."

"Well, thank you. I'm very flattered, but how is it that you recognize me? I mean, usually I'm not much more than a 'byline.'"

"Well, I'm in the business--kind of. I work for *The Salt Lake Tribune*. I did a little stringer work for them and then worked my way up to the crime beat."

"And you are?" Chenault said as he stood, extending his hand.

"I'm sorry. Rachel Potter," she said as she shook

his hand. "And that's my friend Libby over by the door."

Chenault glanced over to see a pretty brunette who returned his nod of acknowledgement with a little finger wave.

"We were just getting ready to leave, but I wanted to come over and say 'Hi,' and introduce myself."

"Well, I'm glad you did," Chenault said. "It's always a pleasure to meet a fellow journalist."

"And again, I can't tell you what a pleasure it is to meet you. I'd, of course, heard of you and your work a number of times, but it was last year when you were nominated for your second Pulitzer that I saw your picture for the first time."

"Of course, I didn't win that one either," Chenault interjected with his roguish smile.

The two nominated stories to which she had referred, the ones that had officially made Chenault a known quantity in the journalism world, were worlds apart. The first had concerned an upper-middle class New Jersey family, of which every member had become addicted to crystal meth. It was a true American tragedy brought to light, demonstrating the fine line between the American dream and the American nightmare, separated only, in this case, by a single breadwinner being downsized.

Chenault's second story just about everyone in the news industry agreed should have definitely won, but in the end it had been edged out due to behind-the-scene forces at work--the same ones that had originally attempted to quash the story. From his earlier days as one of the many faceless D.C. political correspondents, Chenault had made a number of friends and contacts and developed a fairly sizeable network of sources. Using back channels, and by leapfrogging from one source's tip to another, his path eventually led to a former member of the current Presidential administration. The former aide, to protect both his boss and himself, had secretly recorded several pre-war discussions. As it had long been suspected, the story revealed that the current President and his administration knew full well that there was no imminent threat from the latest Middle Eastern regime they had chosen to topple. A ruse from the beginning, its only real goals had been to bring about the dream of a few powerful neo-Cons, and send a message that the United States not only still carried a big stick, but was also now willing to use it. Transcripts of the recording, put into their proper context by Chenault, had been enough to force the already unpopular Vice President to step down as he took the full brunt of the blame, even though it was fully expected he would later be pardoned as "a freedom loving patriot."

Chenault raised his hand to catch the waitress's attention and then turned to Rachel. "I'd invite you to join me, but I'm just finishing up. . .unless, of course, you'd care to join me for a drink at the bar?"

CHAPTER 10

After seeing her friend off, Rachel joined
Chenault for a tonic and lime at the bar, where they
exchanged several more minutes of pleasantries and
a few tidbits from each of their pasts. Chenault
soon found that Rachel Potter was the kind of
woman that most men aspired to meet one day and
then retire from "The Search," knowing that the
grass would never be any greener. Thirtyish, very
attractive--but not intimidatingly so, she appeared to
be make-up free with a healthy, rosy hue to her
flawless complexion, along with blue-green eyes,
shoulder-length honey blond hair, and the lean,
athletic body, perhaps of a former tennis player.
Chenault found her to be bright, funny, and she
seemed to have a certain spunk that guaranteed she
would never be boring, yet there was also a hint of
innocence that suggested she had likely not
ventured too far outside her home state.

After Chenault eventually got around to the

unpleasant purpose of his visit, Rachel pointed out the striking similarities to a kidnapping case she had covered several years back. A young girl had been kidnapped by a man the press had portrayed as a wild-eyed, wandering madman after he'd been caught.

"I remember it quite well," Chenault said. "There was a massive search that went on for weeks. I also seem to recall there were a number of small protests by some groups who pointed out the disparities between the brief, unsuccessful search for a young black girl who went missing around that same time--in contrast to the considerable national exposure for the Utah girl, which they contended was because she was attractive and white."

"I just wanted them to find both girls," Rachel said with a hint of sadness.

"Yeah, me too. But you were saying you thought there were similarities between the story you covered and the Ratchford case? Other than that the girls were roughly the same age, I don't see it. I mean, they caught the wackjob that broke into the first girl's home, didn't they?"

"Is that the way you remember it--that he was a 'wackjob' as you put it?"

"I mean, wasn't he? What, are you going to tell me that he was really just some mild-mannered accountant?"

"No, but he was badly mischaracterized by both the national and even the local press--or at least by *The Deseret News*. The national press just didn't know any better, while *The Deseret* just didn't want it to get out, but most everybody around here had their suspicions, which were confirmed once he was caught. The truth was that he was a fundamentalist Mormon, who'd previously worked in maintenance for the LDS Church headquarters. He was a little down on his luck and had been working as a handyman for the girl's family, but what he did was take the girl, believing that it was perfectly within his rights to take her for his wife. He, like a lot of the fundamentalists who still believe in and practice polygamy, believe that if they feel attraction for an unattached woman, that it's God directing him to take her for his wife."

"You're kidding me. Wasn't the girl like barely thirteen?"

"Doesn't matter to them. When you're raised in a culture that constantly reminds you that you practice the 'one true religion,' and that you're God's true chosen ones, you develop almost a sense of infallibility. After awhile you don't even question your actions or your feelings, believing that God is constantly giving you divine direction."

"That's actually a little scary," Chenault said. "It almost sounds like you're saying they're breeding megalomaniacs."

"I wouldn't be the first to set forth that theory."

"You sure seem to know a lot about the Mormon Church. Is that just from your reporting?"

"You haven't figured it out yet?" Rachel said with a little smile.

". . .You're a Mormon. I feel like an idiot."

"Actually, an ex-Mormon."

"So that would explain the pass on that coffee or drink?"

"I guess old habits are hard to break."

"Or, I guess you could probably say, your 'lack of bad habits' are hard to break. You know, that's one of the many little ironies I've noticed. Mormons supposedly won't smoke or drink, but yet from what I've read, they lead the nation in both white collar fraud and bankruptcies per capita, which seem like, I don't know, propensities a bit counter to the image of a people who bill themselves as upright, stalwart citizens."

"So how did you get to be so up on your Latter Day Saint trivia?" Rachel asked.

"I was working on a piece several years back on various religious zealots from a number of different religions, many of whom had murdered on what they claimed were direct orders from God. Anyway, I was interviewing this one man, a fundamentalist Mormon who'd killed several members of his extended family, based on what he said had been divine instructions from God. While I was at the prison one day, I happened to meet his cellmate, the notorious forger from a few years earlier who sold the Church fake historical documents and then tried to cover it up by murdering a couple of people. Well, some of the things he told me got me interested enough to start researching not only his claims, but some of the other charges made against the Church over the years."

"Like what for instance?" Rachel said.

"Not to be rude, but can you excuse me for just a moment?" he said, as he got up from the bar.

A few seconds earlier, Chenault had glanced over to see Felix Valdez strolling toward them. Valdez, now a cable news correspondent and the host of a nightly news wrap-up, had been a boyhood idol of Chenault, and at one time, the toast of the news industry before his well publicized fall from grace.

"Mr. Valdez. Michael Chenault, *New York Times*. It's a real pleasure to finally get to meet you."

"Michael, love your work--some real hard-hitting stuff. You ever thought about getting into television? I could make a few calls."

As they exchanged pleasantries, Chenault wasn't so presumptuous as to imagine this chance meeting as a "passing of the torch," but he hoped that maybe Valdez saw a younger version of himself. He knew Valdez had been a bit down on his luck over the last several years, and wasn't about to bring that up or offer any condolences to remind him of his troubles. He simply wished to convey that he had been a huge admirer of Valdez from way back, and leave it at that. Valdez seemed to be genuinely flattered, and after Chenault introduced Rachel, Valdez politely told them he needed to be going, since it appeared that one of his sources he was to have met had not shown up. They shook hands, and just before exiting, Valdez graciously signed an autograph for a large, middle-aged woman who thrust a pen and napkin at him as he headed for the door.

Chenault turned to Rachel. "Last item of the evening and then I think I need to call it a night too--I've got an early morning coming up. Take a look at this." Chenault pulled out a pen, and on a napkin scrawled his best memory of the odd character that had been finger painted in blood across the foreheads of the two murder victims. "Do you recognize, or have you ever seen this character before?"

Rachel took the napkin and furrowed her brow slightly as she tried to recall. "I don't recognize this character per se, but I think I know how to find out."

Chenault returned the puzzled look. "So you don't recognize it, but you think you can find out?"

"Unless I miss my guess, this looks like one of the odd letter characters from the old Deseret alphabet."

"'Deseret' as in *The Deseret News*, your competitor here?"

"Actually, they--*The News*--took "Deseret" from *The Book of Mormon*. The alphabet, though, I believe was created back in the mid 1800's in one of the Church's early attempts to further distance themselves from the Gentile population--that's you, by the way," she said with a smile. "It wasn't very complex--partially phonetic--but mostly just created alternative characters from letters in the English alphabet. I think I probably have a copy of it--the old alphabet--lying around somewhere, or I could probably find it on the internet. Let's meet for breakfast, and if you pick up the tab, I just might tell you what it is," she said with a sly grin.

"Deal," Chenault said, returning the smile.

CHAPTER 11

Although Felix Valdez had grown up as a devout Catholic and served as an altar boy up through his teens, once he had gotten his first taste of fame, and subsequent notoriety as a regular at Studio 54 and on New York City's party circuit, he transformed into a man of enormous appetites. Cocaine had been his drug of choice throughout the late '70s and into the mid '80s, followed by a period of self-medication with alcohol after his well-publicized fall from grace. The one thing, though, that had remained a constant throughout his adult life was his near insatiable appetite for attractive young women.

When Valdez had first come on the scene, women virtually threw themselves at his feet as if he were a rock star, and in his own way, in the field of "in your face" investigative television journalism, he was, literally having his choice from among the hundreds of young women who came across his path. Subsequently, two half-hearted attempts at marriage had been extremely unsuccessful, primarily because of his voracious libido and penchant for pursuing and frequently bedding his plentiful, nubile admirers.

Unfortunately, time and chemical abuse over the years had not been kind to Valdez. Along with a paunch and the cragginess that made other men his age seem distinguished, he now appeared bloated and haggard. He was therefore somewhat surprised when the raven-haired tigress whom he'd met at the motel bar earlier that evening agreed to follow him back to his room.

The anonymous source he was to have met earlier that evening had never shown, and to make matters worse, that pompous *Times* reporter who'd been nominated for a couple Pulitzers was at the same restaurant, and he had to endure his patronizing "blah blah" for several minutes. Valdez was almost certain, in fact, that he'd detected an air of condescension on the part of Chenault, which was a laugh, since Chenault worked for the print media--a dying medium at best. Whereas Valdez, he had been riding at the top of the television journalism world for years until. . .

He didn't want to think about what he was about to for the one millionth time, so he decided to make the best of a bad situation and ordered a drink for the gorgeous creature who kept glancing over at him from the end of the bar. Wearing a booze-soaked grin, he sidled over to her, and using a line that had worked on a thousand women before her, said, "Hi. I'm Felix Valdez."

When he awoke several hours later back in his suite at the Salt Lake Hilton, the intoxication of coital bliss had long since worn off, and the old familiar symptoms of a raging hangover were just beginning to kick in, when he felt an object entering his right ear canal. The burning pain was at first excruciating, but as the ice pick nestled deeper into his brain, a strange sense of calm that he'd not known in years swept over him, as his eyes slowly closed and he slipped into unconsciousness for the last time.

CHAPTER 12

From their many years of hunting experience, the Lamott brothers were quite skilled at stalking their quarry in wide open spaces. So in the closed city environment with its numerous buildings, alleys, and side streets, which they could use to either duck into or serve as cover, the stalking of their latest prey was relative child's play. As their glorious prophet had predicted, the meddling New York City reporter had come out to Utah almost immediately. Trailing him from the airport as they'd been directed, they stayed close, but remained undetected.

The young woman who had arrived on the scene not long into the reporter's visit presented The Brothers with a dilemma. With the foreknowledge that the Gentile from New York was to be immediately slain once he had led them to the sacred relic their prophet sought, the fate of the woman was also likely sealed should she choose to remain in his company. Both brothers, however, had it in mind to ask for The Prophet's intercession on her behalf, and even his possible blessing of a union, since the woman appeared to have all the makings of a fine breeder and potential wife.

The Brothers were the product of a union between a much older father and his young niece some forty-three years earlier. Although not mentally impaired, their sociopathic tendencies coupled with their inability to socially interact normally had not made for an active social life growing up, and as a sad result they had been friendless and womanless their entire lives. Over the years, the Lamott brothers had witnessed a number of much older men, many bordering on the decrepit, successfully select attractive, fertile young women to add to their menagerie of wives. Yet they found that whenever one of them made a claim on a young woman who struck their fancy, she would invariably decline with the full backing of her family and the rest of the community. Try as they might, they couldn't understand what it was that others found so wrong with them, or why they seemed to be destined to live alone, or at least with one another. They had even begged their Uncle Hyrum, the aged patriarch of the community, to provide them with wives, but the only choices he had offered were a couple of withered widows, long past their prime, who no one else would bring into their families. Had the women not been well past their childbearing years, the Lamott brothers would have gratefully accepted them, but since part of their calling as Latter Day Saints was to be fruitful and multiply, they declined in the knowledge that they could spread their line well into their later years.

Since they were already pariahs in a community of pariahs, when the phone call came requesting their assistance for a higher calling than just procreating, they gladly accepted. The mysterious, deep-voiced caller identified himself only as "The Prophet," but the things he knew about them and his uncannily accurate predictions made the Lamott brothers true believers. Although never having met The Prophet face-to-face, they fervently believed in their new cause, and in his divinely inspired plan to fully restore the one true faith not just within Utah, but throughout the entire land.

After their initial contact by phone, The Prophet informed them that they were both now members of the sacred Danite order, a secret society that went back to the days of Brigham Young, and whose members were dedicated to the preservation of their faith by any means necessary. The Lamott brothers had long heard tales of the Danites who were rumored to be a covert band of assassins. Their original mission, it had been said, included not only the protection of the second great Mormon prophet, but the use of espionage and surveillance, and if necessary, the elimination of anyone who threatened Young or the church.

The Prophet had laid out his divinely inspired plan to them very clearly, explaining the sequence of events that would need to take place in order to restore the one true faith, and thereby bring about Joseph Smith's original vision of spreading their religion across the land. One of the first steps was, that since the United States, which had been once a great nation, was not only in great moral decline, but on the brink of a massive financial collapse, it first had to be saved. In order to do that, however, certain measures would have to be taken to create the favorable conditions that would then allow the Savior from the secret White Horse Prophecy to be able to ride in on his figurative "white horse" and begin to bring the country back from the brink of collapse. "The Great Restorer," as he was known in the prophecy, after saving the country, would then take the necessary steps that would ultimately lead to the Church taking over the government of the United States, just as the first two great prophets had originally dreamed.

And now with one of their own in the running for the party nomination for President, the time had finally arrived for the plan to be set in motion. The election of Brockston Ratchford would also be the final step towards full acceptance of their once scorned and much maligned religion, and being a Latter Day Saint would come to be regarded as commonplace as being a Methodist, a Baptist, or a Presbyterian. Then once the charismatic Ratchford pulled the country back from the brink of collapse, after allowing divine inspiration to guide him, their faith would come to be celebrated. It would then be just a relatively short matter of time, perhaps within twenty years, before their religion would grow so exponentially that they would then be able to elect Latter Day Saint candidates from every state in the union. They would eventually then be able to go on to control the White House to the point that one day they could establish a benevolent dictatorial theocracy in some form, much like the second great prophet had established in the Utah territory. The Brothers were then told that if they would dutifully follow their divinely inspired instructions, they would play a key role in bringing about this prophecy. For their service to their faith, they were promised by the Prophet they would be amply rewarded with not only untold riches, but more beautiful young wives than they could possibly dream.

The first directive the Lamott brothers had

carried out they believed to have been perhaps just a test of their obedience and loyalty, much as Job and Abraham had been tested by God in the Old Testament of the Christian Bible, since in their minds the order made little sense. The Prophet, though, had assured them that in the fullness of time they would come to understand why it was necessary to eliminate Senator Ratchford's wife, whose beliefs and sincerity of faith had come greatly into question. He further explained that what he had asked them to do was, in fact, a merciful act, because it was only through Blood Atonement that they might have a chance to offer her eternal salvation, and thus save her everlasting soul. As for the young girl, they were instructed to merely care for her until the time was right to allow for her safe return.

The reasoning behind the second directive they received couldn't have been any clearer. A gentile from New York City, who had done nothing but smear their religion and cast vicious slurs against their candidate in his writings, was now on the trail of perhaps the most sacred of all Mormon treasures. The sacred artifact, it was explained, had apparently been discovered by a faithless, ex-Mormon Apostate who had then tried to extort money from the church for its return. The extortionist had been swiftly dealt with by the Prophet himself, but the man would not give up the location of the sacred relic before he had been put to death. It was then believed that this New York writer had somehow received clues to the location of the artifact from the now dead apostate, and it was now the Lamotts' primary mission to shadow this man until this treasure that rightfully belonged to the Church was found and returned. The Prophet had then left the brothers with two final instructions before ending the call. The first, to relieve the man of "That which his eyes should never even lay upon" as soon as it came into his possession. This was followed by the final, thinly veiled instruction of, "And then you know what to do," which left very little to even the Lamott brothers' limited imaginations.

CHAPTER 13

That night as Chenault lay in bed, he pondered the anonymous email tip that had brought him to Salt Lake City, and the more he thought about it, the more it seemed to have been an attempt to draw him into the gathering mystery. The sender, he surmised, apparently knew that he would likely be one of the few privy to seeing the identical characters scrawled in blood across the foreheads of the two unrelated victims. And that could only be due to one of a few possibilities--that the sender, if not involved with the murders, at the very least, had knowledge of both crimes. But for what purpose was someone seemingly trying to lure him in? He also, though, had to consider the possibility that maybe some nervous tipster was just simply trying to help him by showing him the connection between the murders?

The next morning, Chenault met Rachel down in the motel's spacious carpeted lobby, which coupled with the alpine décor of its adjoining restaurant, reminded Chenault a bit of a Swiss lodge he'd once stayed in outside Berne.

"I've got it!" Rachel exclaimed like an excited schoolgirl as she walked forward to meet him.

"Well, do you care to share, or do I have to buy you breakfast first?"

"Now that you mention it, I am kind of hungry."

After being seated in the dining area, the two placed their orders. As their waitress headed back to the kitchen, Chenault turned in his chair toward Rachel, and with a friendly but inquisitive expression said, "So, what is it?"

"It's the letter 'A.'"

"The letter 'A,' as in Hester Prynn's scarlet letter?"

"I don't think that's what it stands for in this case. I think it's for 'Apostate,'" she explained.

"Apostate?"

"As in, someone who's fallen away from the Church--they once knew the true path, but have chosen to turn away. The Church goes so far as to define it as a traitor who's not only betrayed a trust, but an allegiance. Technically, I'm an Apostate, and that's far worse than even being a Gentile."

"Which is what I am," Chenault said.

"Exactly."

"And someone can be murdered just for being an Apostate?"

"Well not every one, obviously. But in the past, yes, some who were considered Apostates have been reportedly, well. . .eliminated. But then again, you do literally take an oath of death if you ever leave the Church or divulge Church secrets."

"But that doesn't make sense in either case. Wasn't Lauren Ratchford likely a devout Mormon?"

Rachel waited a moment to answer as the waitress came over and set her glass of orange juice down and then poured Chenault's cup of coffee before moving on to the next table.

". . .I guess that depends on one's definition of 'devout.' I never knew her personally, but there was some talk around town about her. But you mentioned something about 'in either case.' Is there something you're not telling me?"

"Whoa there, this is my story, remember?"

"Of course, but if I'm going to help you, I'd kind of like to be kept in the loop," Rachel said with a hint of agitation.

Chenault paused for a moment, as his body language let Rachel clearly know she'd overstepped her boundaries.

"I said something wrong, didn't I?" Rachel said.

"I swear to you, I'm not trying to steal your story. I just thought that maybe if I could help you out a little, you might be willing to take me under your wing for a few days, and then if you wanted to toss me a research assistant credit, I wouldn't hold it against you."

Chenault's guarded expression changed slowly to a wry little smile, brought on partially over her witty save, and partially at himself for his brief wave of paranoia that someone might be trying to horn in on one of his stories. He took a sip of coffee, eyeing her over the rim of his mug as she awaited his verdict.

". . .There was a man who was murdered about a week ago in upstate New York. Like the Senator's wife, he'd had his throat slit, and he also had this same character scrawled in blood across his forehead. His name was Martin Koplanski, and as far as I know, Koplanski wasn't a Mormon."

"Not any more," Rachel said.

Chenault was wide eyed. "You've heard of Martin Koplanski?"

CHAPTER 14

"He was a professor at BYU, until he wrote and published a somewhat controversial book, which was also just around the time he renounced the Church."

"And do you know what this book had to do with, or where I might be able to find a copy?" Chenault asked.

"Why?"

"Just professional curiosity."

"I really don't. I more just heard about the story in retelling--it was a bit before my time."

"So what was significant enough about this story that you would have heard anything about it years later?" Chenault said.

"Well, somebody at work one day just happened to mention that what had almost happened to our newspaper had happened to Koplanski."

"I'm not following."

"Well, as I said, Koplanski published a book that

apparently didn't sit well with the powers that be in the Church. In it were a number of things that they--the Church--either so disagreed with, or just didn't want to see the light of day, that they apparently bought up almost all of the printed copies, and then went out and bought the small publisher which owned the rights."

"Which explains why I'm having such a hard time tracking down a copy. I even contacted the Library of Congress, which as you probably know, has a copy of pretty much everything ever published. And their only copy, oddly enough, had been recently checked out."

"And why is that odd?"

"Because they're not a lending library, at least to the general public. Only members of Congress or their staff are supposed to be able to check out a book--or I'm guessing someone with enough clout to get some strings pulled. . . But you mentioned something earlier about something similar happening to *The Tribune*. What was that?"

"Well, a short while back, *The Tribune* published a series of articles about the Mountain Meadows Massacre. The Mormon community got so ticked off about the paper's dredging up its past sins, that *The Deseret* tried to buy *The Tribune* to basically silence the voice of the opposition once and for all."

"I'm sorry, I know I probably should have heard of this, but what exactly is the 'Mountain Meadows Massacre?'"

"Well, the short and the sweet of it is, it's pretty

much the ugliest chapter in the history of the Church. About a 150 years ago, a group of settlers, now referred to as the Fancher party, set out from Arkansas to settle out West. When they arrived in Utah, word soon got back to the early settlement in Salt Lake City about the Gentile intruders, some of whom they considered to be in league with those who'd murdered Joseph Smith."

"I seem to recall that Smith was killed in an armed jail break," Chenault interrupted.

"That's kind of beside the point--and not true by the way. Did you want me to finish the story?"

"I'm sorry. Please continue."

"Anyway, the Mormons formed a welcoming committee of sorts, and with the help of a few local Indians they recruited, set up an ambush, which involved some of the Mormons even dressing up as Indians, complete with feathers and war paint. When the Fancher party stopped for the night in an area now known as Mountain Meadows, the ambush went as planned and the settlers found themselves surrounded. A few were killed, but the Fancher party literally circled their wagons and were able to hold off their attackers for several days. By this time, the few Paiute Indians who'd been involved apparently got fed up and left, since the settlers' head of cattle they'd been promised had been mostly killed off. So, with the Indians gone and the Fancher party successfully holding them off in the gun battle, the Mormons then had to resort to other means. A few of the Mormons, who weren't dressed and painted up like Indians, went in to the Fancher encampment and promised them that they could not only negotiate with the Indians and send them away, but that they could grant the survivors safe passage. There was only one condition they gave them--they told the settlers to show the Indians that they were men of their word, they would need to lay down their arms, and after that, they would then be given an armed escort to the Mormon settlement."

"I don't like the sound of that," Chenault said.

"Well, the Fancher party took them at their word and lay down their arms, and were then escorted single file back in the direction of the Mormon settlement. But then, just as they'd planned, the word was given, and the Mormons turned and fired on them, shooting most of them in the head, but also bashing in a number of their heads, and even mutilating some of them. There apparently was a real killing frenzy that went on. The only ones who were spared were just a few of the very young children who were taken back and raised by the very same people who'd murdered their parents."

"And this is a true story?" Chenault said in utter disbelief.

"Well, not if you ask most Mormons. But yes, it really did happen."

"And if I were to ask 'most Mormons,' what would they say happened?"

"Well, like a lot of things from their history, they've become very adept at rewriting the past.

The older ones, who know about or have heard of the massacre, would probably mostly still be in denial. And the younger ones, well, let's just say that chapter's not going to be in too many LDS history books--it doesn't fit in very well with the all-American family image they've been trying to cultivate."

"And just curious, whatever happened to the men who were involved--the ones who planned and carried out the massacre?"

"Well, there was a cover-up. There was a trial, but only of one man--the step-son of Brigham Young--and that was twenty years after the massacre. Young, of course, disavowed any knowledge or involvement with the massacre, and his step-son was offered up as the sacrificial lamb and executed."

At first, Chenault could only just shake his head in disbelief. ". . .I consider myself pretty well read, and history was even my secondary field in college, but I bet you ninety nine percent of the population has never heard that story before, let alone anything else about this religion and its history. I think most people just think of it as sort of another Protestant denomination--I know I did for the longest time."

"Well," Rachel said with a little smile, "I'm sure if you start digging deep enough, you'll find that story just barely scratches the surface."

CHAPTER 15

As they finished their breakfast, the waitress refilled Chenault's coffee cup and cleared the table.

"So, where to from here?" Rachel asked.

"Actually, this is one of those stories--if it even is a story, where I'm not yet quite sure where I'm headed. It's a little like being lost in the middle of a forest. Sometimes you just have to pick a direction and start walking and hope you run into something."

"And then hope that one thing leads to another?"

"Pretty much."

"Sounds like you have sort of a Zen approach to reporting."

"I guess, but I just call it 'playing it by ear.'" In the back of his mind, however, Chenault was driven by the favorite saying a professor of his had often cited, that *If you looked long enough, and hard enough, that eventually you could find just about anything.* With this workmanlike philosophy,

Chenault had also discovered that if he paid close enough attention along the way, hidden connections would often reveal themselves, and telling patterns would begin to emerge. "You know, though, I was actually thinking about heading over to the LDS Family History Library to do a little research. Want to tag along?"

"Love to," Rachel said.

While Chenault could drive, as a teen there had been little need for him to learn how, since New Orleans was not only made for walking, but had an above average public transportation system. He'd then gone off to school in Boston and moved to New York for work, where he'd made regular use of their excellent public transit systems, and subsequently, hadn't learned to drive until his mid-twenties. So when Rachel offered to not only be his city guide, but to drive to the LDS archives as well, Chenault gratefully accepted. Not only did he enjoy her company, but her offer would also give him a bit more time to go through some of the background research he'd downloaded to his laptop the night before.

Researching Joseph Smith's founding of the religion in Palmyra, NY, their religious persecution in the mid 19th century and subsequent migration to Salt Lake, and the many controversies down through the years, had all been quite easy thanks to the vast information network of the Internet. In the old days, before Google and LexisNexis searches, the material that Chenault had collected in a couple of hours would have taken him days, maybe even weeks, of journeying from one library or museum to another. Now it was simply a matter of a few keystrokes, Googling away, and becoming, if not an instant expert, at least highly knowledgeable on any number of subjects.

The one thing Chenault always bore in mind, however, whenever doing any kind of research, especially from the Internet, was to consider the source. Since almost anyone could write and post pretty much anything he or she wanted to on the web, Chenault always checked several sources to corroborate just about anything he used in any of his stories. This practice, however, was just as much about protecting himself, as it was about getting at the unvarnished truth. He'd learned this hard lesson early on after watching one of his trusted mentors approve a series of articles, going on only the word of one of Chenault's colleagues. The reporter, it later turned out, was little more than a very creative pathological liar, and Don Mills, a highly respected editor with years of experience and accolades, had been forced to retire in disgrace.

About ten minutes into the trip, Chenault noticed an older model, brown pick-up truck in his side view mirror that he was almost certain he recalled seeing several turns back. *It's probably nothing,* he told himself, but then again, people were dying, and someone, he had the faint suspicion, had not only tried, but been successful at drawing him into this little drama, so it never hurt to be overcautious.

"Do me a favor," he said. "Don't pull over or anything, but just gradually start slowing down by taking your foot off the gas."

"How come?"

"Oh, no reason. I'm probably just being paranoid, but that does go hand in hand with a healthy dose of guilt, and since I was raised Catholic. . .Well, you never know when your past sins might be trying to catch up with you."

"And you think Mormons are weird," Rachel said smiling. She slowed the car down gradually, and at first the truck kept coming up on them at full speed, but then quickly slowed down as it drew to within a few car lengths.

"Now use the brakes and take it down to about twenty," Chenault said.

As Rachel slowed down again, the truck picked up speed as the driver extended his left arm out the window to hand signal a lane change and then began to pass them. The driver, a rather rustic looking fellow, glanced ever so slightly over as he caught up and passed them. As he drove past, a beat-up metal camper cover over the rear of the truck came into view, and through the open rear window they saw what appeared to be an even larger version of the driver riding in back staring blankly at them.

"I'm guessing that driver probably wonders if we're either crazy or just obnoxious out-of-town tourists."

"Let him wonder," Chenault said. "I don't know

what it is about that guy, but he kind of reminded me of that trigger-happy farmer at the end of *Easy Rider*."

"I'd say, probably more like one of the extras from the cast of *Deliverance*."

And Chenault had to admit she was right. Their driver had much fleshier features, yet he did have that same haunted, almost animal-like glint in his eyes that suggested. . .well, he didn't want to think about it as he saw the truck pull in front of them, where it stayed for the next two blocks before pulling off at a gas station. Chenault glanced over as they passed by, and what he saw he could hardly believe. The driver looked directly at him and with his hand raised and index finger extended out like a pistol, he pointed it straight at Chenault and then popped his finger up slightly from the imaginary recoil as he said a silent "Pow."

"Did you see what that guy just did?"

"What, did he flip us off?"

"I don't know about flipping us off, but he pointed his finger at me like a pistol and then shot me."

"Well, that's probably the polite Mormon version of shooting the bird, since obscene gestures are pretty much frowned upon around here," Rachel said.

"Oh yeah, shooting me's much more polite," he said as he shook his head in disbelief. For a moment, Chenault pondered the wisdom of investigating such a strange clan of people where shooting someone between the eyes was considered less objectionable than the universal "up yours" gesture, but then laughed it off, realizing more pressing matters were at hand.

"There's something I need to tell you before we get to the library, because we're probably going to have to devise some sort of plan," Chenault said. "Way back when, after my story on the Mormon guy who murdered several of his family members, my editors received an official letter from the LDS Church, which implied in the strongest language possible, short of just outright banning me, that in the future I would have extremely limited access to any of their facilities. Now I doubt if an actual 'watch list' exists, like for Customs and airport security, but it's probably best if I don't press my luck."

"So, what it comes down to is, we need to come up with a way to get you past the front desk?"

"Pretty much. Of course, you know the one thing I've always wondered about that incident is why the so-called mainstream Church would get involved and pay such close attention to a story on the activities of someone who was allegedly just a member of some fringe offshoot of the religion. And prior to that banishment letter, they'd even sent an earlier one demanding retractions of what they alleged were 'outright lies and obscene innuendo used in the smear piece.'"

"I take it that a retraction was not forthcoming?" Rachel said.

"It was not. That's the one thing, though, you definitely have to give *The Times*."

"What's that?"

"If they screw up, and if it's big enough, they'll print it across the front page. And, of course, minor retractions are made daily. But if they stand behind a story, they will not back down."

"Of course, there's the other bigger issue, that maybe even if something is true, that maybe it shouldn't be printed."

"Well, I'm not sure which story you're referring to, but to the extent that lives would immediately be endangered, I agree. But beyond that, I believe the public has the right to know whatever our government and institutions are up to, since the press is, thanks to the Constitution, one of the few checks and balances left now that Congress has seemingly relinquished much of its power to the Executive branch."

"Do you really believe that?" Rachel said.

"That Congress has basically given the White House a blank check? Absolutely."

"No, that we're one of the Constitutional checks and balances."

Chenault smiled, recalling the frequent mantra of one of his political science professors, an activist from the sixties whom the students affectionately referred to as "Red Ernie." "Freedom of the press, baby! Freedom of the press," he quoted Professor Ernest Peterson, who had frequently reminded his undergrads that when the founding fathers drew up

the Bill of Rights, they included it in the First
Amendment for a reason.

CHAPTER 16

Arriving at the five-story Family History
Library, Chenault was somewhat taken aback by
how impressive and inspiring a structure the
building was. Having had a lifelong interest in
architectural and engineering design, to the point of
briefly considering pursuing a career as an architect
while in college, he appreciated a well-designed
building that was not only functional, but pleasing
to the eye.

Unlike the countless scores of undistinguished
glass, metal, and brick boxes most institutions
appeared to erect--and usually just as utilitarian
warehouses to store their records and employees--
this grand repository of historical Mormon artifacts
and records was no run-of-the-mill construction.
The Family History Library was more of an actual
monument to this homegrown American religion,
designed in a style and of a scale, befittingly paying
tribute to the many Saints who had struggled and
fought to build a homeland for its once persecuted
church family. It served as well as a permanent

home to store and protect the many sacred relics, documents, and the venerated family histories which dated back centuries.

One of the chief reasons the Church of Latter Day Saints so revered the ancestry of generations past, Chenault had learned from previous research, was that part of their sacred rituals involved the administering of Baptismal rites to their long dead ancestors. They would also even, on occasion, conduct marriage ceremonies with an exchange of vows between their dead family members. While to outsiders, the practices of baptism and marriage of the dead might have sounded a bit bizarre, the adherents of the Mormon faith reasoned that since many of their ancestors had not had the advantage of being in the Church when they were alive, this was apparently the next best thing.

While the numerous family ancestry centers around the world were held up as first and foremost, for families to be able to research their histories to posthumously bring their ancestors into the "one true faith," the reality had been, Chenault had learned, the centers served as the front line for the Church's recruitment efforts. In concert with almost 75,000 missionaries proselytizing around the world, and multi-millions spent on public relations and television and radio advertising, the LDS Church had more than doubled its membership in the last twenty years to almost twelve million. At their current growth rate, along with their exploding exponential birthrate due to their belief in the glory of procreation, they were on pace to increase to almost one hundred million strong in just over fifty years.

As they'd previously discussed, Rachel and Chenault meandered around the lobby for several minutes, waiting until one of the tour bus groups disembarked and entered the lobby before they approached the front check-in desk. Timing it perfectly, Rachel walked up to the desk and started to check in as if they were a couple, when on cue, Chenault said, "I'll be right back. I need to run to the restroom."

Within moments, a busload of visiting Mormon tourists descended en masse on the lone attendant, a plump, middle-aged blond woman. As her attention was directed to checking in the fifty or so new arrivals, Chenault popped into the bathroom for a moment and then peeked out the door. Seeing the attendant was inundated with the swarm of new arrivals, Chenault slipped out and casually strode down the hall where he met up with Rachel. They then made their way down the next corridor to the library section.

"I tell you what," Chenault said, "I'm going to go through the stacks here first and try to look up a couple of things. Why don't you head on to the family records section and start nosing around."

"And what exactly am I supposed to be looking for?"

"Well if I knew that, I wouldn't need you now would I?" Chenault said with a smile. "Why don't you do this? Since the two people in question both have some Mormon background, why don't you look up both the Koplanski and the Ratchford records and see if anything pops up."

"Well, like what exactly?" Rachel asked with a somewhat puzzled expression.

"There you go asking that question again. I would just say look out for something that catches your attention--an inconsistency, an interesting connection, basically, just anything out of the ordinary."

"Which will tell us. . .?"

"Well, we really can't start asking the questions sometimes until we've found some things that may be possible answers--if that makes any sense."

"Kind of like 'Jeopardy?'"

"Exactly."

CHAPTER 17

Other than the one important bit of information he had failed to share with Rachel, that his main reason in coming to the library was to track down a copy of Koplanski's book, Chenault had been quite truthful when he told her he was not quite sure what they were looking for. His second concern, and the reason he hadn't told her about his search for the book, was to involve Rachel as little as possible for her own safety, since at this point he still didn't quite know yet what he was involved in.

His initial search for the book through the New York City Public Library system had been followed by an equally unsuccessful inquiry through the Library of Congress. He'd then attempted to track down a copy through a number of the library share programs across the country, but had come up empty as well. Only one library of the many he had contacted had ever even had a copy, and the librarian from the small North Carolina college conjectured that theirs most likely had been sold in one of their recent fifty cent book drives. He'd also tried calling Koplanski's widow several times, but she was either not returning calls or had yet to return to the home where her husband had been so brutally murdered.

With the Dewey decimal classification number of Koplanski's book in hand, Chenault went back and forth through several nonfiction aisles guided only by the various category signs, but continued to have no luck. While he really wanted to just head to the nearest library terminal and do a quick search, as an unregistered, and very likely, unwelcome guest, he didn't want to draw any attention which could then lead to an awkward confrontation. As he had found from past experience where he was either an uninvited guest or an outright trespasser, keeping a low profile was usually the best way to avoid any interactions, which could then often lead to further unwelcome contacts and his cover being blown.

He decided to go through the nonfiction section one more time in the event the book had simply been misshelved, perhaps just slightly out of numerical order, when he heard the carpet-muffled footsteps to his rear.

"May I help you find something?" came the very polite male voice from behind.

Chenault jumped slightly, but mostly just inside. He knew the best thing to do was to remain calm and act as if he belonged there. He also knew, though, that in the past when the situation had arisen where he needed to at least give the appearance of being calm, cool, and collected, that had often been when he had become most self-conscious. Having been a late bloomer in the romantic department, that scenario had played out a number of times in his years just out of college, when he had been so excited to be out with a particular woman that he would come off as a bit stiff and completely unnatural. It wasn't until several years later when he had finally developed an inner confidence, mostly acquired from his professional success, that he was finally able to start having some success with the ladies, and now was definitely the time to try to draw on some of that inner calm.

"I was just looking for a book that a friend of mine told me about, and I can't seem to find it in your nonfiction section, so I'm guessing you probably just don't have it. But I thank you anyway."

"It's very likely the book is just out right now. Tell me the author and title and I'll run a quick check to see if we normally carry it," the chipper library assistant responded.

Neatly dressed, with close-cropped blond hair, the young man was one of the many seemingly eternally sunny young Mormons Chenault had run across since first arriving in Salt Lake City. They seemed to be just about everywhere he went--at the airport, at the rent-a-car center, at the hotel, and working in just about every restaurant. They were all certainly pleasant enough, but after less than a day, Chenault joked to Hal over the phone that he was starting to get the uneasy feeling that at some point, like the old *Invasion of the Bodysnatchers* movie, they were all going to turn on him as one, pointing their outstretched index fingers at him, as they let out some unworldly, horrifying screech, identifying him as a Gentile and an outsider.

After a moment to decide the best course to take, Chenault gave the young man Koplanski's name and the title of the book, *The Moroni Deception*, and after about fifteen seconds of typing, the library assistant looked back up.

"Oh, here it is," the young man said. "But you were mistaken about the category--we keep that in our fiction section. And it looks like we do have a copy. Did you want to check it out?"

"I guess I'd like to take a quick look at it first," Chenault said, realizing that it would likely appear suspicious for him to have get Rachel to come back and check out the book. "If that's all right. See if it's something I really want to take the time to read. I'm actually not much of a fiction reader. But I will take a glance at it. Thanks."

"Give just me a minute and I'll be right back."

"Thanks, Duffin," Chenault said, reading from his name tag and guessing it to be one of the unusual Mormon first names he'd heard tales of.

The young man disappeared and Chenault breathed a small sigh of relief. *So far, so good.* He wondered if Rachel had had any luck finding anything of interest at her end in the family history archives. Likely not, but it was still good to have her along. She could also help him by swinging back later to check out Koplanski's book, along with several others to help to conceal its importance. While he still felt a little bad about not revealing the importance of finding a copy to her, if there really was something in its contents that had gotten Martin Koplanski killed, for her own protection, he decided it was best to continue to leave her in the dark.

The library assistant returned a minute later, grasping a red-jacketed book tightly to his chest with crossed hands in a near death grip. Gone was the slightly vacuous smile from before, as he lowered his eyebrows over suspicious eyes, and pursed his lips as if he had a mouthful of lemon juice.

"I found that book you were asking about," the assistant said with the same sour expression.

Chenault didn't like the way he spat out *that book*. "Great! May I see it," he said, extending his hand out. An awkward pause followed.

". . .I'm afraid you won't be allowed to check it out."

Chenault dropped his hand to his side, sure that his cover was somehow blown, since it seemed to be the most likely explanation for the change in the library assistant's demeanor. He guessed it was probably best if he just made a hasty exit before being escorted out of the building, but his curiosity got the best of him. Almost out of professional habit, he asked the question hanging in the air, "And why is that, Duffin?"

"Why is it that it can't be checked out?" the assistant responded, growing increasingly agitated. "Because it's on our list of restricted books. It really shouldn't even be out in circulation. Is that sufficient enough explanation for you?"

Breathing a sigh of relief, Chenault quickly regained his composure. "Well, that's fine. I understand, of course. But would it at least be possible for me to peruse it for just a few minutes. I'm just in town for a few days, and so far I've just found everybody to be so gracious and accommodating. I'll just be right over there at one of the desks at the end of the stacks."

The library assistant pondered the request for a few moments, knowing that he was being gently manipulated. "I'll give you ten minutes, and then I'll be back for the book," he said as he reluctantly handed it over.

Chenault knew he now had a choice to make. As a lover of words and books, and as distasteful as the idea was to partially destroy what was very possibly the last remaining copy of Martin Koplanski's book in existence, he knew in his heart that Koplanski would have consented. His last written words, after all, had most likely been to Chenault, instructing him to "Read my book."

Although Chenault generally liked to "wing it" when he was on a story, the two things that allowed him to do this was to be quick on his feet and to more often than not, be well prepared. In this instance, that meant he had the exact tools and materials stowed away in his trusty blue fanny pack that he would need for the task of removing and transferring the pages of Koplanski's book into his possession.

Chenault made his way down to an empty desk at the end of two long aisles of books, and after seeing no one else around, took a seat. Knowing he had less than ten minutes to complete the task, he immediately pulled several books down from a nearby shelf, searching for one closest in size to Koplanski's. After settling on one with a blue cover, he removed the pages of the book by holding the cover down with one knee, and then slowly pried the center section from its binding. He then took Koplanski's book, and taking care to leave the first several pages intact, removed the remaining pages in the same way. After reshelving the empty book cover, he inserted Koplanki's pages into a Ziploc bag, and then glued the bound pages from the blue book into the spine of Koplanski's hard cover. With no better place he could think of, he then tucked the ziplocked pages down the back of his boxer briefs to slip them past the clerk.

While waiting for the glue to dry, Chenault quickly read Koplanski's brief bio on the inside dust jacket after glancing at his photo. Although he was probably twenty years younger at the time, Koplanski still looked strikingly similar to the round, pink-faced Quaker Oats icon, only with a bushy graying goatee and without the long white locks. After the requisite five minutes, Chenault gave the pages a slight tug to see if the bond held, and then started back to the reference desk.

"Just as I thought, this didn't really hold any interest for me. But I thank you for all your help."

"You're welcome," the assistant said without any emotion, and then looked back down to his computer screen. As Chenault exited, the library assistant glanced over and lifted the jacket cover. He then flipped the pages until he came to the title page. Satisfied that the banned book was back in his possession, he set it aside and returned to his work.

CHAPTER 18

As Chenault made his way down the hallway, he happened to glance over and see Rachel through the mostly plate glass wall. Although she was facing him, she appeared to be so engrossed in whatever was on her computer monitor, she was completely unaware he was on his way to meet back up with her.

God, she's beautiful, Chenault thought, although reminding himself that mixing business with pleasure had never proven to be a good idea in the past. And as much as he tried to remind himself that the story always came first, he was still flesh and blood, and Rachel had stirred something in him that he hadn't felt for quite some time. It also occurred to him, though, that his journalistic mindset of the "story always coming first" was perhaps in large part why he was still single at the age of thirty-seven. He also had doubts she was even attracted to him. The little crush she seemed to have when they first met appeared to be more professionally based than anything else, and after possibly working together for a few more days, they would likely never see each other again.

He walked up from behind and lightly tapped her on the shoulder. "Whatcha got for me?"

Turning partially around in her chair, Rachel glanced back and greeted Chenault with a big smile. "Any luck?"

"Not really. I saw a couple of things that I just sort of scanned, but they really weren't much help. What about you?"

"I'm still on Koplanski's family. But so far, it appears that there may have been a little Latter Day Saint's retribution at its finest."

"How do you mean?" Chenault said looking puzzled.

"Well, I've heard about something like this before, like apparently in the library's genealogy section there's little or no record of any of the family members of the Fancher party that were killed at Mountain Meadows. They've just tried to bury them along with the past, and apparently they've done the same thing with Koplanski. I find bits and pieces about the rest of his family, his wife and his daughter, and even his daughter's family, but Koplanski has apparently been erased from history, at least in the Family History archive."

"You're kidding me. They can really do that?"

"You're forgetting, this is Salt Lake City. They can pretty much do whatever they want here. And once you're excommunicated, you truly are dead to them," Rachel said.

"Well, I'm not sure what conclusions we can draw from that yet, but excellent job. See what else you can find, and I'm going to get started on Ratchford."

As dull as researching a story could sometimes be, Chenault had learned one fascinating thing about the process over the years. He could read back over a file, an interview, or his notes, multiple times, and find nothing of significance, but then a week, a month, sometimes even a year later, come across something else from another source that sparked a connection, and then it suddenly all came together. Although he doubted he was about to have any epiphanies this early on, now was the time to do what was often the tedious scut work, first scanning what could sometimes amount to reams of different materials, then going back over to read and reread the areas of interest he had highlighted. He would then cull much of the rest of the unused material, take notes and file away what he could in his memory, and then hope somewhere down the line it would pay off.

It didn't take Chenault more than forty-five minutes, backtracking from present day, and going back meticulously through state, county, birth and court records, and then high school and college records, to find that Senator Brockston Ratchford appeared to have been born at the age of eighteen. Or, at least, that prior to 1966, there was no record of anyone in the state of Utah named Brockston Ratchford. The explanation for this anomaly he found out soon after. Prior to 1966, young Brockston Ratchford had been raised as Brockston Stepp, before he'd petitioned the court and taken "Ratchford," his mother's maiden name, as his own. He'd then moved to Provo to attend Brigham Young University, after which he'd gone on to marry his college sweetheart, a former beauty queen from Ogden. Chenault asked himself why would a young man just setting out to make his place in the world take his mother's name. *What possible reason*?

Half an hour later he had his answer. Along the way, he came across several stories from seventeen years earlier on Ratchford's first wife, Anetta, committing suicide and leaving behind two sons and a daughter in their early to mid-teens, and a follow-up story a year later after Ratchford had married the family's nanny. Not long after, Chenault came across the most likely reason Ratchford had petitioned the court to change his last name.

Cross-referencing the original last name "Stepp," Chenault came across one Elijah Stepp, convicted on multiple counts of tax evasion and welfare fraud a year before Ratchford changed his name. Stepp hailed from the town of Hildale, Utah, a remote outpost along the Utah-Arizona border, settled by a fundamentalist sect of Latter Day Saints. The *Salt Lake Tribune* article hinted that he was a polygamist, but since that crime hadn't been prosecuted in Utah in over fifty years, it was unlikely that mild embarrassment was what Ratchford was running from, at least back then. Chenault guessed what Ratchford was attempting to break free from in an effort to lead a more normal life, was not just his father, Elijah Stepp, but the entire Hildale community.

And although this old connection with the fundamentalist community wasn't much, it was at least something to go on. This whole business he'd discovered of Ratchford's past history--the name change and leaving the fundamentalist sect to go out and seek his fortune--sparked a memory of one his own father's oft repeated sayings. In an attempt to remind Chenault and his brother to stay out of trouble, the old man would frequently tell them, "You can try to run from your past, but it almost always catches back up with you." Chenault smiled at the memory, realizing that once again, the old Mark Twain adage really was true, "that the older he got, the smarter his father seemed to become." He looked over to Rachel who was still poring over an old document on the other side of the table.

"Maybe it's just a hunch, but it's starting to seem like the signs are pointing to Hildale, Utah, right now."

"Or maybe it's just a lack of any other direction," Rachel said.

Chenault shrugged. "In either case, I think I'm probably going to head down there and ask a few questions."

"So do you have some kind of plan?" Rachel asked. "I mean, I'd kind of like to tag along."

The news that Rachel wanted to continue on gave Chenault a little tingle of excitement, and threw him off his train of thought for a moment as he briefly daydreamed about the possibilities.

". . .I don't know if you've noticed," Chenault said, "but I'm more of a 'wing it' kind of guy, and I've generally found that making definite plans in my line of work is a little like trying to prove a foregone conclusion--which as a journalist, is never a good idea. In fact, very often, I really don't even know what I'm looking for until I find it. So that pretty much just leaves me with trying to go where the story leads me."

"But doesn't that leave you with the feeling that you're just kind of stumbling around in the dark most of the time?"

"Welcome to the world of investigative journalism," Chenault said with a smile.

CHAPTER 19

"So what kind of drive are we looking at?" Chenault called from the back seat as they headed south down I-15, passing through miles and miles of heavily irrigated suburban sprawl.

"You mean, how far? It's probably about a four and a half, five hour drive. Hopefully, we should get in around suppertime."

"And again, you really don't mind me sitting back here?"

"Not at all. If you can get more work done spread out back there, I really don't mind being your temporary chauffer. Besides, most of the time my job just consists of going down to the police station to pick up the most recent arrest log, and then having to listen to a couple of cops, who keep hitting on me, regale me with their exploits of how they ran down some fifteen-year-old shoplifter-- pretty exciting stuff."

Chenault bet the cops were trying to hit on her,

and why wouldn't they? Rachel was one of the most attractive women he had ever met. He liked everything about her. He even liked the way she talked. One of the little endearing things that Rachel did was to pronounce her "t's" in the middle of some words very distinctly. Whereas most English speakers, even the very well educated, tended to pronounce words like "pretty" with a "d" pronunciation in the middle of the word, Rachel clearly and distinctly pronounced the word as it was spelled, almost as a small child might do when first learning to read. In fact, she'd likely picked this little idiosyncrasy up as a child, probably emulating one of her parents.

Enough about Rachel and linguistics, he told himself. *Time to get to work.* Chenault carefully removed the pages of Koplanski's book from the leather attaché case he'd slipped them into earlier, and began to read. Upon coming across the old Robert Burns chestnut, "Oh what a tangled web we weave, when first we practice to deceive," on the page preceding the Table of Contents, Chenault's heart sank a little, as did his expectations for what was to follow. Over the years he had received numerous unpublished and self-published manuscripts from various members of the lunatic fringe bent on uncovering conspiracies from under every unturned stone. Most were full of nothing but disorganized, angry rants against the powers that be--some real, others imagined--which they believed had somehow wronged them or brought misery into their lives. Koplanski's would likely be no different--just another sour grapes manifesto.

Within several minutes, however, just a few pages in, Chenault quickly had a change of heart. In Koplanski's *The Moroni Deception*, Chenault had found the mother lode when it came to separating Mormon fact from fiction. The arguments that Koplanski made were cogent and logical, and the numerous points of historical fact he included were all well documented and clearly very well researched.

Early on in his book, one of Koplanski's most frequent whipping boys appeared to be the Mormon historian and longtime apologist for the Church of Latter Day Saints, Hugh Nibley. In 1961, Nibley authored a book in which he asserted that Joseph Smith had, in fact, never been arrested for "glass-looking" or being a "money-finder." It had long been rumored that Smith had once been tried and convicted for fleecing a number of his neighbors by charging them to locate hidden money and lost treasures through the use of his magic seer stones which he claimed would guide him to the treasures' hidden locations. Apparently not believing that any evidence would ever surface to the contrary over 130 years later, Nibley went on to say that if it could ever be shown that Smith had actually participated in such activities, that this would be damning evidence against Smith's claims of being a divine prophet. He further added that confirmation of these charges would bring the very legitimacy of the entire religion into question. Unfortunately for Nibley, and perhaps even more unfortunately for Smith's legacy, the court documents were discovered in 1971 and proved fairly conclusively that Smith had, in fact, been tried and convicted for such activities. The documents included not only arrest warrants and the court transcripts, but the legal bills from four separate charges filed against Smith.

Koplanski wrote:

Sadly, though, the Mormon Church has since taken possession of these items and likely buried them deep within their vaults, never to again see the light of day, in the hopes that they might once again be forgotten.

Koplanski took on Nibley's next argument in a somewhat lighthearted manner by bringing up the somewhat odd case Nibley frequently made. Nibley maintained that it was highly unlikely that a young and relatively uneducated Joseph Smith could have written the entire 300,000 word Book of Mormon all by himself without having had some sort of divine inspiration.

"To Mr. Nibley's charge that Joseph Smith, having had little formal education, was too big of a nincompoop to have written the Book of Mormon all by himself without having had some sort of divine inspiration (or golden cheat sheets), I would just simply state that after over thirty years as a

*college professor, I can confidently respond that in
just about every year I have taught, I have had
students make both witting and unwitting attempts
at just this sort of thing--it's called plagiarism.
Furthermore, these same plagiarists, who were far
less intelligent than Smith's defenders would have
us believe that he was, more often than not,
borrowed far better material than Smith ever did.
And as it has been repeatedly, and in my opinion,
fairly conclusively shown, between lifting numerous
ideas and passages directly from The Holy Bible, as
well as liberally borrowing from at least three other
sources, all written around that same time, Smith
(who should perhaps be given his due credit for the
invention of the concept of "cut and paste") merely
demonstrated that he was the consummate lazy
school boy, content with claiming others work as
his own."*

Chenault read on and found the contents to be
not only highly informative, but at times rather
entertaining, as Koplanski skewered one Latter Day
Saint sacred cow after another with his wry sense of
humor mixed with a healthy dose of skepticism.
One small, but rather revealing claim that Koplanski
lead the reader to draw his or her own conclusion
about was the fact that Joseph Smith had
maintained, at least after the second printing and
thereafter, that he was only the "translator." In the
original printing, however, Smith had previously
noted himself as the "author" and "proprietor." That

Smith claimed authorship originally, but then later changed his account, Koplanski clearly found very telling, along with noting that one of the very first things Smith did after writing *The Book of Mormon* was to incorporate.

"A business decision if there ever was one," Koplanski noted.

Another of Smith's claims Koplanski addressed was that he had always maintained he had translated the plates from "reformed Egyptian," a language and alphabet that still had yet to be discovered. Yet for some not so mysterious reason, Koplanski noted, the texts all came out sounding much like the Old English from the *King James Bible*, with all the "thee's," "ye's," and "thou's." Some readers eventually noted that the two sounded so similar that it was soon discovered that, in fact, vast passages from the *King James Version* of *The Bible* had been copied virtually verbatim and spread throughout, comprising almost one eighteenth of *The Book of Mormon*. Koplanski then went on to further question the veracity of Smith's claim that *The Book of Mormon* had been originally written in the 1st Century. He did this by pointing out that the near identical *King James Version* passages included within *The Book of Mormon* also contained the same italicized words that the *KJV* translators had inserted into the *King James Version* when it was completed in 1611, some 200 years before Smith discovered and translated the Gold Plates.

Koplanski then followed the Bible revelation with a well documented story about the creation of *The Book of Abraham*, which although not included in *The Book of Mormon*, was nonetheless, an important and well regarded doctrine in the Church of Latter Day Saints. Smith's central claim was that he had translated *The Book of Abraham* from an ancient scroll that had been given to him as a gift. The truth in his story was that there had, in fact, been an ancient Egyptian scroll in Smith's possession that had been purchased from a traveling Egyptian-themed side show. Where his story fell apart, however, was that when the scroll was later actually translated, it was revealed to be nothing more than ancient Egyptian funerary rites.

After a while, though, it almost seemed to Chenault as if Koplanski had grown weary from his own barrage of attacks. His writing began to fall into a pattern of simply enumerating one reason after another why the religion and its many tenets stood not just on shifting sands, as Smith and his defenders dodged back and forth between explanations of how things came to be, but in many cases, more like quicksand, as the numerous, fairly obvious fabrications came crumbling down upon closer scrutiny. For instance, Koplanski noted, albeit with a preface that

"Although scientific discovery does not typically come into the proving or disproving of a religion, since the latter is based largely on one's belief

system, the one claim that science has definitively been able to disprove since Joseph Smith first made it, is that American Indians are not the descendents of the children of Israel, as he claimed in the "translated" Book of Mormon. American Indians have, in fact, been shown through genetic testing to be the descendents of the children of Mongolia, most likely from southern Siberia. "

Yet despite pointing out the religion's numerous other inconsistencies and historical inaccuracies, outright falsehoods, and catching Smith in almost certain plagiarism, Koplanski, ever the fair-minded academic, still asserted that all of it was still just anecdotal and circumstantial, and not true evidence, at least not strong enough to upend an entire religion.

" The only way to truly prove or disprove Smith's claims is to prove or disprove the existence of the Gold Plates, upon which their entire religion is ultimately based. And until the alleged plates are found, and their authenticity is proven (or disproven), the Mormon religion will always have the advantage over their detractors who have the burden of disproving a negative--an impossible task. Still, how fortunate has it been to Smith and his followers that the plates so conveniently disappeared? "

Finishing the chapter, Chenault glanced at his

watch to find they'd been on the road for almost two hours. As he turned to look out the window, the stark contrast between the passing scenery hit him like a slap in the face. Gone was the suburban greenery of central Utah, replaced by an arid, desolate and near featureless landscape of orange and brown soil, along with the occasional outcropping of dark boulders, with only wisps of sagebrush to remind him that they were still on planet Earth.

From a travelogue he'd come across, Chenault seemed to recall reading that the red rock country of southern Utah appeared that way because of its high concentrations of iron oxide or rust, which coincidently, it mentioned, was the same reason that the planet Mars had a reddish tinge whenever it was viewed. He found this other-worldly coincidence somehow apropos, given that the more he learned about this unofficial State religion and its many oddities, the more he felt like a stranger in a very strange land.

CHAPTER 20

"The Senator wants to know exactly what's being done to find his daughter," Evan Fiske bellowed, as he leaned over in a position to best direct his voice down at the speakerphone on his boss's large mahogany desk. Listening in to the call, Senator Brockston Ratchford leaned back in the plush leather chair behind his desk with his fingers interlaced across his chest.

"And his wife's murderer?" Agent Patterson's voice shot back out the speakerphone.

"Well, obviously," Fiske said, not use to dealing with a government employee who was possibly as sharp-witted as he was.

"Well, I'll be honest with you--at this time we don't have a lot to go on."

As Ratchford leaned forward in his chair, Fiske lowered his head and bent down to hear the next question he was to ask

". . .Well, what do you have?" Fiske asked.

"Well as I said, really not much. And what we do have we can't really release while we're still in the middle of an investigation."

"And I'll tell you right now, I don't give a flying fuck about your normal investigative protocol!" the ferret faced Fiske exploded. "This is not a normal investigation. Comprende? The Senator's a very powerful man and in case you hadn't heard, he's running for the President of the United States, if that means anything to you."

"Yes, I'm well aware of that fact. But as I said before, I'm really not at liberty to discuss any aspects of this case, especially since it doesn't regard you, Mr. Fiske."

"And in case you haven't guessed, I'm speaking on behalf of the Senator. He's sitting right here, as a matter of fact, listening to all your babbling."

Ratchford leaned forward toward the speakerphone. "Detective. . ."

"Special Agent," Patterson's voice interjected.

"Special Agent, what exactly is it that you're holding back, or should I say why are you holding back? Should I be concerned--am I considered a suspect?"

"Again, Sir, I apologize, but I'm not at liberty to say. If you would like to speak with one of my superiors, I'll be more than happy to put you in touch with them, Senator."

"No, that won't be necessary," Ratchford said. "I think you've told me just about everything I need to know. Instead of going out looking for the depraved criminals who did this, you're wasting your time considering me as a possible suspect."

"With all due respect, Sir, that's not what I said."

"In case you haven't checked the Senator's whereabouts for the night in question," Fiske chimed in, "He was with me two thousand miles away at a D.C. fundraiser that evening."

"We're well aware of that fact as well, Mr. Fiske."

"Then why in God's name are you people wasting your time on investigating me as a possible suspect?!" Ratchford roared. "Do you have any idea what this could do to my campaign if this ever got out?"

"Sir, again, I never said that you were considered a suspect. I just said I was not at liberty to discuss whether you were or not, as well as any other aspect of the case," Patterson said, observing that at the other end of the line, both Ratchford and Fiske seemed to be more concerned with Ratchford's reputation and campaign than the investigation.

Fiske, sensing it was time to do some damage control after his and the Senator's double-barrel barrage, quickly interjected, "I think what the Senator's trying to say--and obviously he's very distraught over this entire matter, so you'll have to take what he says with an understanding of the emotional trauma that he's just been through--is that anything you can possibly do to expedite this investigation, and anything you can possibly do to share any new information that comes to light, well.

. .let's just say that the Senator would be eternally in your debt, if you follow my meaning."

After a brief pause, Patterson's voice trailed off out of the speakerphone, ". . .I'll do what I can."

"That's all we ask. We'll be in touch." With that, Fiske reached over to the phone and ended the call.

CHAPTER 21

Late that afternoon, the shadows from the desert crags began to create an almost strobe-like effect as they passed from light to dark and then back again, making it almost impossible for Chenault to continue reading. After he had Rachel pull off the road, Chenault got out and stretched for a minute and then hopped into the front seat. Rachel then pulled back onto the lonely highway.

"Just curious, since you seem to have your finger on the pulse of most everything that goes on around here, but what do you know about Brockston Ratchford?" Chenault asked.

"Just that he's been Utah's favorite son for quite some time now."

"Yeah, I gathered that. When he first got nominated I did a little more background research

on him, since he just seemed to kind of come out of
nowhere. That's where I found out that the good
Senator made most of his fortune from a Salt Lake
City investment house, where virtually everybody
who was anybody in the state of Utah invested with
him as if he could somehow foretell the future. But
the thing was, while he did well for some, he lost a
lot of money for others, but of course he and the
company always made lots in commissions no
matter how the clients did."

"That's what you have to love about
stockbrokers--even when they're losing your
money, they're still making it for themselves,"
Rachel chimed in.

"Yeah, but that's not what struck me so much
about his story--how he made his fortune, but why
this weird allegiance to him? His first two
investment houses quickly went belly up, so
apparently he wasn't as clairvoyant as advertised,
but still investors kept flocking to him in droves to
give him their money."

"You know, now that you mention it, his success
story almost has a ring of familiarity about it. Have
you ever heard of the Dream Mine?" Rachel asked.

"No, what's that?"

"Well, around the turn of the last century, a man,
I forget his name now, anyway, he claimed that the
Angel Moroni--the same one who first visited
Joseph Smith--had visited him in a dream. His
story went that Moroni took him out to a nearby
mountain which opened up for them, and Moroni

proceeded to show him a vast cavern filled with gold. Later he said Moroni showed him the exact spot to start digging on the outside of the mountain, and promised him that one day just before the Second Coming, the gold would be struck which would allow the faithful to comfortably survive throughout the Final Days. Anyway, there was never a lack of investors or true believers, all, of course, Mormon, and the mine proprietors could always fall back on the claim when no gold was struck, that the Final Days weren't quite here yet. And that's been going on ever since, and has actually had several reincarnations as recently as the 1980's. If I'm not mistaken, there have actually even been several groups who have set up a so-called City of Refuge near the mine to wait out the Final Days."

"Please tell me you're making this up," Chenault said.

"I wish I was, but no, it's all on record. In fact, I imagine there's probably a mining company out there right now that would more than happy to sell you a few shares in a new operation to start digging away for Moroni's hidden gold."

"Unbelievable. But anyway, back to Ratchford. I just think most people are a little more financially savvy than that today, so I just can't see in this modern age of cynicism, half the state of Utah investing their hard earned money with somebody with as mediocre a track record as his. It's got to be something more."

"Like what then?"

Chenault just shook his head. "I have no idea. But just maybe, if we're lucky, the town of Hildale might have a few answers."

CHAPTER 22

Realizing it was unlikely, from what they had heard and read, that there would be any sort of restaurant where they could actually sit down and enjoy a meal in Hildale, they decided to pull over at the next truck stop diner. Just as advertised on the tattered, decaying billboard they'd passed five miles back, they arrived at "Hal's," a nondescript, mostly block building located off to the side of the road in what could only be described as the absolute middle of nowhere. Upon stepping out of the car, they were both immediately engulfed by the noxious diesel fumes that seemed to hang in an invisible cloud around the dusty rest stop.

"That…is nasty," Chenault said. "Hopefully the food's at least a step above the air quality."

"There's only one way to find out."

"Have you never eaten at a truck stop before?"

"I can't say I've had the pleasure," Rachel replied.

"Well, you may be in for a pleasant surprise. You usually get one end of the spectrum or the other. It may be some of the nastiest, greasiest food you've ever attempted to swallow, or if they have a good short order cook who knows what he's doing, some of the best home style food you could possibly imagine."

"I'm impressed. You struck me a bit as one of those haute cuisine food snobs who wouldn't be caught dead in a place like this."

"Some of the places I've been, you wouldn't believe where or what I've had to eat. And," he said smiling, "I'm from N'awlins, and good food is good food, an' it don't matter where dey make it."

"Oh what, is that like your real accent?"

Chenault shook his head with a little smile. "Just talking about food sometimes brings out the Cajun in me, I guess."

As they stepped inside the large corrugated metal and concrete block box that comprised the diner and the small convenience store area in front, they sensed that all eyes were on them as they made their way to their table. Even after they were seated in their booth by the window, the four truckers seated at the tables around them continued to eye Rachel hungrily until Chenault came to her rescue, loudly clearing his throat and snapping them out of their brief fantasies and back to their meals.

"So how does it feel to be the belle of the ball?" Chenault asked.

"Not too special. In fact, I kind of get the feeling

if you slapped on some lipstick and high heels, they'd probably be eyeing you in the same way."

"Is that what you'd like me to do? I never would have guessed that about you," Chenault said with a mischievous smile.

"You're terrible," Rachel said, returning the smile.

". . .And you're the opposite," Chenault said just above a whisper as he gazed back at her.

"And what would that be?"

"If you don't know, you'll have to go check your thesaurus," he said with a sly smile.

Just then a skinny, middle-aged, pink-uniformed waitress walked up with pen and pad in hand and snapped them back to reality with her shrill voice. "So you all decided what you wanna order?"

Chenault first looked back over at Rachel with a resigned smile and a chuckle, hoping to convey to her that *Bad timing is the story of my life,* without actually having to say it in front of the waitress who'd just walked in on their "moment." After ordering chicken-fried steak with mash potatoes and gravy for himself and a Western omelette for Rachel, Chenault went over and put a couple of dollars in the juke box, and then sat back down as an old Tom Petty song started up.

"Okay," Rachel said, "I have to ask. What's with the old Navy pea coat? I'd have guessed you being from New York, that you were 'fashion forward,' except that from the looks of that jacket,

I'd say it's seen its better days."

Chenault thought about it for a moment before replying. Hal Sikorski was the only other person he had ever told, but there was just something about Rachel that made him want to open up to her.

"Obviously, as you've noticed, it's not a fashion statement. It's really more. . . I guess the only way to say it is--a tribute to a fallen friend and comrade. I was a sophomore when I joined the student paper, and that was the first time I met James Ellison, the senior editor of *The Harvard Crimson.* Not only did he welcome me aboard, but he was really encouraging, and I guess even though he was just two years older, he became kind of a mentor. After graduation, James took a job with *The Washington Post* and in his first overseas assignment as a war correspondent, he was one of the first journalists killed in the early days of the first Gulf War. Ever since then, I kind of took to wearing the same kind of jacket that James could always be seen wearing around campus. So that's it."

"That's really nice," she said, as a faint, but warm smile passed over her lips.

The fact that she was clearly moved by his explanation made Chenault feel even closer to her and he couldn't remember ever wanting to kiss anybody any more than he did at that moment. But he caught himself and snapped out of it, as he kept in mind that Rachel was only along as a temporary assistant, and if he made any sort of grand romantic gesture that went unreciprocated, the remainder of the trip could be quite awkward. Besides, she lived and worked in Salt Lake City and seemed to otherwise be quite content there; she wouldn't be interested in pulling up roots and moving to New York. *Or would she?*

As they ate their meal, Chenault sensed it was probably best to turn the conversation back to their work, rather than trying to recapture the moment from a few minutes earlier when there had been some mutual sparks, since those kind of moments usually just happened rather than were created.

"So while I was camped out there in the back seat, I came across quite a few interesting tidbits about your prophet, or I guess I should say 'your ex-prophet,' and just wondered if you had ever heard about any of them? So apparently, while going back to retrieve the Gold Plates a second time after he lost his first translation, Smith wound up having to wrestle what he later described as a 'frog demon.'"

"No, I'd never heard that," she said with a chuckle. "Although it sounds a little made up."

"Well no, he actually relayed that story several times himself. But speaking strictly just towards Smith's credibility, the one account I came across that really stood out in my mind as being sort of emblematic of the charges made against him over the years, particularly in regards to his alleged translations of the Gold Plates, was that back in Smith's day, it apparently had become all the rage to haul mummies and ancient scrolls back from

Egypt and then tour them around the country. Somebody apparently presented Smith with a set of these old scrolls which he took home and proceeded to translate. You know what the translation became?"

"No, what?"

"*The Book of Abraham*--which although wasn't included in *The Book of Mormon*, it did form part of the church doctrine and was canonized by the Church."

"I never knew that."

"But see, here's the thing though. These same scrolls were later actually translated, and it turned out they were really nothing more than some obscure Egyptian funeral rites. Now that doesn't bode very well for his earlier claims on the original translation of the plates, since it appeared he just kind of made up things as he went along. Speaking of which, I guess you're probably pretty familiar with the story of Smith's discovery and translation of the plates."

"Well, just that as a teen he was supposedly visited by the Angel Moroni who turned the Gold Plates over to him, or at least told him where to find them, and that Smith then later translated them into *The Book of Mormon*. Isn't that about right?"

"I guess that would be the concise Mormon version."

"So what am I leaving out?"

"Well, to slightly reword a line from one of my favorite movies, 'Can you handle the truth?'"

CHAPTER 23

"So let me get the rest of this straight," Rachel said, as Chenault started in on his slice of apple pie the waitress had just set down. "Because some of this stuff I'm familiar with, like that Christ supposedly visited America, and that Moroni was a white Native American angel who told Smith that the native Americans were originally from Jerusalem, and that the bad tribe had wiped out the good tribe in a war, and that God then turned them red as punishment, and those are our current Native Americans. But I'd not heard that before about some skeptics hiding some of the original pages of *The Book of Mormon* to see if Smith could reproduce or exactly re-translate the pages."

"Yeah, and whether he guessed what they were up to or not, he fell back on the explanation that since God was so upset with him for losing the pages, that he wouldn't be allowed to use the Lehi plate again, but would now have to translate from the Nephi plate," Chenault said. "Which would then explain why even though the stories would be similar, the translation wouldn't be exact."

"So kind of like, he was always one step ahead of his skeptics?"

"Well, that's one way to look at it, I guess. But then he really didn't help make his case when the first publication of *The Book of Mormon* came out and he had himself listed as not only the 'author,' but as the 'proprietor,' and it wasn't until later printings that he backtracked and listed himself as just the 'translator.'"

"So, any more shockers?" Rachel said between sips of water.

"Well, let's see. I don't know about shocking, but apparently Smith was tromping around Missouri at some point and came across a pile of stones and announced that the pile was the remains of Adam's altar, and that the Garden of Eden was right there in the middle of Missouri. Now I've been to Missouri, and I mean, it's okay, but it's no Garden of Eden. Also, I believe I recall there was something about his maintaining that Jesus and Lucifer were brothers, and that you can actually become a god yourself and eventually live on the moon or your own planet."

"Yeah, I guess that is pretty crazy. But you know if you really stop and think about it, it's really no crazier than a virgin birth or raising the dead and walking on water. . ."

"Or a talking burning bush or parting the Red

Sea?" Chenault chimed in. "I guess no matter what the religion is or how seemingly outlandish the beliefs or stories are, it all comes down to a simple matter of faith."

"Of course, the craziest has to be Scientology," Rachel said, "who I read the followers believe something along the lines that millions of years ago aliens were dumped off in their space ships into Earth's volcanoes, and then were blown up with hydrogen bombs, and now their evil spirits reside in us."

"Yeah, I'd have to agree--that one pretty much takes the cake. But back to your Latter Day Saints, you know what one of the other things I'm finding is?"

"What's that?" Rachel said.

"Well, there are a ton of anti-Mormon sites on the internet. A few of them, as you might expect, have been put up by Southern Baptists and the like, who mostly preach that *The Book of Mormon* and the Mormon religion are a perversion of Christianity and therefore an abomination in the eyes of God. But what I'm finding, though, is that most of these sites have been put up by ex-Mormons, who by far appear to be the most critical--almost all from their own personal experience. Their accusations against the Church include everything from covering up widespread molestation, to using extortion, to being a brainwashing cult. A number of the sites also have to do with support groups for recovering Mormons, or those who are thinking about leaving.

You know, you don't really have too much of that kind of thing with Presbyterians and Methodists. It really does just make you wonder what all goes on inside that Church. Is there anything you can reveal or shed some light on? Why exactly did you leave?"

"Truthfully, I'd rather not go into it--at least not now. It was a very personal and painful choice and one I'd really rather not relive on the spur of the moment at a truck stop. Maybe one day."

"I'm sorry. I shouldn't have asked."

"Don't apologize. You didn't know. And I'm sorry I snapped at you. . . Maybe one day when I'm feeling up to it I'll tell you."

"I won't bring it up again," Chenault said, imagining the painful memories that he had probably dredged up. "And also, I know I can sometimes come across as a bit of a know-it-all, so if I ever start prattling on about something that you really don't have any interest in, please just let me know."

"Too late," Rachel said.

"I'm sorry. I guess that's just the curse of the Ivy Leaguer--this compulsive need to try to enlighten the. . ."

"I was just kidding," she said with a sly smile.

"I knew that," Chenault said with a mock straight face.

"Sure you did, Harvard boy. Sure you did."

CHAPTER 24

From high up on a red rock mesa, Cloyd Lamott centered the crosshairs of his telescopic sight squarely on the back of Chenault's head as he stepped out of the truck stop café. The scope he peered through was securely mounted on his newly purchased .300 Winchester Magnum, a high powered rifle capable of dropping a 700-pound elk in its tracks from five hundred yards away. At the three hundred yards distance he estimated himself to be, it would be very much like shooting a fish in a barrel. At present, however, he was only sighting in his future intended target, waiting for the word to be given that the sacred relic had at last been found so that he could finally drop the meddling Gentile outsider in his tracks. Gently squeezing the trigger, Lamott fired off an imaginary round as he imagined the man's head exploding from the impact.

Earlier in the day, Lamott had been pleasantly surprised when he found himself traveling due south, headed towards the very place he knew as home and still thought of as his sanctuary. And even though he and his brother had left Hildale as outcasts, he knew in his heart that one day, after they had helped The Prophet accomplish the divine mission he had set out before them, they would return and be welcomed as the twin town's favorite sons.

After having been spotted by the reporter back in Salt Lake City, Lamott had rented an all-wheel drive Bronco with the prepaid credit card he'd been sent by FedEx a week earlier. It was the same card he'd also used to purchase the scope and rifle, along with a GPS tracking device that he had attached beneath the rear bumper of the man's rental car the night before. This time, however, Lamott made sure to stay far enough behind so that the car the reporter and the woman were in was nothing but a tiny speck on the horizon ahead of him. He would not make the same mistakes this time. In fact, he still couldn't believe what a fool he had been to look directly at the man earlier that day and then further acknowledge him by stupidly gesturing at him. If he had only just kept looking straight ahead and ignored him for the moment, he wouldn't have to play this long distance game of cat and mouse. His preference had always been to be close in for a kill, gutting his quarry first when he could with the jagged blade of his hunting knife, and then slitting his victim's throat. He and his brother Delmer had killed a number of times before, all necessary, as explained by his Uncle Hyrum, to not only cleanse the community, but to keep down the population of young men who wouldn't stay away after having been excommunicated and run out of town. He and his brother had then buried them in shallow, unmarked graves strewn across the desert outside Hildale, where they were now all but forgotten.

Their uncle had explained to them not only the importance of keeping the male population down-- so that there would be more wives for those deserving few--but that everyone of the young men it had become necessary to dispose of had shown some proclivity for worldly perversions. And since their behavior had been a clear indication that they questioned their faith, Blood Atonement was therefore the only way to save their immortal souls. And even though the Christian *Bible* clearly stated in one of its passages that "Thou shalt not kill," as it had been explained to Lamott and his brother, that for an enlightened few, when carried out in the service of the Lord, to either protect the faith or bring lost souls back into the fold, that to lie, to steal, and even to kill were at times permissible. And since God's laws took precedence over the laws of man, as both The Prophet and his Uncle Hyrum had explained, it was very clear to Lamott that killing the Gentile was in the service of the Lord. Not only that, but justified retribution for the man's hatred of their faith which he had so clearly demonstrated by not only his slanderous attacks, but by his unbridled greed. Just the sheer folly of his seeking what would surely be the Church's greatest treasure for a few pieces of gold was such an affront that surely death was too good for him.

Lamott also had to admit to himself that the other reason he so looked forward to snuffing out the life of the Gentile, was that he would be eliminating the one person who appeared to be his competition for the hand of the young woman whom he found himself becoming increasingly attracted to. This was just an even further sign that this union was sanctioned from above. In his conversation earlier that day with The Prophet, he had even requested that he be allowed to let the woman live so that he could later take her as his first wife. After careful deliberation, The Prophet had consented and granted permission to let her live, provided that all went as planned, and then as a reward for Lamott's devotion to their cause, promised the woman to him as the first of his many wives.

The one other concern that had been weighing heavily on Lamott had been leaving his brother behind in the motel with the young Ratchford girl. Partly, because all of their lives, he and his brother had been virtually inseparable, but even more so because of his concern for his brother's past inability to control his desire for young females. And since The Prophet seemed to know just about everything about them, this meant that he could probably see into their hearts as well, which was most likely why he had issued the dire warning of what would happen to them if the young girl was so much as even touched. Maybe after some time had passed, The Prophet would eventually change his mind and consent to let his brother take the girl as his bride. Perhaps they could all even live together in the same house at first, until they started having more and more children. Then after that, after they had proved their desirability as husbands and fathers, even more women would eventually accept their invitation into celestial marriages with them. It was all finally going to happen for them, just as they had been promised.

CHAPTER 25

When they pulled into Hildale, Utah that evening, the sun had already been down for several hours. The illumination from the nearly full moon was enough, however, to reveal what Chenault had come across in some of his earlier research that Hildale was a dilapidated little desert town that had seen its better days a half a century earlier. Many of the few remaining small buildings that had once been businesses were now boarded up, and most of the streets were unpaved. If there were ever a more fitting description of Hildale than "a ghost town with people living in it," as it had been described in one of Chenault's travel guides, he couldn't think of it.

Hildale, along with Colorado City, located just across the state line in northern Arizona, were situated along a desolate stretch of highway, nestled at the foot of several towering, red sandstone formations. Both towns seemed to have materialized out of the ether, springing up out of the chalky, rust colored desert. As was the intention of the two founders almost one hundred years earlier, the locations were so remote that they, their followers, and their progeny would be able to continue the practice of polygamy out of the glare of any public scrutiny.

Further research by Chenault revealed the disturbing fact that most everybody in the two small towns were related to either one or both of the towns' two founding fathers. As a result, there was an extremely high rate of a rare genetic disorder that caused severe mental retardation, which was the sad result of too shallow a gene pool brought about by the many intermarriages that had taken place between closely related cousins. As for the institution of marriage, placement marriages had become so commonplace that teenage girls had come to be referred to as "poofers" in the community. One day they were living out their lives, living with their families and attending school, and then "poof," the next day they were gone, married off with little or no advanced notification and moved into their new, often much older husbands' households. It struck Chenault that the girls really were not so much child brides as they were indentured servants, and in some of the more reprehensible cases he'd heard and read about, little more than sex slaves.

The lot for many of the young men was just as bad in some cases, and unimaginably, worse for others. Since there were too few brides for the young men in the town, there became an oversupply, and the solution had been to ship a number of them off to like-minded colonies in either Mexico or Canada. Others were sent elsewhere to work for polygamist-owned businesses with their paychecks going directly back to the church--that was for the lucky ones. Those not so lucky were simply run out of town or dumped off on the streets of Salt Lake City to fend for themselves. Many of these "Lost Boys," as the media had come to refer to them, resorted first to drugs, and then later to prostitution just to stay alive.

While looking for a place to stay that night, the only thing Chenault found still in operation was a rundown eight-unit motel, somewhat ironically named "The Buena Vista." The ramshackle motor inn appeared to be just as down on its luck as the rest of the town, with peeling paint visible on just about every surface, and the doors and windows boarded up on several of the rooms. The only good news was that with only two other cars in the parking lot, there appeared to be plenty of vacancies.

After checking in and going to their separate rooms, Chenault read Koplanski's book for an hour and a half before crawling into bed. As he lay there under the musty sheets, he pondered a number of the other odd things he'd come across as he gazed up at the dark orangish blotches on the room's water-stained ceiling. Like, how had Mormons come to believe that Gentiles, or anyone else who wasn't a Latter Day Saint, were literally devils? Was that perhaps a part of their fairly well known persecution complex, which was mostly a holdover from the days when they really had been unmercifully persecuted some 150 years earlier?

And how was it that even though the Church had proclaimed that the practice of polygamy was to be abandoned, that the custom had survived over 100 years later. It had not only survived, but, in fact, had thrived within certain fringe groups, and even appeared to have been tacitly condoned by the current Mormon powers that be, who showed not just a casual indifference to it, but had failed to prosecute anybody in the state of Utah for its practice in years. Several state officials had even gone as far as publicly defending the practice in statements decrying that it was a violation of their Constitutional rights to practice their religion as they saw fit. Perhaps then, the polygamy ban a hundred years earlier had really been nothing more than part of a public relations strategy to move them into the mainstream of American society. The bottom line was that what was portrayed as the public face and what really went on behind the scenes Chenault was finding, were often completely divergent. And as he had learned over the years from something his father had once said, "If you really want to know someone, don't just listen to what he says--watch what he does."

CHAPTER 26

The next morning Chenault was awakened by the pitiful wheezing of a vehicle in the motel's parking lot as its driver made one futile attempt after another to start it. Each attempt became shorter and fainter than the last, and each high pitched, drawn out wheeze was followed by a sad sputtering and then silence. Normally, a minor annoyance like that wouldn't have bothered Chenault in the least, and back in the West Village would have merely been drowned out by the din of a thousand other city sounds. In the quiet stillness of Hildale, however, where it was otherwise virtually silent, the lone sound from the single vehicle began to grate on him like grinding of a dentist's drill.

After several minutes of this, Chenault decided to finally peek out his window and see whom the persistent person or persons were who could not, or would not accept the fact their vehicle simply was not going to start. Pulling the curtain aside a few inches, he glanced out to the parking lot to see what he and his friends growing up in New Orleans would have referred to as a "beater"--an ancient, rusted-out, moss green sedan with the hood and passenger side door painted with a dull gray primer. Unable to make the driver out, Chenault closed the curtain and headed back to the bathroom to begin his morning routine.

Shortly after cutting the shower on, he heard a knocking at the door, and presuming it to be Rachel, wrapped a towel around his waist and stepped out of the bathroom. Upon opening the door, he found himself face to face with a big rawboned man, whom Chenault guessed to be in his late forties, dressed in a tee shirt, denim jacket, and brown work overhauls, and peering out through pale blue eyes from under a faded John Deere cap. His face was deeply lined and weather-burned, and the contrast made the shaggy, dirty blond hair spilling out from his cap appear almost golden.

". . .Can I help you?" Chenault finally managed to get out, feeling somewhat awkward standing there half naked in front of a total stranger.

"Yeah, as matter of fact. You think you could give me a jump?" the man said.

The question caught Chenault slightly off guard, much like the man's appearance at his door, but after processing it in his half awakened state, he finally replied, ". . .You got jumper cables?"

"As a matter of fact, I do."

The man's name was Rulen Sparks, a local man who, although he didn't go into much detail, was apparently a bit down on his luck. After giving him a jump following a brief exchange, Chenault accepted Spark's invitation to join him at the one remaining diner in town for breakfast, figuring that he might just turn out to be a potential source.

Before heading out, he lightly rapped on Rachel's door just in case she was still asleep. A few seconds later, the door opened and Rachel, already showered and dressed, stepped into the doorway looking quite refreshed despite her equally depressing and dingy room.

"Good morning. How'd you sleep?" she asked.

"Well, it wasn't exactly the Ritz-Carleton, but luckily, once I shut my eyes I'm usually down like a log. I'm going to join my new friend over there for breakfast and see if he has any interesting tidbits he might be willing to share, and wanted to see if you'd care join us."

Rachel grimaced slightly. "I'm actually feeling a little bit queasy--maybe the aftereffects of our truck stop cuisine--so I think I'll take a pass. I'll just wait here for you until you get back."

"Alright," Chenault said, trying to hide his minor dismay that she didn't want to at least come along. "I'll leave you the keys in case you change your mind or get to feeling better."

On the ride over to the diner, the dusty, red dirt streets and several ramshackle buildings that comprised the town of Hildale turned out to be an even bleaker scene than Chenault had envisioned from the night before. Why anybody would possibly live there of their own choosing was beyond Chenault, but assuming Sparks was likely a lifetime resident of the sad little community, he kept the question to himself.

"Something just occurred to me," Chenault said. "Won't we probably need to get another jump when we get ready to head back?"

"Old Bessie usually don't need but one jump a day, and she can sometimes even go two or three days without needing a new charge."

Despite Spark's assurances, after seeing how long it took the '78 Cutlass to start even after being jumped, Chenault was glad he'd left the keys with Rachel, because he could already foresee having to ring her up in an hour or so for a ride back.

Passing several of the townspeople along the way, Chenault felt almost as if he had stepped back in time. Most of the locals making their way along the dusty dirt streets appeared to be dressed in 19th Century prairie garb, and looked more like extras from an episode of *Little House on the Prairie* than citizens of the 21st Century. The women and young girls were all in long prairie dresses and white cloth bonnets, while a few let their long braided hair spill down their backs. The men and boys were dressed just as modestly, most in long dark pants and starched buttoned-up shirts, with a few in matching dark jackets. Chenault had also heard the tales of some of the more devout Mormons wearing sacred, some even said "magical" underwear underneath their clothing, and for some odd reason that fleeting thought wound through his mind.

After getting out of the car to cross the street to the diner, Chenault noticed that the few pedestrians around seemed to go out of their way to avoid walking anywhere near him. Some even actually appeared to cross to the other side of the street just to avoid having to walk by or make eye contact.

"Yikes. What's that all about? I take it they're not too fond of out-of-towners?"

"Actually, they're not. But it's not you they're avoiding--it's me. See, I'm being shunned."

CHAPTER 27

"I understand if you don't want to talk about it," Chenault said.

"Oh no, I don't care if the whole world knows about it. In fact, you say you're a newspaper reporter--you ought to write something about it; like how my whole life's been pretty much taken away from me, 'cause I stood up to some fake little prophet after I saw him for what he really was."

Just then a husky man wearing a white apron stepped out from behind the counter and set a menu and a glass of water down in front of Chenault and walked away without saying a word. Chenault started to say something about the man's appearing to ignore Sparks, but Sparks shook his head not to say anything. It struck Chenault that the place wouldn't last a week back in New York, or anywhere for that matter, with its abysmal customer service. Not to mention, it was completely devoid of any atmosphere, aside from several yellowing fly strips littered with dead bugs hanging from the ceiling, and a framed portrait of an apparently glowing Joseph Smith hanging on the cheap plywood paneling lining the room.

After the man was out of earshot, Sparks leaned in and said under his breath, "That's my cousin, Levi. Just play along. Order two of whatever you're having, and I'll pay you when we get back outside. That way he can maintain he still shunned me if anybody takes notice." He then subtly gestured with his head in the direction of a young couple sitting two tables away from them.

"But he still won't talk to you?" Chenault said, as it occurred to him that if Sparks was telling the truth, then the more likely reason Sparks had invited him along was not so much a friendly gesture or show of hospitality, but that he needed to find someone who could order his breakfast for him.

Sparks shook his head. ". . .That's the whole deal. I've been excommunicated. I'm supposedly an 'Apostate' now. Even though I been a dedicated Mormon all my entire life, that sawed-off little so and so trumped up some charges against me after I got on his bad side about a year back, and it was right then I realized he wasn't speaking for God. He was just a mean, little old man who let his position go to his head. And now he's took my house, and is reassigning my wives to new husbands along with all our children."

"That's insane," Chenault exclaimed in disbelief.

"Maybe in your world, but not here."

"And there's nothing you can do about it?"

"I can stand up to him--I already have. But I can't stand up to the whole town who follows him like sheep. Rules is still rules that me and mine have to abide by."

"But I don't understand. How can he just kick you out of your own house?"

". . .I built the house with my own hands, along with the help of a lot of family and now former friends--everybody pitched in. But like most everything else around here, it was built on church-owned land. But you don't think nothing' about that when you're building it. You don't think that anything could ever go wrong. You just think that since you're a part of the church family, you're just getting a free piece of land to build on. But that's when they got you, and that's when the intimidation really starts as far as keeping people in line. And every once in a while, they make an example of somebody to show everybody else what can happen--how you really can lose your home, your family, your friends--your life, if you just get a little out of line. And this time they picked me."

Chenault placed his double order and they continued to chat during the course of the meal as he tried to feel Sparks out a little more before getting to the more pressing questions that he had regarding Brockston Ratchford's origins. About halfway through breakfast, Chenault noticed that the young couple who had not uttered a word the entire time they were there, suddenly got up, tossed some cash on the table, and after exiting, took off briskly down the street. Since he wasn't sure if their behavior was odd, or perhaps completely normal in Hildale, and not wanting to give Sparks any cause for concern, he said nothing.

Perhaps out of concern for his own welfare, and uncertainty about Chenault's motives, Sparks began to ramble, relaying mostly bits of unimportant or irrelevant hearsay about the goings on around town, and never quite getting to his point. Throughout it all, though, Chenault sensed Sparks was feeling him out, deciding whether or not he could be trusted. After a while, however, Sparks began to recall some of the better times before his expulsion, reminiscing over his eleven children and his two good wives, and a third wife, whom over time he had grown less and less fond of.

Chenault realized that Sparks probably didn't get to talk to very many people, and after having been betrayed and abandoned by his own church, family, and lifelong friends, he probably trusted no one. Yet despite Spark's recent misfortune that would have devastated most people in similar circumstances, there still seemed to be a glimmer of hope that shone through his weather-beaten exterior. He also observed that despite Spark's bad grammar and somewhat limited vocabulary, likely the result of a very limited formal education, it belied an intelligence of a much wiser man than his words revealed. After a while, as Sparks began to open up about a number of more important things, Chenault decided that it was now finally time to ask his first real question.

"So did you ever hear anything about Senator Ratchford growing up around here?

"Yeah, Brock Ratchford was from around here--though he didn't go by that name back then. Most people don't know that--he was a Stepp then."

"By here, you mean in Hildale?"

"Yep, right down the street. He grew up in that big house a couple blocks down--the one with the green trim and shutters. His father, Elijah, was the spiritual leader of the town at the time."

"Spiritual leader? What--like the minister?"

"Mister, the Church don't have ministers, they have prophets. In fact, he was something like, what some outsiders might consider something along the lines of the Pope. He was the only one around here who supposedly had direct communication with. . ." He then gestured upward with his raised thumb. "They got the same setup in Salt Lake, only on a lot grander scale as you might imagine."

"And he ran everything?"

"With an iron hand I heard. Just like that little so and so who trumped up charges against me."

"Again, I'm very sorry. Have you ever thought about maybe just moving away from here?"

"Now why didn't I think of that? And where am I gonna move? Everything I ever owned, everyone I've ever known and loved, is all right here. The so called life I'm living now. . .I might as well be a dead man--or a ghost--that's about the way they treat me."

"Don't say that."

"Oh, don't worry. I ain't going to kill myself. That would give 'em too much satisfaction. You know, get excommunicated and you wind up killin' yourself. They'd love that. . .Was there anything else you wanted to know?"

"Did you ever hear about anything that might have distinguished Ratchford while he was here, something out of the ordinary?"

"What do you mean? Like that supposedly he had 'the gift.'"

Even though it sounded a bit hokey, Chenault had to bite. "The gift of what?"

"The gift of foresight. He could supposedly tell what was going to happen before it actually did."

"Well, it didn't seem to help him too much in the beginning when he set out to build his financial empire," Chenault said.

"Mister, it wasn't about that. Manna--that's a fool's proposition."

"Then what was it about?"

Sparks paused for a moment, deliberating whether or not to share the next piece of information. ". . .They say. . .they say that he foresaw himself as the President one day. In fact, it wasn't much talked about, but it was even said that he claimed as a boy that he had a vision that the Angel Moroni visited him and told him that the spirit of the prophet lived on in him."

"The prophet?"

"Joe Smith. And that it was his place in history to succeed where Smith had failed."

"And where did Joseph Smith fail?"

"When he ran for President."

"Joseph Smith ran for President?"

"Read your history books--it's right there. And hell, what's so spectacular about that? Didn't that one feller who owned the religious TV network and a couple of them Black fellers who said they were ministers run for President?"

"Yeah, but they didn't start an entire new religion."

"Well, that's their problem now isn't it?"

"Yeah, I guess it is," Chenault said, smiling at the little injection of levity. "Was there anything else he had in this vision, other than that he was to be President one day."

"Oh yeah--that he would be the one to save us all from a moral and economic collapse, as well as the one to finally unite the country under the one true faith, just as Joe Smith originally set out to do. O' course, that's all just part of what they call "The

White Horse Prophecy," which has been around for years, and which I see it for what it is now--just a lot of hooey. But o' course, you know what happens if enough people believe in somethin'?"

"No, what's that?"

"They make it true. You ask any of the true believers around here, and they'll tell you, Brockston Ratchford is Joseph Smith incarnate."

"What about other Mormons? In Utah and elsewhere?"

"Let's just put it this way, if they don't believe it, they're not telling anyone. And for that matter, if they do believe it, they're not telling anyone, at least when it comes to outsiders. We're real good at keepin' secrets. We Mormons have a long history of what we call the 'wall of silence.' It wasn't no Italian mafia that invented that. Whether it's Church secrets or something like this, they won't talk about it with any outsiders. In fact, they got oaths of death for such things. You spill the beans, and you've taken a vow to die."

"Yeah, but I think the Freemasons have similar oaths of having their tongues and eyes plucked out and their entrails ripped from their body."

"The difference is, though, Mormons take it serious."

"And you're not afraid of telling me some of these things now?"

"Well hell, I figure since I'm shunned and excommunicated, I ain't a Mormon no more, so I really don't give a damn."

They wrapped up the conversation by Sparks answering several of Chenault's earlier questions, like explaining how he and the other husbands provided for their large families in a town with few jobs. It turned out it was simply through the well-honed practice of welfare fraud, which they referred to as "bleeding the beast." The practice consisted of a husband legally marrying only one of his wives, while the rest were just spiritual unions and therefore not legally recognized. This then enabled those women, referred to as "sister wives," and their children to take full advantage of the numerous state and federal programs like Food stamps, welfare, and Medicaid, all the while, of course, sharing the monthly checks with their husbands. There was even one reported case of a family that had taken in over a million dollars in a ten year span, an anecdote that Sparks actually seemed to take some pride in telling. The other dirty little secret he revealed was that the practice of polygamy was likely much more widespread than just the confines of their two small towns.

"You think we're the only polygamists in this state, the only ones who follow the old ways? We're just the only ones who are proud of it and are visible to the public, even though we're tucked away in this godforsaken armpit in the corner of the state. But I bet you there are far more members of the so-called mainline church who just keep it secret, who keep their second or third wife hid away like a mistress. I mean, why do you think that the state of Utah hasn't prosecuted anybody in, hell, forever? It's like what the Army's got with them homosexuals--it's basically 'don't ask, don't tell.'"

And if it were true, that actually wasn't a bad analogy Chenault thought, as he got up from his chair and tossed fifteen dollars on the table to cover their tab. As Sparks went over to the front counter to grab some toothpicks, Chenault stepped out of the diner and immediately caught something out of the corner of his eye. Looking down the street to his right, he saw a rather sizable procession of townspeople making their way up the middle of the street and moving briskly towards him.

"We need to get out of here," Sparks said, as he came out the door.

They moved quickly across the street and hopped in his car, but when he turned the key, the only sound that it made was a faint and very brief, high-pitched metallic whine from the engine and then silence. Chenault and Sparks looked at each other for a brief moment and then climbed out of the vehicle to face the grim-faced mob. Leading the procession was a small, wiry old man with a puckered face, spider-webbed with fine wrinkles, who was dressed in an almost formfitting dark suit, starched white shirt, and a black bolo ribbon tie, which completed his 19th Century ensemble. About five feet away from reaching Sparks and Chenault, the old man came to a halt and the rest of his entourage, including the young couple from the diner, followed suit.

Despite being physically unimposing, an intensity burned in the old man's eyes that spoke to the fact that he believed he was not a man to be trifled with as he eyed Chenault for several moments, sizing him up, before finally saying, ". . .What business do you have in our town?"

"The last I checked this was a free country, and I don't have to seek permission or explain myself to anybody."

"See, that's where you're wrong, mister. The church owns most of the property in this town, including right where you're standing, and I run the church. So if I took a liking, I could say you two were trespassers, and if I wanted to, I could even have the sheriff arrest you or run you out of town. Isn't that right, sheriff?"

A chunky man in a beige uniform stepped out from the mob. "That's right."

"So that's the way you want to play it?" Chenault said.

"Son, we're not playin' here. I'm deadly serious," the old man said.

"I think you misunderstand me. That's just an expression. . .back where I come from." Chenault looked to the sheriff. "Do you not have any laws here, like in the rest of America, that protect people who are just minding their own business, like myself and my friend here?"

The sheriff started to speak, but the old man cut him off. "This is not America here. This is God's land, and we operate under God's laws--and here I

say what those are. You are a Gentile and an
agitator, and the more you talk, the less inclined I
become to show you any leniency since you are
clearly ignorant of our laws and our ways here.
Sheriff, I'm thinking seriously about. . ."

At that moment the old man went silent as the
roar of a car engine racing up the street from behind
Chenault grew increasingly louder as it drew
towards them. Just as the old man was pulled back
to safety by several of his flock, the silver Volvo
that had been barreling towards them screeched to a
halt in a cloud of dust.

"Hop in!" Rachel said, as she leaned over from
behind the wheel.

CHAPTER 28

Following Rachel's lead, they jumped in and shut the doors. They then proceeded to slowly but steadily make their way through the crowd, parting the mass of angry onlookers who reluctantly, but eventually, stepped aside. They appeared to be almost home free until a scowling young man stepped forward and smacked the car's hood hard with his hand. With that act of defiance, the rest of the mob then transformed into an angry gauntlet and everyone else soon followed, loudly hitting and kicking the car, and slapping the windows and windshield with a cacophony of blows. Just as they managed to reach the edge of the mob and began to pull away, they heard a hard crash as a rock bounced off the rear window, leaving an ugly spider web crack.

"Guess it's a good thing I got the insurance," Chenault said.

"What happened back there?" Rachel asked as

she gunned the engine and sped away.

"I honestly don't know," Chenault said. "One minute we're having breakfast and the next minute we're on Hildale's most wanted list. . .Thanks for getting us out of there."

"Don't mention it."

"It's all because you were talking to me," Sparks said from the backseat.

"And probably the fact that I'm an outsider," Chenault added. "That's a hell of a town you got there."

"And the sad part is, a year ago I probably would have been part of that bunch."

"And who was that guy anyway--the old man?" Chenault said.

"That Mister, was Hyrum Lamott. He's the one I was telling you about."

On the drive back to the motel, it occurred to Chenault that some of the information he'd just been given about Ratchford back at the diner, he probably could have gotten from no other place--or no one else in the world for that matter. And despite the fact that he occasionally even referred to himself as a "lapsed Catholic," and had never been particularly religious, in that moment, it really did seem more than just a stroke of luck that the one man in Hildale who would ever reveal some of Ratchford's dirty little secrets, literally came knocking at his door.

"Thanks," he said, looking back towards Sparks in the back seat.

"For what?"

"Just for opening up the way you did. You told me some things I probably couldn't have gotten from anybody else, even if I'd stayed here for a month."

"Well, I'll just warn you, Mister. I don't know exactly what you're looking for, but you need to be real careful about where you go poking around, asking questions about such things."

"And why's that?"

"I take it you never heard of the Danites?"

"No," Chenault said a bit dismissively.

"Well let me educate you real quick then, because it's not a matter to be taken lightly. The Danites, or the 'Armies of Israel' as they were also known, were a secret society that was originally formed by Joseph Smith himself back when he was still in Missouri. They started out as his bodyguards, but then became vigilante assassins and carried out the bidding of those in power in the Church, and eliminated any enemies the Mormons had, sometimes even killing Apostates who'd left the Church."

"Just curious, but do you know how they supposedly killed most of their victims?"

"By 'Blood Atonement.' They'd slit their throats like cattle."

"And by Blood Atonement, they could supposedly give their victims eternal salvation, is that right?" Chenault asked.

"Yeah, as a matter of fact, it is. But how'd you

know that?"

"Just a lucky guess, and the fact I know of two Mormons--well one was an ex-Mormon--who died exactly that way in the last week," Chenault said as they pulled into the motel parking lot. As soon as he said it, he instantly regretted sharing the last bit of information with Sparks.

". . .I never really wanted to believe the stories were true, but I guess you just confirmed it."

"It's probably just coincidence," Chenault said, as Sparks opened his door and got out.

Sparks leaned down and looked Chenault directly in the eye through the open window. "Mister, you and I both know that's not the case," he said, his voice weakly trailing off, as he then started towards his motel room.

After Sparks was out of earshot, Chenault looked over to Rachel. "I didn't want to say anything in front of him, but a couple of the folks in that crowd back there were clearly the byproduct of too shallow a gene pool."

"How do you mean?"

"I mean, I kind of feel bad pointing this out, but a few of them made that banjo playing kid from *Deliverance* look like a member of the Mensa Society."

"So you're implying that inbreeding appears to be the favorite past time around here?"

"Well, I don't know about that, but. . ."

"It's okay," Rachel said, cutting him off. "It's just when you're brought up in a religion and you can actually get a pretty fair picture of the way it was probably practiced just a hundred years ago, it kind of makes you think."

"I can imagine. Not to change the subject, but. . .even though we've been here less than a day, I think it's pretty clear we've already overstayed our welcome, and I think I've probably found out about as much as I'm going to. So probably, I'm thinking, we ought to head over to Colorado City and see if there's anything else we can dig up there, and then get the hell out of here. How does that sound?"

"Sounds like a plan," Rachel said with faint smile, along with what appeared to be a slight look of relief.

On their way out of town, they drove Sparks back to his car, only to find that "Old Bessie" had had just about every piece of glass smashed out of its windows, windshield, and headlights. After scraping the broken glass chunks from the driver's seat, Sparks connected the jumper cables and sure enough, the car started right up.

"You sure you're going to be alright?" Chenault said.

"Yeah, I'll be fine. After you leave, they'll just go back to what they was doing before--pretending like I don't exist. I'm used to it by now."

On the short drive over the Arizona state line to Colorado City, Rachel asked, "So what'd you find out from Sparks?"

"Well, let's see, along with some more

background on Ratchford's family, like that his father once held the same position that Hyrum Lamott now seems to hold--spiritual dictator over the town, that ol' Brockston apparently believes he has this special gift where he can foretell the future. And that right there might explain why everybody and their brother were investing their money with him. That, along with that he supposedly claimed Moroni visited him as a boy and that not only did he see himself as the successor to Joseph Smith, but that he foretold he would be elected President one day to save the country. The part that's even scarier than his delusions of grandeur are that apparently, according to Sparks, quite a few others--and not just in Hildale-- have bought into it. So have you ever heard about any of this stuff?"

Rachel rolled her eyes. "If you ask me, I'd say that's probably more just wishful thinking on the part of the locals here. It probably makes them feel more important about themselves that one of their own is running for President. I'd say I was in the Church long enough to know or have heard about any such ridiculous things. I mean, think about it. How crazy does that sound--that the entire Mormon nation is secretly conspiring to get this guy elected no matter what? I can hardly stand most of them now, and even I don't buy into that."

"I don't know," Chenault said. "The way he told it, it wasn't like he believed it--in fact, he was kind of skeptical. It was more like he was just relaying what he had heard over the years."

"My advice would just be, whatever you take out of here, take it with an extremely large grain of salt and don't use it is as a primary source. These people are so isolated and out of contact with the rest of the world here, there's really no telling what they think the rest of the world believes, or where they come up with some of their crazy ideas--that's all I'm saying."

Chenault cocked his head to the side for a moment as he thought about what were likely sage words of advice. "You're probably right. I just still got the feeling, though, that Sparks wasn't just making this stuff up off the top of his head."

"You sure about that?" Rachel said.

"But for what purpose would he make it up?"

"Did you happen to give him any money or anything?"

"Yeah, I picked up his breakfast and gave him a few bucks, but it wasn't for his story--it was just to help him out. I mean, he certainly never asked for anything."

"Maybe he just felt he needed to give you something he thought you could use to pay you back, even if he had to make it up."

God I hope not, Chenault thought. *That's all I need is to be accused by Ratchford of letting facts get in the way of a good story.*

The rest of the day in Colorado City proved to be fruitless, as it appeared the word had preceded them that a couple of outsiders were nosing around asking questions. Chenault soon found that he literally couldn't even get the time of day, when as a lead in, he would hold up and point to his wrist, and ask whoever happened to be passing by if they had the time. He had hoped that this old trick might lead into a conversation, but of the twenty or so people he asked, not a one would respond.

Driving back through Hildale the next day on their way back to Salt Lake City, they noticed a crowd of people standing outside a large home up ahead. As they drew closer, it appeared the townspeople were all looking up at something on the home's wraparound porch, but which was too shaded for Chenault to make anything out.

"Slow up, if you don't mind. See what's going on over there?" Chenault said, as they slowed to a crawl. At first, the attraction that had drawn the crowd appeared to be a man swinging from one arm from a beam under the porch roof, but as they slowly drew closer, they saw a mop of dirty blond hair from the back, and then the purple, bloated face of Rulen Sparks as he hung by his neck from a twisted bed sheet.

"No!" Chenault cried out. "Stop the car!"

Chenault raced through the crowd, pushing people aside as he bounded up the porch stairs and grabbed Sparks just below the waist. "Somebody cut him down!" Chenault pleaded, as he struggled to hold up the deadweight of Spark's swaying body, but nobody moved to lift a finger. As it slowly sunk in that the body was not only completely lifeless, but already partially stiff from the rigor mortis that had set in, he slowly lowered Sparks' body and released it. Seeing Hyrum Lamott standing in the front of the crowd, Chenault stormed down the stairs towards him, only to be blocked by three men who stepped in front of him.

"You did this," Chenault said, looking past one of the bodyguards directly at Lamott.

"How could I? I'm just a frail old man," he said with the hint of a smile.

"Whether you had this done or you drove him to it, you as good as murdered him."

"Now I don't think that would even hold up in your court of law," Lamott said.

For a moment, Chenault was at a loss for words. ". . .You people disgust me."

"We'll just have to live with that," the old man said with a twisted smile. "Now why don't you just hop back in your car with your pretty lady friend and skeddaddle on out of here? And don't worry--we'll dispose of the trash."

The words Chenault wanted to say, and the things he wanted to do to Hyrum Lamott at that moment would have all been for naught, and as he moved back through the crowd, he tried to look directly into the eyes of whoever was in his way to convey his utter contempt, but no one would look up or over to meet his gaze. As he got back in the car, he looked over to see two women standing back from the crowd, each with several children clutching at their dresses, and all of them with tears streaming down their faces. Chenault gestured towards them with a subtle glance to catch Rachel's attention.

". . .If only Sparks could have known how much he was still loved," Rachel said, more trying to console Chenault who was clearly taking Sparks' death very personally as he just sat there shaking his head in disbelief.

After several moments contemplating Rachel's remark, Chenault finally replied, ". . .But then maybe that's what drove him to it--if he did do it--because he knew he'd never have what he had with his family ever again."

Little else was said after that on the long and somber drive back to Salt Lake City.

CHAPTER 29

Shortly after reaching the outskirts of Salt Lake City that evening, they were greeted by the beacon-like glow reflected off the gleaming, majestic LDS Temple illuminated ahead in the distance. Chenault, who'd elected to drive most of the way, barely said a word the entire way back, but was finally driven to break the silence with one of the several questions that had been weighing on him since they'd left Hildale.

"You think there's anything to that Danite story Sparks was going on about?"

"Not really. The Danites may have once existed, but now they're nothing more than just a boogeyman story some parents tell their kids to get them to clean their rooms."

"You don't think that it's more than just coincidental that the day after he tells me about them, he winds up dead?"

"Not to be coldhearted or insensitive about it," Rachel said, "But it's actually not that uncommon for some people who have basically lived and breathed the Church their entire lives, and then get excommunicated, to take their own life. Their life as they knew it is essentially over. They have no more friends or family--or a business or job in some cases. They're basically thrown out into the world with nothing, and a lot of them just can't cope or see their way to starting over."

"But see that's the thing--he told me just the day before he had no intention of killing himself, almost more out of spite than anything else, because he said it would give them even more power to lord over all the terrified sheep in that town."

"So you're saying you think he was murdered?"

"Well, there'd probably be no way I could prove it in that twisted little town, but I imagine if I made a few calls to the right people, the Feds could swoop in and probably get to the bottom of whatever the hell's going on there. I mean where do I start? Child brides and statutory rape? Incest?

Welfare fraud? Corrupt law enforcement? Rampant polygamy, all topped off with a possible murder?"

"You know they actually tried that once."

"Tried what?" Chenault said.

"Years back, they swept in and took most of the husbands off to jail."

"And what was the end result?"

"Not only did it backfire, but it created all kinds of public sympathy for them, especially after the statewide press portrayed it as the government tearing apart innocent families and attacking their religious beliefs. So now, they're pretty much just left alone."

"That sounds about right," Chenault said, with a look of disdain. "Especially after Waco and Ruby Ridge, and those other massive PR debacles. It seems about the only thing the Feds have the stomach to take on now is something that's either going to be low profile or a slam dunk, and none of the things going on in Hildale would fall into either of those two categories." He peered off into the distance for a few moments. ". . .I just feel like. . .I need to do something more."

Even though he had only spent a couple of hours with Rulen Sparks the previous day, Chenault had come to empathize with Sparks and his sad plight, so much so, that he now felt a palpable loss, and deep down wondered if he somehow wasn't partly responsible for what had happened. He kept trying to tell himself that Sparks was just another source and that bad things sometimes just happen, but somehow that didn't seem to keep Spark's purple, bloated face from haunting him. Chenault had interviewed young Marines before, who on the very next day had been blown to bits, but that was in a war overseas, and unfortunately par for the course. But this was just a man he had met and had breakfast with, a man who if anything was minding his own business, and the more he thought about it, the surer he was that Rulen Sparks had been murdered. And not only that, but that it had been meant to serve as a message to him--to stop poking around into matters that didn't concern him. Why they'd not gone directly after him was likely because his murder would have been a relatively high profile death, which would have brought in an outside investigation, while Spark's staged suicide would just be another anonymous death in an otherwise anonymous town.

In retrospect, he was now doubly glad that he and Rachel had left that alien world behind, where things not only didn't make sense, but where somebody else clearly had the upper hand. The most obvious candidate was Hyrum Lamott, but trailing behind in a close second was a man with much more to lose should Chenault decide to continue on the investigative track he was now on-- the junior Senator from the state of Utah, who just happened to be running for President.

When they reached his motel, Chenault drove

down to the underground parking and wound around until he located Rachel's late model, cream colored VW Beetle. As they both retrieved their overnight luggage from the trunk, Rachel looked over to the glum and silent Chenault, who still appeared to be lost in thought.

"It was a real honor getting to work with you these past few days," she said.

Chenault worked up a faint smile. "Likewise. You were a big help--more than you know. If there's anything I can ever do for you--like a reference or something, or if you ever get up to New York, please look me up." He then leaned in and gave her a friendly, but brief kiss on the cheek. "Take care."

Ten minutes later, Chenault was up in his room getting ready for bed when he heard a faint knocking. Since he wasn't expecting anyone and there was no peephole, given recent events, he kept the chain on the door as he opened it part way. There stood Rachel.

"What are you doing here?" he said softly, as he unlocked the chain and opened the door.

"Just earlier, when you were talking about Sparks, and obviously feeling terrible, I just felt like maybe I should have said something--like, it wasn't your fault, if that's what you're feeling."

"Thanks, but. . ."

Rachel then opened her arms and leaned in to Chenault to hold and comfort him, and in return, he held her for all he was worth, feeling like he never wanted to let her go as she pressed her warm body against his and cradled her head to his shoulder. Eventually, he felt her pull back a little and he released his grip from the small of her back, but she pulled only far enough away to look up at him.

"Also, as you've just seen, I'm not real good sometimes at expressing my feelings and. . .if I didn't tell you in these last couple days how I've come to feel about you, I know I'd regret it for the rest of my life. I know I probably haven't shown it much--I guess maybe it's part of my upbringing and all that guilt that was laid on us growing up about the evils of premarital sex and sometimes even just dating. But I really am very attracted to you, and I didn't know if you maybe felt the same way."

Chenault was indeed taken a little aback, because up until that moment he had thought, despite the occasional flirtatious spark that had seemed to exist between them, that Rachel's interest in him was mostly just professional, since none of their flirtations seemed to ever amount to anything else. They seemed just to be simply that--meaningless flirtations.

He definitely could not deny the fact, however, that he found himself very attracted to her, more so than to anybody else for a very long time, but her declaration just seemed so out of the blue that he was taken a little off guard. But then he reminded himself, that despite the fact that she was a beautiful thirty-something-year-old woman, because of her strict upbringing, she probably never really had learned all the little things one does in course of the normal courtship process--the little "accidental" touches, the laughing at the other's bad jokes, the over touching to emphasize a point. In fact, he had almost even felt as if there was an invisible barrier around her, which is why when she had done none of those little things, or had responded to any of his subtle attempts, he had, in turn, kept his distance. But as Rachel dropped her veil, openly sharing her attraction and even her feelings for him, he could no longer hold back, and as he took her in his arms and pressed his lips to hers, an indescribable warmness enveloped his body.

Forty-five minutes later, as Chenault lay back on his pillow and watched several small beads of perspiration drip gently down the side of Rachel's exquisite right breast, it occurred to him, as much as he hated to admit it, that what had just happened between them had seemed somewhat perfunctory, at least on her part. The old adage about "sex being like pizza," popped into his head, *That even when it's bad, it's still pretty good*, didn't quite hold true for Chenault this time. He had wanted it to be earthshaking and amazing, and to bond with her in those special, passionate moments, so that it would leave no doubt that what had just happened between them was destiny. But it was not to be--at least this time.

He tried to tell himself it was probably because of Rachel's self-professed inexperience, but then wondered if there was not a more likely reason.

After having been thrown into circumstances together and dancing around each other for so long, maybe now they were just forcing the moment and trying too hard to make it work. He then heaved a sigh and shook his head, mentally kicking himself for overanalyzing what had just happened. *Just enjoy the moment and see where it goes* he told himself.

"What are you thinking about?" Rachel asked.

Chenault looked over and smiled, as he gazed down upon her flawless face and body.

". . .Just you."

"And what are you thinking about me?"

"Just how incredibly beautiful you are."

"Is that all?"

"That's all," he said with an assuring smile.

Rachel suddenly appeared quite self-conscious and seemed to hesitate over what she was about to say next. ". . .I'm sorry about. . .I guess I was just a little nervous the first time."

"You were fine," Chenault assured her. "And hopefully, we've got a lot of time together ahead of us and we'll learn everything we need to know about each other--in that department," he said with an encouraging smile.

Reassured, Rachel seductively bit her lower lip with a smile as she gazed over at him and said, "Well then, I'm ready for my next lesson if you are."

CHAPTER 30

An article appeared in *The Washington Post* online the next day, noting that the previously floundering campaign of Senator Brockston Ratchford had recently taken on new life. Most pundits had been predicting that Ratchford was about to drop out of the race due to his extremely low poll numbers and limited name recognition around the country. This was due in large part, the article pointed out, to his overall failure to capture the imagination or interest of the American public. But with the murder of his wife and kidnapping of his daughter, Ratchford had been on virtually every television newscast across the country, as well as on the front page or cover of every newspaper, magazine, and tabloid.

The article went on to point out that while Ratchford had previously failed to connect with a national audience, he now had not only the sympathy, but perhaps more importantly, the ear of an entire nation, and would remain headline news until his daughter was found. At his most recent press conference, Ratchford vowed before a sympathetic nation to "press on" with his campaign and "be strong," as well as promising that he would continue to hold daily press conferences announcing whatever progress was being made in the ongoing investigation.

The article then went on to note that the Democratic Party, which had apparently learned nothing in their years out of power, again appeared to be on the verge of nominating a candidate who would be virtually unelectable in a national election. This time around it appeared to be either a highly polarizing and abrasive congresswoman from Connecticut, or the Hispanic former Secretary of Housing, whose sexual appetites were legend and would be ripe for a whispering campaign by whomever he faced. Thus, it very much appeared that whichever GOP candidate got the nod, he would be a virtual shoo-in come election time.

The article concluded noting that should Senator Brockston Ratchford go on to be elected, the Mormon religion would then finally achieve the acceptance they had been seeking from a society that had long viewed them with suspicion. Their very well-planned, and well-financed public campaign of transforming themselves from a rebel band of bearded polygamists, to the clean-cut, God fearing, family-first bunch had been the first step in transforming public opinion. The final step would be the nomination and election of Brockston Ratchford to the highest office in the land. A number of pundits and historians had, in fact, already predicted that Ratchford's election would likely do much the same for the LDS faith as Kennedy's election had done to demystify Catholicism for the American public.

Chenault knew and respected the writer of the article, Jonathan Burke, a former columnist at *The Times*, and found his insights and opinions to be a close reflection of what he had been batting around, but had yet to put into words. As he saved the article to his thumb drive, Chenault made a mental note as well, to file it away for future reference.

CHAPTER 31

For the past two days, Maria Alverez had gone by Room 207 to carry out her daily cleaning duties at the Salt Lake City Hilton, only to find a "Do Not Disturb" sign posted on the door handle. It was not until the third day, after one of the guests complained about an odd smell, she became a bit suspicious and finally knocked. When no one answered, she took out her passkey card, and upon opening the door was met with an overwhelming stench that almost knocked her backwards.

Salt Lake City police arrived on the scene soon after, and for the next several days, the mysterious death of Felix Valdez was the lead story across the country, briefly bumping the Ratchford murder/kidnapping off the front page. An autopsy had yet to be performed, and the only detail leaked was that Felix Valdez's nude body had been found lying in bed in a puddle of blood. Gruesome images of his discolored, bloated body, secretly captured by an anonymous rescue worker on his cell phone, followed soon after over the internet.

When Chenault heard the news, his heart sank a little. Not only had a boyhood hero of his passed, but he was reminded of his own mortality as well. He was not, however, surprised by the news. Valdez had not looked well when they had met, and it was very likely that years of drug and alcohol abuse had finally taken their toll. When Chenault later heard about the photos that had been secretly shot and released over the internet for the entire world to see, he was disgusted. Although deep down, he wondered if Valdez, at the twilight of his career, might not have run similar photos on his own little watched nightly news wrap-up in an attempt to boost his own anemic ratings.

CHAPTER 32

When the anonymous tip came into KSLC, the CBS Salt Lake City affiliate, the station manager, who also doubled as the news director, first suspected the tipster was nothing more than a prank caller. If the lead was legitimate he reasoned, why had the caller not directed it to local law enforcement or even the FBI? The kidnapping of Senator Brockston Ratchford's daughter was long past being just a local or regional news item of interest. ABC's Nightline had resurrected their day-by-day count they had used so effectively to make a name for themselves during the hostage crisis in the late '70s, and a daily update of the Emily Ratchford kidnapping was part of their nightly lead-in. A number of international correspondents were on the scene as well, reporting back to their home countries the compelling story that had all the shocking sensationalism of the OJ murder trial and the JonBenet Ramsey investigation rolled up into one.

The station manager had not actually spoken with the caller. The station's receptionist had fielded the call and directed it to one of the news people who was prepping for that evening's news cast. The seasoned newswoman had a hunch, however, and after conferring with the station manager, they contacted the FBI and the SBI, as well as the Salt Lake City Police Department. The station reps had then worked out an agreement that they would have exclusive coverage of the SWAT team's assault and hopeful rescue of Emily Ratchford, but would not televise it live to keep from tipping off the kidnappers and endanger her any further. They also had the added backup that if the story turned out to be just a hoax, or a complete bust, they would never have to air it and no one would ever be the wiser. If it was true, however, they all knew they likely had the story of the year, and they would capture it all live, or at least slightly tape delayed. The rights alone, to be aired over and over for weeks to come on stations around the world would net the station millions, not to mention the accolades that would likely follow.

CHAPTER 33

When Delmer Lamott heard the light rap on his motel door, he at first didn't give it a second thought. His brother had gone out earlier for a few groceries while he stayed behind to look after the girl. He had, in fact, spent most of the afternoon just watching her. Her ripening young body had just begun to show the full promise of womanhood, and he suspected that within just a year or so that she would make a fine breeding vessel. As tempted as he had been to give the blossoming girl a first-hand lesson in the "birds and the bees," he knew that if he gave into his desires and defied the instructions of The Prophet, that as promised, God would strike him down in an instant.

The Prophet had been very clear in his instructions to them--the girl was not to be harmed, let alone touched, other than to allow her to go to the bathroom and occasionally feed herself. The rest of the time she was to be handcuffed to the bed by both wrists, although folded velvet was to be loosely wrapped around each wrist before being shackled. As they'd been further instructed, a satin blindfold had been loosely tied around her head, and to avoid having to gag her, she'd been told that if she ever cried out, her entire family would be killed. She meekly obeyed and spent most of her waking hours lightly sobbing, which was drowned out by the steady drone of the television that was left on throughout the day.

As he went to open the door for his brother, Delmer Lamott had a sense for a brief moment that something wasn't quite right--just as the door came smashing in and two black-garbed men in body armor charged in to attack him. Lamott threw the first man past him, sending him crashing headlong into the dresser as the second one drew back to smash him in the head with the steel butt of his compact assault rifle. But Delmer, although a large man, had an animal-like quickness and struck first, smashing his left elbow into the side of SWAT team member's head hard enough to knock him out. As the snipers on the building across the street sighted in their target, the last thing Delmer Lamott saw as he glanced down was the convergence of several red dots of light on his chest--just before it exploded.

Watching the events unfold from a block away, Cloyd Lamott felt what seemed like part of his soul being ripped out of him as he saw his brother crumple into a bloody pile. Whoever had killed his brother, and more importantly, whoever had betrayed them, would pay with their lives--he vowed it.

To the viewers watching the successful assault and rescue on the news that evening, it was almost like watching a perfectly choreographed scene from an action blockbuster. Every detail went as planned, including the happy ending with the tearful reunion between father and daughter. Reality television didn't get any better than this and actual events had fortuitously wrapped up by 3 p.m. Mountain Time which allowed the story to appear as the ten minute lead-in on every television newscast across the county.

"A dramatic, but happy ending to an otherwise tragic story in Salt Lake City," or some variation was the teaser most newscasts enticed their viewers into watching that night's 6:00 local news, while the networks were already preparing their one hour specials for that night. Interviews with the cast of characters followed, from the two SWAT team members who had led the charge, to one of the snipers, to the station manager who went into great detail about how he had decided not to air the rescue live so as not to further endanger the young girl. Rounding out the story was a grateful Brockston Ratchford who went on and on about the fine job everyone involved had performed, before he closed with what sounded very much to Chenault's seasoned ear like a prepared final statement.

"Although my daughter, Emily, appears to be in good health, she still has been rushed to the hospital to be treated for any possible injuries. And lastly, I'd just like to say, even though I did lose my beloved wife in this terrible tragedy, there's still a happy ending, because my little girl--my beautiful little girl, has been returned to me. Good night and God bless."

CHAPTER 34

As Chenault finished watching the two hour prime time special, "Rescue in Salt Lake City," later that evening, he was left strangely unmoved. The range of emotions that he normally would have expected to have felt from such an otherwise moving story were nowhere to be found. His reaction, or rather his lack of reaction, in fact, made him wonder for a moment if maybe he had just gotten so jaded from a career in which he'd just about seen it all, that was he now just incapable of experiencing such emotions?

He quickly realized, though, his lack of empathy was due to only one thing--it was simply just a matter of now knowing too much about Senator Brockston Ratchford to completely buy his

performance and the story. There was just
something too pat about it, almost as if it had been
scripted by some hackneyed Hollywood writer.
Everything just fell too perfectly into place.

However, as much as Chenault distrusted
Ratchford--and politicians in general--he still
couldn't believe the man would have gone so far as
to having his wife murdered and his daughter
kidnapped simply as a publicity-grabbing ploy.
Still, something about it--and he couldn't quite put
his finger on it--just didn't feel right, or as his friend
and editor, Hal Sikorski, would have put it, "It just
didn't pass the smell test."

All the little things he had learned and pieced
together about Brockston Ratchford over the past
few days, along with the so-called facts that were
being reported on this story were not only not
passing the smell test, but were starting to reek. His
altered family tree and true upbringing in the
fundamentalist Hildale community. His mysterious
business success and the allegations of his
"visions." The Mormon community's silent but
unwavering support of him. And the alleged
suicide of his first wife and subsequent marriage to
Lauren Ratchford, who at the time was the family's
nanny, and who fourteen years later then is
murdered by the kidnappers of his daughter--
kidnappers who never even bothered to ask for a
ransom, but who just seemed to have holed up,
biding their time, waiting for something--
instructions maybe. The girl hadn't been assaulted

or harmed in any way early reports seemed to indicate--she had basically just been held against her will for six days. And then there was the murder of one of Ratchford's chief rivals for the party nomination. It all just didn't add up--or did it?

CHAPTER 35

Miles Bender, the night manager of the Desert Flower Motor Inn, sat behind the front check-in desk in the tattered, moss green recliner he had rescued from the curb a month earlier, skimming a year-old copy of *People* magazine as he smoked a cigarette. Bender at one time in his life had dreams of rock and roll stardom, which later turned into the goal of at least making a living as a working musician. Eventually, however, he settled for the life of a roadie with several semi-famous bands before hurting his back, which then led him to drift in and out of a number of dead-end jobs. Even though he was now in his late forties, he continued to dress as he always had, in torn and faded jeans that were too tight for him, and a sleeveless, threadbare Pink Floyd concert tee shirt that barely concealed his now basketball-sized gut.

Just as he flipped the page to find out who the top five celebrity couples were the previous year, he heard the dainty tinkle of the bell above the front entrance. After taking one more long drag on a half-burned Camel, he looked up to see a vaguely familiar looking man swing himself over the four foot high check-in desk. Before Bender could finish saying, "What the fuck do you think you're. . ," the man pounced on him and dragged him by his neck to the back room where Bender and the other night managers would occasionally catch a catnap.

Cloyd Lamott had gone back to the motel that night to track down the night manager who had checked them in several days earlier, and the one he presumed had betrayed them. Although not quite as large as his brother, Cloyd Lamott still possessed an uncanny strength and dragged the two hundred pound man in back as if he were a child. As the man kicked and clawed from his air supply being cut off, Lamott continued to hold him tightly, as he reached down to his right hip to feel along his belt for his hunting knife. At just the thought of the kill, Lamott's bloodlust was now running so high he could barely hear the man's screams as he drew the jagged seven inch blade from its sheath.

As when he leapt upon a fallen deer to slice open its throat, Lamott felt a tingling inside his body that ran right down to his groin. Only when it came time on a hunt to slit the soft underside of the deer's neck, he did it with an impassioned precision. This time was much different, as he plunged his knife into the screaming man's chest, stomach, and kidneys, again and again. Finally, after grabbing a hold of the man's short ponytail, he bent the man's head back and started sawing just below his Adam's apple. Slowly at first, so that the man, whose screams were now silent, would know what his fate was to be, and then faster and faster, as he sawed through the final juncture until he met no more resistance.

As he tossed the night manager's head to the floor before exiting, the man's earlier pleading and screams echoed in his head. *"Why?! Why are you doing this?!"* Lamott, now covered in blood from his chest to his toes, briefly considered the possibility that the man might have been innocent, but then just as quickly dismissed the notion. As he had been taught since he was a small child, as a Latter Day Saint, all of his decisions and actions were directed by a higher power, and God would never lead him astray.

CHAPTER 36

The next day more details were released about the dead kidnapper, who was revealed to be one Delmer Lamott, a forty-three-year-old fundamentalist Mormon who had allegedly kidnapped thirteen-year old Emily Ratchford to be his child bride. Although he carried no identification, he had been tracked down from his fingerprints which were on file for several arrests for voyeurism, all charges of which had, strangely enough, been dropped in every case.

The first thing that struck Chenault when Delmer Lamott's mug shot flashed across the screen was an almost déjà vu feeling that he had seen this man before. And then it hit him--the large man in the back of the beat-up pickup truck that had seemingly shadowed them on their way to the Family History Library. The very same one in which the driver of the truck had made a rather suggestive gesture towards Chenault, as in suggesting that he would have liked to have put a bullet between his eyes.

The second thing that immediately struck Chenault was the last name--Lamott. Since Hildale was a town of less than five thousand, the odds were extremely high that the kidnapper, Hyrum Lamott, and very possibly Brockston Ratchford were all closely related. On top of that, probably no one else in the world knew about this connection at this point but Rachel and himself, Hyrum Lamott, and now very likely, Brockston Ratchford--if he hadn't already known.

And then there was the odd fact that even though there had apparently been no sexual assault, or anything else that would lead to the conclusion that the dead kidnapper was simply looking for a young wife, this whole thing was now being turned into a story about a crazed polygamist looking for a child bride. Seemingly, déjà vu all over again, because the last time something relatively similar had occurred, as Rachel had pointed out, it had actually been a polygamist looking for a child bride, but then it had later been spun into simply a "crazed sexual predator" story. Ratchford's fellow Utah Senator had even gone so far as to play up this somewhat misleading aspect by using the kidnapped teenage girl as the very public face of his new "Sexual Predator" law.

Chenault thought he was starting to notice a pattern, at least when it came to actual events and how they were reported, or rather portrayed, by the local media and law enforcement. What was presented to the public, and perhaps even more importantly, to the outside world as fact, seemed to be more often than not a case of misdirection.

Can they really be that hard up to protect this glossy public image they've built up? Chenault asked himself, realizing he'd probably just answered his own question. Based upon his own behind-the-scenes knowledge, along with the many contradictions and details that made very little sense, he was beginning to doubt if anything being put out regarding the current story was even remotely close to the truth.

The news segment ended with a familiar mug shot filling the screen, confirming Chenault's earlier suspicions, as the newscaster announced in a voice-over, "Cloyd Lamott, the brother of the dead kidnapper, is also now considered a suspect in the case. The FBI, along with local authorities, has now launched a nationwide manhunt for Lamott, issuing an All Points Bulletin. They warn that Lamott is likely armed and considered to be extremely dangerous."

It occurred to Chenault he could release a story about the likely Ratchford-Lamott connection, but that unless he could absolutely prove a connection beyond just the family tree, it would likely just be dismissed as a smear attempt against Ratchford and be quickly forgotten. On the bright side, however, his diligent research had finally begun to pay off, and hidden connections were slowly but surely starting to emerge.

He called Rachel on her cell. "Did you just see that?"

"I did," she said at the other end.

"And are you thinking what I'm thinking?"

"Like, that Hyrum Lamott might have been behind the murder-kidnapping of Ratchford's wife and daughter?"

"Because I bet you a million bucks he's related to the kidnappers."

"In that town, how could he not be?" she chimed in.

"But could he really be that stupid that he'd think no one would make the connection?"

"Assuming it was him, he probably never thought they'd be caught, so no one would ever make the connection," Rachel reasoned.

"But would it have been because of some grudge against Ratchford--some longstanding blood feud-- or for some other reason his depraved mind came up with that we can't even fathom? Like, did he maybe even somehow think this would help Ratchford?"

"By what, putting him on the front page and getting him some sympathy votes?" Rachel tossed out.

"You never know. Whatever the case, there's not a lot I can do to prove anything at this point, especially if it involves going back to that insane place, where the only guy in town who would even talk to me wound up dead. But I'm sure my new friend, Agent Patterson, would probably cut me a deal with an exclusive if my lead pans out. And I still haven't entirely ruled out Ratchford. Even though it's a long shot, he might have somehow still had a hand in it, and him--him I can still go after."

CHAPTER 37

Knowing this might be his best and last chance to ever get Brockston Ratchford alone again, particularly if he went on to get elected, Chenault made a point to be at Ratchford's next press conference. The first time Chenault had met Brockston Ratchford several years earlier, the Senator had been quite charming and even ingratiating. After introductions, he had opened the interview with the same self-deprecating joke he'd used a hundred times before to break the ice at American Legion posts and retirement centers across the country.

"I know one of the questions you're probably going to ask me about is where do I stand on same sex marriage. And to that I would just simply respond, I believe that marriage is between a man and a woman--and another woman."

With neither of them having an axe to grind, the entire interview had been quite amicable. The

Senator had later even had a member of his staff send Chenault a short "Thank you" note, thanking him for his flattering portrayal in the piece, which had been a gentle introduction to several of the Republican politicians considering a run for the Presidency in the next election.

The second time they met about a year later, however, the tone of the meeting had taken a decidedly downward turn. Chenault had been granted a brief interview, and as he approached the Senator to reintroduce himself, Ratchford had quickly cut him off by saying, "Yeah, I know who you are."

It had only gone down hill from there. By Ratchford's curt responses and prickly demeanor, it quickly became clear to Chenault that the Senator was no longer a fan. Chenault suspected that Ratchford begrudged him for either his having been instrumental in bringing about the resignation of the Vice President and embarrassing the Senator's political party, or for the perceived attack on the highest office in the land during a time of war. Chenault skillfully probed both these possibilities in the interview, but neither seemed to be of particular concern to Ratchford.

It was not until Chenault got the response to his final question regarding whether the Senator believed he had a good chance of becoming the first Mormon to be elected President, that the source of the Senator's antagonism became much clearer.

"Well, if I don't, I guess I'll know who I have to

blame."

Prior to the previous Vice President stepping down, due in large part to Chenault's war exposé, and then falling on his sword to save the entire administration, he had made it very clear that he wouldn't seek the Presidency due to health concerns and family commitments. With his removal, there had then become a power vacuum--an opening for the President to insert a less controversial and much more palatable politician to slide in to the role of "President in waiting" for the final year of office. The likable and moderate James Hillendale, with his appointment then became the only obstacle in the path of Senator Brockston Ratchford from becoming the next President of the United States, and one that he had clearly not counted on. So by Ratchford's behavior, it had become fairly clear to Chenault that, at least in Ratchford's mind, he held Chenault personally responsible for creating an opening for Hillendale, and thus making it that much harder for him to win the Presidency.

The Sheraton Grand Ballroom was not all that grand, but the main building it was housed in was centrally located with plenty of parking, and so for those utilitarian reasons, frequent use was made of it by anyone with an inclination to hold a press conference. Chenault saw no point in arriving early because he knew it would do him no good to try to corner Ratchford, who was surrounded by handlers, and it would also now appear Secret Service agents. Chenault also figured that it was unlikely Ratchford would call on him from the press corps, nor were the questions he wanted answers to ones he particularly wanted to ask in a public forum. As Ratchford stood in front of a sea of microphones, answering questions mostly about the health of his daughter and how his family was coping, Chenault slipped to the edge of the crowd. He then moved forward and up to right of the stage, seeking out Ratchford's longtime aide and confidante, Evan Fiske, who as usual was impeccably dressed in a dark tailored suit and red power tie.

As long as Chenault had known Brockston Ratchford, he had known Evan Fiske, and from that first time he had met the man, he had never particularly cared for him. He was also fairly certain the feeling was mutual. While Fiske had at one time been seemingly helpful, that was, in fact, part of his job--to schedule, to screen, to protect, to placate, to field questions he would and would not let his boss answer. But perhaps what put Chenault off the most about him was the very weird, Svengali-like vibe Fiske gave off--controlling to the point of creepiness. Chenault had occasionally even wondered if Fiske was not so much Ratchford's political handler as he was his puppet master.

The last several times Chenault had requested an interview, even one just over the phone, Fiske had turned him down flat without even an explanation. He predicted this time would be different. After reaching Fiske, Chenault handed him a slip of paper. He glanced down at the handwritten note and after a few seconds, shot Chenault an icy, clench-mouthed glare, as a thick blue vein protruded across his forehead. He then dutifully sliced through the campaign entourage which allowed him to pass, and walked over to the podium. Leaning in towards Ratchford, Fiske whispered something in his ear. By Ratchford's initial tight-lipped expression, Chenault could tell that he was less than thrilled to hear that his least favorite reporter was on site, but he quickly recovered with a big gleaming smile as he leaned into the podium.

"Well folks, that's all for today. If we have anything else--any updates, my press office will send out a release and post it on our website. I also want to thank everybody out there across this great land of ours one more time for their prayers for my daughter's safe return and for my family. Again, thanks for coming out, and God bless."

He then drifted slowly back toward the rear exit behind the podium, waving and smiling, as several reporters shot more questions at him that went unanswered. Upon reaching the exit, he quickly turned and slipped back into an antechamber just off the main ballroom.

"The Senator would like to speak with you," the grim-faced Fiske pronounced, practically spitting out the words. He then escorted Chenault through a hallway that connected to the antechamber behind the ballroom where Ratchford stood reviewing some notes. Several of his staff along with two

Secret Service agents stood nearby as Fiske walked Chenault up to Ratchford.

"Leave us be," Ratchford said.

"Pardon," replied the tall, dark suited, black Secret Service agent, who had the good sense to take his sunglasses off indoors, unlike his more compactly built white counterpart.

"Clear the room. Just leave me and Mr. Chenault--and you," he said, motioning with his head at Fiske, who nodded in understanding.

"Just for good measure, why don't you pat him down first? We'd prefer any recording devices Mr. Chenault might have be made unavailable to him during the interview," Fiske said with a remnant of a smile, in his play to get the upper hand back.

The two agents obliged, separating Chenault from his fanny pack and his small handheld recorder which they then set out of reach on a nearby table. After about thirty seconds the room was cleared, leaving just Ratchford and Chenault to stare at each other as Fiske stood off to the side.

"So we meet again, Mr. Chenault."

"The pleasure's all mine, Senator."

"First off, this is all off the record, is that understood?"

"Well, I'd kind of hoped to get your. . .I mean that is usually the whole point of requesting an interview. But okay, we'll let this remain off the record for now."

"Then first, let me ask you this? What is it exactly that you seem to have against me? Is it because I'm a Latter Day Saint, or do you just have a prejudice against people of faith in general?"

"I'm afraid I don't follow what you mean, Senator."

"Let's just cut the bullshit, son. Very classy. You threaten to bring up my family connections with Hildale and Colorado City if I don't meet with you. I would have thought a man from *The Times* would have been above such a third-rate, chickenshit stunt. In fact, in some legal circles they might even say what you just did amounts to extortion or blackmail. But if it's so important to you to find out--yes, I did originally come from Hildale, and no, I'm not proud of that fact."

"Not proud, or politically embarrassed?"

"What difference does it make? I'm not my Father. The practices that were carried on there. . ."

"Don't you mean, 'that are still carried on there,'" Chenault corrected him.

"In any case, are practices I don't observe or condone."

"Then why run from it?"

"I think you already know why. It's hard enough running as a member of the LDS, let alone being tied to some lunatic fringe offshoot."

"I don't know. I've met a few of them, and they all seem to be quite proud of you. One of them even happened to bring up the White Horse Prophecy. You're familiar with that aren't you, Senator?"

Ratchford glared coolly at Chenault for a

moment. ". . .If you ever bring up any of this, I will sink you. Personally, professionally--I will find any skeletons that are out there in either yours or your family's closet, and if I have to make something up, I'll do that too."

"Are you threatening me, Senator?"

"The Senator does not make threats, he just makes promises. That way we keep it all legal," the smirking Fiske interjected.

Chenault glanced over at the Senator's smiling lackey with a look of disgust, and then looked back to Ratchford. "So let me understand this? Pretty much, you're saying you basically will say or do just about anything to get elected? Is that about right?"

"Son, you ask any candidate that question, especially someone who has not only the cojones, but the ambition to run for President, and if they were to tell you the absolute truth, every one of them would tell you the exact same thing. And I think you know what the answer is."

"I'd like to believe that's not true."

"Son, you can believe whatever you want, but we're through here. So why don't you scurry on back to your hole."

No words came to Chenault as he gathered his belongings and headed for the exit with his figurative tail between his legs. It occurred to him that he had accomplished absolutely nothing with the brief interview that Ratchford had controlled from the beginning--and then he had a fleeting thought.

Chenault had learned long ago that in dealing with public officials well versed in the art of evasive answers, sometimes it was just as important to elicit a reaction, or sometimes even a non-reaction, than to get the person to actually answer questions in an interview--questions they frequently already had prepared answers for, or would simply just answer with bald face lies. What he now had in mind he knew was risky. If Ratchford didn't show his hand, Chenault could already envision his reaction. Ratchford would lash out at him, and rightfully so, with a tidal wave of unbridled anger and self-righteous indignation. *How dare you! Get this insensitive piece of filth out of my sight, and have him banned from all of my appearances from here on out.*

And then it occurred to Chenault that maybe he was simply smarting at having just been humiliated, and he was only trying to lash back out at Ratchford for handling him so effectively and sending him on his way like a wayward child. But then the fact he was second guessing his instinct to attack, mostly because of what Ratchford's family had just been through, was the reassurance he needed to remind himself that he wasn't just some knee-jerk attack dog from the press. He did still have a conscience and could be compassionate when need be, but he also still had a job to do, and unlike an increasing number of his press brethren whom he had observed cozying up to various candidates, he wasn't in this business to make friends. Brockston Ratchford was running for the highest office in the land, and now on top of everything else Chenault had come across, he seemed to be a less than honorable man. Chenault's gut told him to go for it, and he rarely went against his instincts. *Besides, what's the worst that could happen now?* he asked himself. He knew it was unlikely he would ever be granted an audience with Ratchford again, and after what he just pulled, there was a better than even chance that he would be banned from future press conferences anyway. This would likely be his last chance and he had to take it.

Just before the reaching the doorway, Chenault stopped and turned around. "Oh Senator, I almost forgot. My condolences on your wife's passing." He paused for a brief moment and then leapt past the point of no return. ". . .You seem really broken up about it." He then waited for the explosion.

"Son, unlike you, I'm not someone who lives in the past," Ratchford said. "I've moved on."

"Can I quote you on that?"

"No, you may not. No, I tell you what--why don't you go ahead and print that, that "I've moved on." And then when I come out at the next press conference, all teary eyed and say 'How I can't believe they would print such horrendous lies about me, right after my poor wife was so brutally murdered,' I'll make you look like the biggest piece of shit since--I don't know when. So go ahead. Go for it."

Chenault now had more than he could have hoped for. Nothing that was printable--at least not yet--but enough to know that this man, even if he wasn't directly involved in his wife's murder was, at the very least, completely unworthy of office and more calculating and two-faced than just about anyone he had ever met.

"Senator, I have just one more thing to say to you. Don't you ever call me 'son' again. I had a father -- he was a good and honorable man. Something I don't believe that you would begin to know the meaning of."

"Please, spare me," Ratchford retorted out of earshot just as the door shut behind Chenault, and just as Fiske could have sworn he caught a glimpse of a small, dark object clenched tightly in Chenault's right hand, roughly the same size as the micro recorder Chenault had retrieved a minute earlier. He could have also almost sworn that Chenault had a slight grin on his face as he turned and exited.

"What is it?" asked Ratchford, sensing Fiske was on edge.

Fiske paused for a moment. ". . .Nothing I can't take care of."

CHAPTER 38

After checking in with the front desk clerk that evening to see if any messages had been left, Chenault turned to see two rather boyish looking young men, both dressed in ill-fitting, slightly oversized suits, converging on him. His first fleeting impression was that they were a couple of Mormon missionaries, the kind often seen peddling their bikes in pairs all over the world. The fact, though, that they were here in Salt Lake City, an unlikely recruitment ground, and that at least by their swagger, they appeared to be quite full of themselves, led him to the more probable conclusion--greenhorn cops.

"Michael Chenault?" the first one asked with an air of self-importance.

"That's right."

"We'd like to speak to you for a moment," he said, as he held his hand out to direct Chenault over to the side lobby.

Chenault decided to play along and accompanied them out of the thoroughfare of the hotel lobby into a marble-tiled foyer in front of the elevators.

"Can you tell us where you were on the night of November eighth?" the young cop said, which by his tone and delivery suggested that he'd probably watched way too many cop shows growing up.

"What year?" Chenault said, trying to keep a straight face.

"This year, smart ass. Last Tuesday night."

Pretty sure he already knew the answer to the question he was about to ask, Chenault went ahead and asked. "Who wants to know?"

The young cop whipped out his badge. "Salt Lake P.D. I'm Detective Nielsen and this is Detective Kimball," he said glaring back, clearly annoyed that his authority was being challenged.

"Can you tell me what this is about?"

"Just answer the question," the previously silent Kimball said.

Chenault thought for a moment, wondering if he should further antagonize the two by asking them if they weren't going to first read him his rights, because anything incriminating he could have possibly answered, a good lawyer would easily be able to have dismissed. He decided to save that card for later--just in case.

"...I'd just arrived in town that day, and I had dinner at the City Bistro that evening. I met a young woman there, and we talked until about 10:30. After that, I went back to my motel room."

"With the woman?" Nielsen said.

"Not that it's any of your business, but no, I was alone."

"Too bad. She could have been your alibi. Isn't it then true that you met Felix Valdez at the restaurant earlier that night, and that you had words?"

"We had words? Who told you that?" Chenault shot back.

"Let's just say we got an anonymous tip," Kimball said.

Ratchford and Fiske flashed through Chenault's mind. These two really would probably say or do just about anything, and this was likely their little power play to show just how far their reach and resources extended.

". . .So what were you arguing about?" Kimball said, following up.

"We weren't arguing. I'd never met the man before. I introduced myself, we spoke for a few minutes, and then he left."

"So he just came in, talked to you for a few minutes and then left?"

"I know how that sounds, but he said he was there to meet somebody who apparently stood him up, so he just left. And why does any of this even matter?"

"Did it occur to you that since you were probably one of the last people to see Felix Valdez alive that you might give us a call?"

"Actually, no it didn't. Of course, I'd heard that

he'd died, but I didn't know when, and from what they reported in the news, it sounded like he'd had a brain aneurysm. So no, I didn't think it was important that I notify authorities that I had met a boyhood idol of mine for less than two minutes, and that three days later when he died of a brain aneurysm, that I should contact somebody."

"Well Mr. Valdez didn't die of a brain aneurysm, and it wasn't three days later. Autopsy reports completed the other day showed that he'd probably had what was very likely an ice pick inserted into his right ear canal, which was then used to scramble his brains. And forensics further indicated that it likely occurred on the night that you just happened to meet him. You, of course, wouldn't know anything about that, would you?"

Chenault typically had a lot of respect for cops, but not for lazy or incompetent ones, and as best he tried, he couldn't hold back. "Oh yeah, that's right, I forgot. . .You know, you guys, I know you're just trying to do your job, but gimme a break. And why don't you do that--your job. I mean, what possible reason or motive would I have for murdering Felix Valdez? And have you checked with the cab driver that probably drove him back to his motel, or the doorman that opened the door for him? I mean, if people who last saw Felix Valdez alive is your only criteria for making ridiculous, unfounded charges, then those two sound like prime suspects to me?"

"Yeah, but you were the only one who we got a tip about," Kimball said.

"Yeah, well I just gave you two new tips. And I'd say that by your powers of deductive reasoning, that the doorman did it. In fact, have you even talked to the doorman or the night watch yet to see if they possibly saw anybody or anything suspicious that night?"

Realizing that not only was Chenault likely not their man, but that they hadn't even questioned the doorman about whom he might have seen, the young detective's face started to turn crimson as he retorted, "You don't have to get snotty."

"I don't know. This is the second time in a week that I've had cops show up at my doorstep hinting that I'm somehow involved with some gruesome murder. I'm a reporter. I'm not some crackhead or mobster, or some other 'usual suspect,' so yeah, I think I have a right to be a little on edge when groundless charges keep getting directed my way by cops too lazy to maybe look at the actual evidence, or for some possible motive first before coming around. I mean, let's just say for the sake of argument that I did it. Do you usually find that it works to just go up to the first person you can loosely tie to the crime and then get a confession? Is that the way it works here in Salt Lake City? Your criminals are just so honest they either confess or just turn themselves in?"

The detectives had had their fill of being dressed down and started off.

"Just make sure you stick around town for a few more days in case we have any more questions,"

Nielsen said.

"You're kidding me, right?"

"No, I'm not," the angry young detective shot back, his feelings clearly hurt.

Chenault realized that this was likely his punishment for crossing the line and making them look foolish, so lesson learned. But he also knew that if he hadn't gone on the offensive and just let the two steamroll him, the way they were apparently used to dealing with most of their suspects, he'd likely be headed to booking. He would have then had to contact a lawyer, and deal with the rest of the rigmarole associated with having to defend oneself against spurious charges.

"Just out of curiosity, do either of you have a father or an uncle in the department?" Chenault called out to the departing junior gumshoes.

Nielsen glared back at Chenault first before he snapped back, ". . .Why do you ask?"

"Oh, no reason." It had just struck Chenault that he couldn't imagine anyone with as little on the ball as these two, not only slipping through to join an actual metropolitan police force, but reaching the rank of detective at such a relatively young age without the forces of nepotism at work. The young detective's defensive response pretty much confirmed his suspicions.

Chenault decided he'd stick around a day or two longer than he'd planned, on the slim chance the two tried to pull a power play of their own and track him down again. It would also give him a chance to do a little more local research, as well as get to spend some more time with Rachel, and then he would be off on the next flight to JFK, because as best as he recalled, "Stick around town for a few more days" didn't carry a lot of legal weight.

CHAPTER 39

With some time to kill, it occurred to Chenault that one of the things he had yet to cross off his "to do" list was interview Walter Sneed, one of the gate guards from Brigham Acres, the Ratchford's gated community. Before now it would have been nearly impossible, since up until recently, Sneed had been surrounded by either a gaggle of ravenous reporters shoving microphones into his face, or by a battery of stone-faced police officers trying to shield Sneed from these same reporters. From the gray, exhausted look of Sneed after he'd finally been released from police custody, it appeared he'd been kept up for hours on end, during what was likely a several day barrage of interrogations by various law enforcement agencies.

Chenault reached Rachel on her cell. "So, you want to tag along? See if this Sneed, the gate guard, might know more than he thinks he does?"

"I would, but after being out of town for a few days, there a couple things I need to take care of. But I would like to know what you find out."

"Well then, I guess I'll talk to you later," he said, before ending the call.

With the understanding that Sneed only worked nights at the Brigham Acres front gate, Chenault called Sneed's home number--mainly just to find out if he was there, but got an automated message that the number had been disconnected. This was followed by the expected news, after calling "Information," that Sneed now had an unlisted number. With that temporary dead end, he decided to take a chance and head over to Sneed's home, but upon arriving at the modest, white clapboard bungalow, saw there was no vehicle in the drive. *Just dandy,* Chenault thought.

Guessing that Sneed was likely trying to keep a low profile until things blew over, Chenault decided, albeit somewhat reluctantly, to try to call in a favor from Patterson. Reluctantly, because in the *quid pro quo* arrangement he had with most of those he'd dealt with in law enforcement, Chenault hated to go to the tap too early, since he'd often found them to be quite chintzy with the information they would supply in return. Since he was usually only interested in getting crucial inside information about a particular case--or "leaks" as they were usually referred to after the fact--just finding out where the security guard might be hiding out would be an easy one for Patterson to give him, but a favor which he would likely hold over Chenault's head the next time he came around.

"Special Agent Patterson," the FBI agent answered.

"You get my email?" Chenault said, as he began the conversation by reminding Patterson of the most recent tip he'd sent on the possible Ratchford-Lamott-Hildale connection. "I never heard anything back from you."

"Yeah, I got it," Patterson said.

"And?"

"And what? The two came from the same backwater town as Ratchford. So what?"

"And you don't find that more than a little bit odd?"

"Not really," Patterson said in a rather blasé tone. "It was just a couple of more than likely, inbred brothers, out looking for child brides, and we've got one dead and the other one on the run. You know, you reporters are always thinking there's some sort of conspiracy afoot--I guess it's what sells papers."

Chenault had the perfect sarcastic response to Patterson's charge that *The Times* was basically no better than a checkout line tabloid, but he decided to let it go in favor of getting down to business. "I've got a small favor to ask."

"Well, ask away," Patterson said. "Though obviously, I can't promise you anything."

"I'm just trying to track down Walter Sneed, the guard at the Ratchford's gated development, and

I'm not having much luck so far."

"That's an easy one. I take it you haven't checked the front guard house yet?"

"But I thought he only worked nights," Chenault said.

"He does, but since the murder, he's been coming in on his days off. Partially, to hide out from the press, but more than likely to show the residents there how truly dedicated he is to his job if his employment there ever comes to a vote. So what do you need with him anyway?"

Still mildly irked with the agent's earlier comment, along with the fact that Patterson had clearly done nothing with anything he'd given him, Chenault said, "I'll let you know," as he pressed the "End call" button on his phone.

On the drive out to Cottonwood Heights, the Salt Lake City suburb where Brigham Acres was nestled away, Chenault had plenty of time to draw up a plan of action as to how he would play it when it came to questioning Sneed. His thoughts, however, seemed to keep drifting back to his encounter earlier that day with the two junior detectives.

Just by the fact that the department had sent those two, it seemed fairly evident to Chenault that someone up the chain of command had little faith in their so-called tip. That, or perhaps with the high profile Ratchford case still ongoing, very little time and resources were being diverted to the Valdez investigation. The fact it had been reported that

Valdez's watch and billfold were missing, and that he'd been found nude in his motel room bed, it had likely been assumed that Valdez had been involved in a late night transaction gone bad. Noticing over his many years on the job that cops were generally loath to spending much time solving cases where they had viewed it as "the victim probably had it coming," Chenault even doubted if the case would ever be solved. *Too bad*, he thought, *No matter what Valdez got himself into, he deserves better.*

In the back of his mind, it had been Chenault's plan all along to at some point meet Walter Sneed in person. It wasn't so much that he wanted to ask Sneed many of the same questions that he'd probably already been asked a hundred times before, because from what he had seen and read in Sneed's interviews, he mostly already knew the answers that he'd get. He did, however, want to get his own feel for the veracity of Sneed's story, and see if there was a slim possibility of getting the beleaguered guard to shed any more light on what did or didn't actually happen that night. Knowing that Sneed had been portrayed by the media as everything from a person of interest in the case to an incompetent boob who had left his post the night of the murder, he thought the empathy card might play well to get his trust. He also knew, however, that it might be an uphill battle since he was reasonably sure that the surprise interview would likely start out quite contentious. Normally, Chenault didn't like using "blindside" interviews, but he felt that in this case he might be best able to catch Sneed off guard by just showing up on his doorstep to get his most honest reactions and answers.

The second prong of attack was just to get Sneed talking. Even if he wasn't able to extract any usable information early on, it was still important to build rapport with a reluctant source, and to get him talking about almost anything. As he'd found from his years of conducting probing interviews, usually once they started talking, it was sometimes hard to get them to stop.

As Chenault approached the main entrance, the ten foot high, stucco-covered walls that wrapped around the entire front portion of the development for as far as the eye could see, appeared nearly impenetrable--with the exception of the wide open front gate. As Chenault coasted up to the guardhouse, he spotted a slightly rotund man in a khaki uniform stand up in the booth. The mustachioed, fiftyish Sneed, who looked as if he could have come straight from central casting, held out his left hand in a gesture to halt.

"Can I help you?" he inquired gruffly.

"I hate to bother you at work, but I tried calling you earlier at your home number," Chenault said as politely as he could.

"And why would you do that?"

"I just wondered if I could maybe ask you a few questions about the night Lauren Ratchford was killed. My name's Michael Chenault and I'm a. . ."

"I already told you people--I wasn't there that night."

"What people?"

"Aren't you a cop?"

"Do I look like a cop?"

Sneed looked him over. ". . .Not really. So who are you?"

"As I was trying to tell you, I'm just a reporter."

"Then I got nothin' to say."

"What, did the police or your employer tell you not to talk to the press?"

"No, but you people are the ones who's trying to make me look bad by laying all the blame on me."

"Nobody's blaming you. And why would they do that anyway--blame you? How was it your fault?"

"Because I wasn't there that night," Sneed said, wearing his shame like a sign around his neck. "I thought I'd made that clear about a million times, and you people finally stopped asking me about it-- until now!"

"I'm sorry. I've just been out of the loop for the last several days, and I'm sorry to ask you this again, but where were you that night?"

"I was off, God damn it! I get off two Friday nights a month, and the one night I'm off, the Senator's wife gets butchered, and I get made to look like some fuckin' dipshit."

Sensing things were starting to take a downhill turn, Chenault noticed the tell-tale outline of a cigarette pack protruding from Sneed's shirt pocket, and patted himself down as if looking for his own pack. Coming up empty, he looked up to Sneed. ". . .You got a smoke?"

"Yeah, sure." Sneed reached to his pocket and popped out a cigarette to Chenault, who lit it and then held out his lighter to return the favor. As Sneed leaned in toward the open window to get a light, the strong, sickly sweet stench that emanated off of him from the previous night's binge pierced Chenault's nostrils. Sneed took a long drawl and then waved a large silver Mercedes-Benz through the gate.

"Am I in the way here?" Chenault asked.

"No, no, you're fine."

"So, on one of the two nights you're off each month, the Lamotts just happened to come by on that night?"

"It's like the cops said, 'Just bad timing--pure coincidence.'"

"The police actually said that, that they thought it was just 'pure coincidence?'"

"Yeah. I mean, what else could it be?"

"Well, off hand, I can think of a couple other more likely possibilities. How about the fact that I'm guessing most of the residents know you're off these two nights a month."

"Well yeah, maybe some of them have noticed, but you don't think it was someone who lives in here who could have told them, do you?"

"Well, why not? Rich people generally hire other people to do their dirty work, don't they?"

"Hey, if you're getting at what I think you're getting at, then you're dead wrong. There ain't no way a man--especially a man like that--would have something like that done to his own family."

"And I hope you're right. Of course, I didn't actually say anything about it being Ratchford. Why would you think that, or what would cause that to pop in your head?"

"I just thought that was what you were kind of gettin' at."

Chenault shook his head. "No. Just making a general observation about rich people. Let's see, and I was also wondering, why is it that there wasn't somebody scheduled to relieve you on your nights off? Why was there no one to fill in for you?"

"It's like most gated communities--it's just for show. There's usually no one even here during the day. Everybody's got their gate code to come and go as they please. At night, it's just me and a buddy who switches off with me every other day, and we take turns coming in about 6:30 in the evening, and stay for a twelve hour shift."

Chenault nodded in apparent understanding. "Here's something a little off the subject, but I'm just curious about. And you don't have to answer this, but--would you vote for Ratchford?"

"For President?"

"Yeah."

"Well, to tell you the truth, I don't know. Believe it or not, I'm not Mormon."

"Yeah, I kind of picked up on that."

"I was raised Southern Baptist, but moved out here a few years back looking for work. They--the Mormons, mostly seem to be hardworking, God fearing people--real family oriented, but I still get a funny feeling around a lot of them sometimes, like they're all in this private club that thinks for some reason that they're better than the rest of us."

"Yeah, but I imagine most people could probably say they find that to be true for just about any pious group. But what about Senator Ratchford, himself?" Chenault said.

"Well, Senator Ratchford, you see him on TV and in interviews, and he seems real warm and friendly, like a man you can really trust. But you meet him in person, when there's no cameras around, like when he's driving back and forth through my gatehouse--and he wouldn't give you the time of day. He's kind of a. . ."

"Kind of a prick?"

"Well, you know I don't like to use that kind of language, but yeah, he's not in person like what he appears on television."

"So more like a 'hypocrite'?"

"I don't know about that. He just doesn't seem like who he appears to be, if that makes any sense."

"Perfect sense. Off the record, I know you probably hear things around--people talking. Did you ever hear, I don't know, maybe something about the Ratchfords were maybe having a few problems? You know, like any marriage has."

"Well, you know I don't like to gossip, especially about people who are basically signing my paycheck, but you know that wasn't his first marriage? Supposedly his first wife, well you know. . ."

". . .Committed suicide?"

"Oh, so you know about that. But did you also know it was supposedly a little fishy?

"How so?"

"Well, you know my memory's a little bit cloudy on that. And uh, times are tough right now for a working man--if you know what I mean."

The mere fact Sneed had tossed out the "pay for play" offer had Chenault just about mad enough to smack the cigarette out of Sneed's crooked mouth. He had never subscribed to checkbook journalism, and he wasn't about to start. After a moment to cool down, he opted for the more civil and lawsuit free approach, and icily stared down the ethically challenged rent-a-cop.

"   Did you just ask me for money?"

"Well, if you're just gonna put it out there like that--yeah."

"Congratulations. You've just put everything you told me earlier into doubt, so I won't be able to use a single thing you've given me, or perhaps more importantly, could have given me."

"I don't get it," Sneed said with a puzzled look. "When I lived back East when I was younger, cops used to pay me for tips all the time."

"Yeah, and how much of it was the truth, and

how much did you just make up to earn a buck?"

"Well, I see what you're sayin', I guess. But don't nobody have to know except between me and you."

"Well see, that's the difference between what I can use as a reliable source and what cops can. And I could go into a whole host of legal and ethical explanations as to why, but I'm already wasting my breath and you probably wouldn't get it anyway," he said, just before he gunned the Volvo and whipped it into a doughnut around the guardhouse. He then sped out the front entrance making his way back onto the highway, leaving the befuddled guard standing open mouthed by his faux rock-covered gatehouse.

As Chenault headed back towards town, he got Rachel on her cell and relayed most of his encounter with the guard to her. "I mean think about it--there are really only three logical explanations," he said. "The first is that just by sheer dumb luck, the kidnappers just happened to come bopping along on the one night that the security guard was off. The second, and even least likely, is that they would have had to stake out the place two months or more to figure out the pattern that this one guard had off two Saturday nights out of the month."

"Why not just one month?"

"Because they would have had to have seen a repetition of the sequence. That it wasn't a matter of the guard just happening to be off, or possibly calling in sick on one of the nights. And based on what I saw of those two guys in the truck, neither one struck me as being a master of deductive reasoning."

"And so what's the third explanation?"

"The most obvious--they had to have had inside information to know to go on that particular night."

CHAPTER 40

As he sometimes had a tendency to do when once promising leads didn't pan out, and dead ends seemed to become the rule rather than the exception, Chenault started to doubt himself. Maybe, he told himself, it was time to do a gut check. Maybe all of the little coincidences and tragedies didn't necessarily add up to the conclusion that Brockston Ratchford was behind any of what had gone on. Maybe Ratchford was just another opportunistic politician, who after being beset by a family tragedy, had just happened to have made the best of it with a cynical campaign, and whose leading opponent had just happened to have been gunned down. *It happens*. Still, Chenault knew in his gut that Ratchford was not who he portrayed himself to be, but all he had at this point to go on was conjecture and a jumble of seemingly unrelated leads and hunches, none of which made for a publishable story.

There had been more than one story in his past that he had backed off of, and which he was later glad that he had. He, in fact, found he needed to rely on his own best judgment in such matters, because his editors at *The Times* trusted him so implicitly because of his reputation and past accolades, that they probably would have run with just about any story he presented to them. This virtual blind trust had thus become a double-edged sword. To pursue and then go with a story where it later turned out there was little to nothing there, would not only make him a laughingstock and the butt of a hundred jokes told by catty journalists envious of his success, but would essentially amount to professional suicide. Maybe he could get a job teaching journalism at some small Midwestern college whose name no one had ever heard of, or even a job as a reporter in some backwater town. But it would be unlikely he would ever again reach the heights he had attained at such a relatively early age, and most likely he would never work in journalism again--especially after libeling a presidential candidate who had a very good shot at winning not only the nomination, but the general election to follow.

It wasn't helping matters that he had recently been receiving a stream of emails and text messages from Hal, essentially telling him to "wrap it up."

Since Chenault had given no prior indication that he was anywhere near wrapping it up, this seemed to essentially amount to someone, somewhere, who was well above Hal Sikorski's pay grade, telling Chenault to back off.

Is this coming from brain trust or higher?

Chenault texted.

Just wrap it up

was all Hal wrote back.

Ironically, this was just the sign that a disheartened Chenault had been looking for. If someone up the chain was exerting pressure to drop the story, there was the likelihood that this person was receiving phone calls from even higher places. Chenault knew he'd never get a straight answer, and that he'd be fed something along the lines of, "Legal was getting nervous," or that some unnamed, oversensitive executive, in the interest of fairness, didn't want *The Times* accused of being anti-religious or Mormon bashers.

The one thing Chenault did know now was that he was going to proceed ahead at full steam, and that even if he did actually get called back, he would just continue ahead on his own dime. If he got to the end of the investigation and still didn't have enough to make any of his suspicions stick, then it wouldn't see the light of day--so no harm, no foul.

Am proceeding

Chenault texted back.

Seconds later, his cell phone rang.

"Michael, I'm telling you this as a friend--just drop the story. We're getting a lot of heat from above, and they're just not that convinced anything is there. And you really haven't sent us or told us anything concrete."

"I gotta tell you, Hal, I'm really surprised. I know there've been other news organizations that have quashed stories, but I never thought *The Times* would attempt to bury one--especially as a result of outside pressure."

"Now you don't know that, and neither do I. And as I said, you really haven't given us anything--so there is no story."

"Okay Hal, just for the sake of argument, what's the bottom line here?"

"The bottom line is, if you continue to pursue this story, you do it without the approval of *The Times* and their legal protection. And if any harassment or libel charges are made, it probably means your job."

"You're serious?"

"I'm afraid so, pal."

Chenault just shook his head in mild disgust. ". . .Tell me you at least went to bat for me." There was a brief pause.

". . .I went to bat for you," Hal said, his voice weakly trailing off.

"I hope it was with a little more conviction than that."

"Michael, unlike you, I have a wife and two kids to support. I therefore pick and choose my battles very carefully. This was not one I could win. If you keep going, I wish you luck, but please keep me out of it." The phone line then clicked.

For the first time Chenault was in uncharted waters. Always before, just to say, "I'm with *The Times*," not only commanded instant respect, but opened all sorts of doors that never would have been available to him otherwise. On top of that, without the behemoth that was *The New York Times* at his back, along with the backing of their vast legal department and all the rest of the resources that came with that affiliation, Chenault at that moment had never felt more alone.

He started to reconsider his earlier position. *The easiest thing to do is just walk away.* He had yet to substantiate a single hunch or lead, and he'd frequently gotten the feeling on the assignment that he was getting nowhere fast. He even started to tell himself that sleazier politicians had probably gotten away with far worst. But in the end, maybe it was his recalling the early lesson that "Sometimes doing the right thing was often the hardest thing" that his father had instilled in him, or maybe it was a bit of his mother's ornery stubborn Irish heritage coming out, but Chenault knew that there was a story. And he also knew, that some way, somehow, he would bring it out.

This man--this politician, who was somehow a master of portraying himself as a pillar of society and the consummate family man, was crooked to the core. Chenault knew it in his bones. And if he did nothing to stop him in the only way he knew how, he knew he'd have no one but himself to blame if Brockston Ratchford was elected on the following November 6th.

CHAPTER 41

The next morning, as Chenault was stepping into the elevator to head down for breakfast, his cell phone rang. Checking his caller ID, he saw it was Hal. His first reaction was to ignore it, since it was likely just another call berating him to get on the next plane back to New York. But as best as he could recall, he and Hal were still friends, so somewhat reluctantly, he stepped off the elevator and flipped open his phone.

"Hello," Chenault said in a flat, emotionless tone.

"Hey, Michael. Sorry I was a little short with

you last night, but as you can imagine, we've been under a lot of stress around here with all the calls we've been getting."

"Is that what you called to tell me?"

"Hey, I'm apologizing here."

"Yeah, well it sounded more like an explanation. You kind of told me I was on my own last night and then hung up on me."

"I didn't mean to hang up on you. I had just thought we were finished. Look, I think I've maybe got something for you. I've been checking your mail like you asked, and you got a small package in the mail yesterday. I opened it up this morning and it was an 8mm video tape."

"And?"

"And, I could tell you what's on it, but I just had it digitally transferred earlier by the graphics department, and it's headed your way right now in a MPEG file."

"I take it it's worth my time to watch? I was just heading out."

"Have you ever known me to waste your time? Wait, don't answer that."

"I'll watch it and give you a call back. But can you just give me a hint as to what cinematic masterpiece I'm about to see?"

"Just Martin Koplanski addressing you and Felix Valdez in his final farewell performance."

"I'll talk to you later," Chenault said, snapping his phone shut as a million thoughts raced through his head. Had Felix Valdez been on the same story trail that he had, only to wind up with an ice pick in his brain? Had Valdez perhaps been lured in the same way as he had been, and why had he and not Valdez been allowed to live?

Chenault debated whether to give Rachel a call to come back over and watch the video. The night before, they had talked it over and come to the decision that she would assist him for a while longer, perhaps even accompanying him when he made his way back East. She had convinced her editors that they were on to something big, and that even though *The Times* would ultimately break the story, *The Tribune* would reap plenty of accolades as well for her participation.

Up to this point, Chenault had thought it probably best that the less Rachel knew, the better-- to lessen her involvement--especially with regards to Koplanski, and whatever it was he once had that very likely got him killed. Since, however, she was going to continue working on the story, it was probably best if she did see the video, since anyone with an interest in Chenault would likely assume she knew everything as well. Rachel, however, had slipped out of the motel room early that morning to grab a few things from her apartment, before heading over to *The Tribune* to tie up any loose ends. In the end, Chenault decided to go ahead and watch it, and if there was anything pertaining to the story, he'd share it with her later.

After connecting to the motel's WiFi, Chenault searched through the email on his laptop until he found the most recent one from HSikorski@NewYorkTimes.org with "Koplanski video" in the subject line. He then saved the file to his hard drive and hit "Play."

As the video began, the withered haunches of a skeletal old man draped in gray sweat pants were seen slowly shuffling away from the camera. The man then turned around and sat down. Martin Koplanski wore an old, discolored white v-neck tee shirt, and his gaunt and deeply lined face was covered with a wispy white beard. His head was almost completely bald, with the exception of a with a few thin patches of white hair, which suggested that the rounds of chemo he had likely undergone had been successful at killing most of his hair, but not his cancer. Yet despite Koplanski's near cadaverous appearance, there still appeared to be a mischievous twinkle in his eyes as he looked up and to his right on the camera's viewfinder to make sure he was framed and in focus. He then edged forward in his chair and moved around until his face almost filled the 17 inch screen. It was then he began to speak.

"If you are seeing this now, then apparently the worst has happened to me, and at my direction this video is being sent to you by someone, who, well, I'll just say who is very close to me."

Even though he looked near death, Koplanski's voice was still clear, and although it wasn't strong, his voice wasn't as weak as one might have expected from his frail appearance.

"Mr. Valdez and Mr. Chenault, you two are the only ones who I believe can take on this. . .this mission, if you will, to find what I have hidden from those who would, well, . . accelerate my death. And whom I might add, would happily kill you for these 'artifacts,' as I'll refer to them, if they knew that either one of you were on the right track or actually had them. I believed possibly that I could negotiate with these people, and I thought I was doing the right thing by my family. I wanted to look out for my wife and my daughter, and my daughter's children for a long time to come, but if you are seeing this, then apparently I badly misjudged the people I was dealing with. I guess I probably should have reread my own book and taken a lesson from the so-called White Salamander affair, that they'll never again negotiate for what they believe is theirs. They were never to be completely trusted, but then I should have known that. I mean, it was old Brigham Young himself who once uttered the words, 'We have the greatest and smoothest liars in the world.' I suppose even, it's like the old fable, the one with the frog who gives the scorpion a ride on his back across the pond, only to be stung halfway across. I apparently was the foolish frog to think that the scorpion could change its nature. The saving grace is, they will not find the artifacts without the few clues I am about to give to you two--and only you two--about where I have hidden them. Ah, but what is 'them' you might ask. If you have read my book, and I trust that you have by now, I frequently allude to the very foundation of this religion. That's all I'll say for now."

He can't be talking about the Gold Plates thought Chenault. *Even some of the faithful doubt they exist.*

"Now you may or may not know of my experience with this religion and its practitioners--I made very little mention of it in my book. I only imparted one historical fact after another, and then provided my own perspective, which was one that was obtained over my many years as a practicing Latter Day Saint, before my disillusionment, and before I finally pulled my head out of the sand and opened my eyes as an historian. They say that we are the worst haters of Mormons, we ex-Mormons, or Apostates as we're sometimes referred, but I never hated the people, that's the God's honest truth. Just all the lies that this so-called faith was founded upon and the machinations of their twisted leaders. Some might ask, 'How you can say you hate someone's religion and not the people who practice it?' Well, I would just say to that, the same way that a dyed-in-the-wool Democrat can say he hates Republican policies and their leaders, but not the good people--most of them the salt of the earth-- who make up its rank and file."

Chenault checked his watch. While portions of Koplanski's diatribe were mildly interesting, it so far didn't sound like he was going much of anywhere with it.

"Anyway, I'm rambling now, I know,"

Koplanski said. "But if you still have any question as to the legitimacy of this Church, just let me put it this way--if you hear or read about one isolated incident, you can file it away as anecdotal or an aberration, or just something that doesn't entirely represent the whole. But then, when you list and see a number of these things together, one after the other, and throughout the years, you begin to see that they're not just aberrations, but a fully developed pattern. From its very inception, when Joseph Smith allegedly first received the Gold Plates from the angel Moroni and then reportedly translated them into *The Book of Mormon,* up until today. The first curious thing I noticed was that Joseph Smith immediately went out and had his new church incorporated, a rather odd act for such a pious man, I think you'll agree, who alleged himself to be a prophet of God. And also very curiously, in the very first printing of *The Book of Mormon,* Smith had himself listed as being the author, as well as identifying himself as the 'Proprietor.' It wasn't until the second and subsequent printings that it was changed to 'Translated by Joseph Smith.' I could go on and on, but if you've read my book as I asked you to, you will see that when you add up all these cold, hard historical facts, that without the Gold Plates, it all comes tumbling down like a house of cards. The Gold Plates that even Smith's eleven original witnesses couldn't fully agree on their description, and which was even later revealed that they had only spiritually witnessed them--whatever that means. I mean, why would it take 'faith' and 'spiritual eyes' to see them if they're sitting in a bag right there in their lap? And of course, some of these so-called witnesses later went on to recant their testimony and were, of course, excommunicated. However, the fact remains, that Joseph Smith, and now myself, are the only ones to have ever actually seen the artifacts, be they real, or be they--let's just say, less than authentic.

So perhaps you're thinking that since I now despise this religion so much, after what it did to my life and to the lives of my family, that even if I found actual proof of the existence of these artifacts, that maybe I wouldn't necessarily want this proof to come out just out of spite. And you might be right. However, the fact remains that I'm still an historian, and one who specialized in religious history at that. So, I guess anything is possible. But then again, maybe what I found proves that there were, in fact, something along the lines of what Smith claimed, but not quite as authentic as he would have had us believe. And which if this revelation ever came out, would fairly well completely discredit the religion. But only I know what I have at this point, and hopefully one or both of you gentlemen will also see what I have found, and I will leave them in your care and to your discretion to do with them what you will.

I hope you understand that when it comes to the artifacts, that I'm not playing coy, or trying to be mysterious just for the sake of being mysterious.

There is a method to my madness, and I've set up a
series of safeguards to keep their final location from
those who would, well--kill for them. One of you,
Mr. Valdez or Mr. Chenault, whichever of you who
proves to be most tenacious, . ."

Or not been murdered flashed through
Chenault's mind.

". . .needs to go see my wife--my lovely Marie--
and ask her for a box of my best smokes." With the
bony index finger and thumb of his skeletal hand
wrapped around it, Koplanski brought a large thick
cigar up to his dry, cracked lips and took a long
draw. The end of the cigar glowed bright orange as
Koplanski briefly closed his eyes as he savored it.

". . .I know, I know. But what's it going to do,
kill me?" he said with a mischievous grin. "I
acquired a taste for these several years back after
my long bout with Mormonism. Anyway, as I said,
you need to go see my wife. And no, don't bother
to ask her over the phone, you'll need to be in
Palmyra anyway. You'll understand why later. I
wish you the best. And please be careful. And take
it from me, if you ever sense that you're in any
danger, you need to just walk away--because they
will kill you for them."

CHAPTER 42

Evan Fiske rapped lightly on the door of Brockston Ratchford's wood-paneled study before he eased it open and peeked in.

"Come on in. Close the door, if you would," Ratchford called over from across the large room where he'd been reading the latest *Time* magazine article on his campaign.

Fiske closed the door behind him and strode over towards Ratchford who sat up in the plush, high-backed leather chair behind his massive desk.

"So, have you given any thought to what we talked about the other evening?" Ratchford said, just as Fiske began to take a seat in one of the straight-backed chairs opposite Ratchford's desk.

"Sir, in answer to the question you posed the other night, I slept on it, and I really think that it's probably not a good idea at this point to bring out the nanny. . ."

"Amelia," Ratchford interjected, filling in the

name for him.

"It's probably best at this time not to bring out Amelia with your family--especially at any of the media events. I know you think the concept of your family appearing 'whole' plays up the whole 'strong family' angle and all that nonsense, but keep in mind, your wife has been gone just a little more than a week. You're polling so well right now there's absolutely no reason to bring in any outside factor, and especially one which we can't really predict with any certainty how it would play out in the press--though I'm thinking this soon--probably pretty negatively. In fact, I think it's probably best to replace her for the short term with an older, more matronly nanny, sort of a grandmotherly figure. And then, who knows, maybe down the line, when we need a bump in the polls, or to get you back on the front page, maybe then we'll think about bringing Amelia back and play up the romantic angle of it--single mom with three kids, she comforts you in your time of grief, and then who knows, maybe some wedding bells shortly before the election. It'll be the modern-day Brady Bunch."

Ratchford just shook his head in admiration, chuckling to himself. "You are one calculating son of a bitch."

"You like it?"

Ratchford smiled. ". . .You're gonna get me elected President, aren't you?"

Fiske looked Ratchford directly in the eye. "You can count on it."

CHAPTER 43

A half empty bottle of champagne, along with a bowl of strawberry remnants and some leftover whipped cream, rested on the night stand next to Chenault, who was leaning back against the headboard as he read. Rachel, wearing nothing but one of Chenault's Oxford shirts rolled to the sleeves, sat next to him as she checked the email on her phone. It was the end to an otherwise almost perfect evening as Chenault, finishing the final passage of Koplanski's book, could only just smile and shake his head with a deep admiration for Koplanski's work.

"Rachel, you've got to read this sometime," he blurted before he could catch himself.

"Read what?" she said, glancing over.

Chenault grimaced slightly, ". . .Uh, Koplanski's book."

"Oh, so you finally found a copy?"

"I kind of borrowed it from the Family History

Library."

"Really? So that's what you've been reading this whole time?"

"Well, not the entire time. I was getting some other stuff done. But I think I have a pretty good idea now why Koplanski told me to read his book."

"And when would he have done that?" she said, as she turned to him wearing a puzzled expression clearly meant for his benefit.

"Oh yeah. I kind of left that part out too."

"Which part?"

"The part where Koplanski sent me a letter-- probably right before he was killed."

"And what did the letter say?"

"'Read my book.' That's all it said."

"He wrote you just a three word letter, and didn't say anything else?"

"Well, he did sign it. But I think you'll agree that three word letters carry a lot more weight when the writers of them have been recently murdered."

"Well, aside from wondering why you never told me about this until now, why do you say you now see why Koplanski told you to read his book?"

"First, before you dwell on it any longer," Chenault said, "I didn't tell you about it, and the importance of the book, because, I don't know if you've noticed, but people around us seem to keep getting killed."

"So you were shielding me from this bit of information for my own protection?"

"Well, yeah. That's pretty much it exactly."

"I don't know if I buy that. I think you're somehow still worried that I'm going to try to scoop your story, and the fact that you still don't seem to trust me after, well you know. . .."

Chenault drew in a deep breath, trying to recall if indelicately dealing with a lover's hurt feelings was one of the many reasons he was still single, and in retrospect, he was pretty sure it was.

". . .Rachel, I promise, you're making too big a deal of this. Of course, I trust you. What do you want to know?"

"Just--why he told you to read his book?"

"Because it pretty much tells me what he was probably killed for. And where he probably found it, which validates its authenticity."

"And what is 'it?'"

"Well, the central premise of Koplanski's book seems to be that with all the credibility problems and wild claims, and other mumbo jumbo swirling around Joseph Smith, that the legitimacy of the entire Mormon religion rests upon the authenticity or existence of the Gold Plates--since Smith's entire story and the Book of Mormon are based upon their translation. I mean, here's the passage that Koplanski opens with, which incidentally, he borrowed from Smith's nephew who was President of the Mormon Church at the time, and who was actually writing in defense of the church and the authenticity of his uncle's story." Chenault turned to the first page of the prologue and began reading.

'Mormonism must stand or fall on the story

of Joseph Smith. He was either a prophet of God, divinely called, properly appointed and commissioned, or he was one of the biggest frauds this world has ever seen. There is no middle ground. If Joseph was a deceiver, who willfully attempted to mislead people, then he should be exposed, his claims refuted, and his doctrines shown to be false.'

"So, if the actual plates were ever found," Chenault said, "even the doubters could no longer ridicule the religion, and it would likely grow explosively worldwide. It would be along the lines of finding 2000-year-old videotapes of Jesus walking across the water, or raising the dead and resurrecting--there would no longer be any room for doubt."

"Yes, I suppose. But without them, wouldn't the religion pretty much just carry on as before? I mean, there are still millions who believe they at least once existed.

"I guess so, but see, that's not the only other option," Chenault said.

"So what's the third option?"

"It's the one that Koplanski--who keep in mind, was a complete skeptic at this point--seemed to be leaning towards the most in his book. And that is, that the plates did in fact exist, but that they were nothing more than just a prop that Smith had cobbled together before concocting his religion. Smith had this whole story that God had instructed him that no one was permitted to actually lay their eyes on the plates, 'Lest they be destroyed' is the quote I think I kept running across. Of the alleged original witnesses, several of them later recanted, and then later it came out in the story that they were only 'spiritual witnesses,'" he said, taking the liberty to emphasize "spiritual witnesses" with air quotes. "But there were, in fact, quite a few people who did swear under oath that they held them in their laps after the Plates had been placed inside a cloth sack. So then, there had to be something in that sack with some heft to it, so it felt like they were at least in the shape, and close to the weight of what Smith had described."

"So 'them' are the Gold Plates?" Rachel said.

"Or some facsimile thereof."

"And where did he supposedly find them?"

"Well again, it's only speculation, because he wrote the book years ago, but if you put it all together--well, first listen to this. Keep in mind when I'm reading this passage, that Koplanski's farm, where he later supposedly found what he keeps referring to as 'the artifacts' was just north of the town of Palmyra.

After Smith first announced his discovery of the Gold Plates, he was reportedly the recipient of much unwanted attention--likely from his former treasure hunting associates, as well as the local criminal element. The Gold Plates, either real (giving the Religion the benefit of the doubt), or a prop (from which he would go on to propagate his masterful hoax) would not have been safe almost anywhere on the small Smith farm. His patron at the time, however, a Mr. Martin Harris, a farmer of some means, and reportedly the scribe of the first 116 pages of The Book of Mormon (as Smith supposedly translated the plates from the bottom of his hat with his seer stone) owned a sizable farm, some 320 acres, just north of the town of Palmyra, and less than 3 miles from the Smith farm. It is my contention that the plates (be they completely authentic, or simply a mere prop) might one day be discovered on what once comprised Martin Harris property.

"And don't tell me," Rachel said, "Koplanski's farm was on what was once the Harris property."

"Very good," Chenault said with a smile. "You get a gold star for the day."

CHAPTER 44

Chenault's memories of growing up in New Orleans were filled with the ancient rituals and vivid religious iconography of his father's Catholicism, along with the fiery Old Testament passages frequently quoted by his mother. Although Mama Chenault had converted when she'd married, she had still retained a good bit of the Pentecostal fire and brimstone with which she'd been raised. Surprisingly, though, her most oft quoted passage, and the one that had sunk in most deeply in the young Chenault was "Judge not, lest ye be judged."

Given that in the Big Easy, where there were a multitude of things to potentially be judgmental about, from drive-through bars, to drag queen strippers, to just about everything that happened during Mardi Gras, it was a wonder his mother had remained so tolerant. And through it all, Chenault had also developed a "live and let live" philosophy, one which he credited with leaving himself open for new experiences throughout his life. From migrating to the chilly climates of Massachusetts for college, to later moving to live and work in a place even his mother had always made a point of referring to as "Sin City," Chenault had always tried to remain open-minded in his life as well as in his work.

He'd even made a concerted effort throughout his career to keep his political views to himself, and had never been in the business of pushing one political candidate over another. That wasn't his job. That's what spin doctors, sound bites, and thirty-second campaign commercials were for. In part, he held to this philosophy because he wanted to be thought of as fair-minded, thus allowing him journalistic access to candidates of all political persuasions. He also wanted to never give any one cause to accuse him of being a member of the so-called, and as far as he had determined, rather fictional "liberal media" establishment.

But this time was different--it was now time to take a stand. The more he found out about Brockston Ratchford and the very questionable foundations of the religion that Ratchford purportedly subscribed to, the more he questioned whether Ratchford was even fit to be the Chief Executive of the most powerful country in the world.

Although Chenault was of the mind that anyone, including Brockston Ratchford, had every right to believe in whatever he or she wanted to, he had to draw the line at a candidate, who from everything he'd learned, apparently believed that his election was predestined, and therefore ordained by a higher power. With these delusions of grandeur, Ratchford would then ultimately would take no responsibility for his actions, and would likely defend whatever he did in office, at least in his own mind, as being "God's will." But what was perhaps even scarier, was that by his own admission, Ratchford would say or do just about anything to get elected, which lead Chenault to only one conclusion--that the man was not only morally bankrupt, but possibly delusional--a potent combination usually reserved for deranged Third World dictators.

It also bothered Chenault that Ratchford's religion even seemed to have a not-so-hidden political agenda, which appeared in large part to be to propagate the religion, seemingly for reasons beyond just increasing their tithing base and their vast financial holdings. Even just imagining the nightmare scenario where the theocracy that Joseph Smith had dreamed of had become the law of the land, had Chenault tossing and turning in bed that night as he wrestled with the decision on what his next move would be.

There seemed to be several paths before him. He could stay and try to prove that Brockston Ratchford would stop at nothing to get elected, which perhaps even included having some involvement in the murder and kidnapping of

members of his own family. He could also keep
feeding tips to Patterson in the hope that FBI and
the joint agency task force could somehow tie them
all together and make a case. Unless, however, he
could provide them with some sort of "smoking
gun," or an eyewitness who would actually testify
against the powerful Senator, Chenault seriously
doubted that Patterson or anyone else involved with
the investigation had the nerve to follow through
with a full inquiry of Ratchford. They all knew that
in a high profile case like this, if any one of them
made a single misstep or an unsubstantiated
allegation against Ratchford, their career would not
just be in jeopardy, but over. This then meant that
without conclusive proof to even just initiate an
investigation, absolutely nothing would happen to
Brockston Ratchford, and the political juggernaut
he now appeared to be would just keep rolling along
all the way to the White House.

Chenault, who had never been very religious in
his adult life, was even beginning to wonder if there
might not be some grain of truth to the charges
made early in the campaign by some evangelical
Christians, who at one time had called Ratchford
everything from the "Anti-Christ" to "Old Scratch"
himself. While he didn't necessarily buy into these
charges literally, he had come to the conclusion
from everything he had learned, that the election of
Brockston Ratchford would very likely be one of
the worst possible outcomes for the country as far
as not only affecting U.S. policy, but also by

extension of its power--the world. In the lone possession of this inside information that he'd uncovered, as well as an insight into Ratchford's true character, which it was also unlikely any other reporter in the world had, Chenault realized that there was now much more at stake than just getting a story. It now felt something more along the lines of being his sworn duty to do just about whatever was necessary--short of knocking the man off--to prevent the election of Brockston Ratchford.

CHAPTER 45

"I'm spinning my wheels here," Chenault told Rachel the next morning. "I think Ratchford's dirty. In fact, I know it in my bones, but so far, neither the FBI or I have a single solid thing on him. So unless some buried body pops up from his past, this guy's going to wind up getting elected."

Rachel sat up in bed and leaned back against the headboard as she gave the matter some thought. ". . .What about where you have Ratchford on tape saying how he's 'over his dead wife' and 'already moved on'?"

"I thought about that. And while it makes him look like an incredible asshole, that's nothing the

FBI could really use. And releasing it this early, well, . .it would probably be forgotten by next week."

Chenault knew that to do any damage to Ratchford's credibility, he needed to be patient, to wait until after Ratchford had either peaked or was going into the final stretch. That would be the time when the recorded quotes might do the most damage, to show what kind of man Ratchford really was, but released too early there would be way too much time for damage control, counter attacks, and plenty of time for the public to completely forget about it. Sadly, it was one of the things Chenault had noticed throughout his career covering politics-- that otherwise intelligent voters seemed to have remarkably short memories for candidates' transgressions, especially for candidates of their own party.

"There is, however, a Plan B," Chenault went on. "It was actually something you said the other night that got me to thinking. I don't even remember exactly what it was now, but it has to do with going at this from a different angle, since it seems like we've gone about as far as we can in the story--at least from this end. But if we head back east to Palmyra and are able to get to the bottom of the Koplanski story, and find that the murders are indeed connected as they appear to be, then hopefully, that will lead us back around to making whatever the connection might have been here, and figuring out just exactly what went on between

Ratchford and the Lamotts-- if anything. Of course, it also occurred to me, since I haven't been able to stop thinking about them since I got the video from Koplanski, that if we can find the plates that Koplanski supposedly stashed away, and they do turn out to just be a prop as he seemed to keep hinting, that could just as effectively derail Ratchford's campaign if it's shown that's he's basically nothing more than a 19th century Scientologist."

"You don't think that's a bit of a stretch?"

"Not really. If I--if we, can find the plates and they do turn out to be just as Koplanski speculates throughout his book--just a prop and the foundation of a hoax that ultimately became a worldwide religion, then Ratchford's judgment will not only be shown to be questionable at best, but his credibility, I believe, would be absolutely shot. It would be such a black eye to his campaign that I don't know how anybody, even within his own party, would be able to take him seriously."

"But what if, let's say, the plates turn out to be real?"

"Well, of course, I would. . .unveil them, I guess. I mean, it would be on par with producing the original Ten Commandments tablets, but. . ."

"But you don't really believe they're real do you?" Rachel posed with a skeptical grimace.

"It doesn't really matter what I believe--it just matters what they turn out to be. But if they do turn out to be real, I'd more than likely wait before bringing them out so it wouldn't give Ratchford any added boost before the election--and then hope for the best in the meantime. So what do you think?"

". . .I say let's find them."

CHAPTER 46

Before making their way to Palmyra, New York, Chenault decided that after all Martin Koplanski's widow, Marie, had been through, it was probably a good idea to call ahead. First, to let her know that he and Rachel were headed her way, rather than just showing up unannounced on her doorstep. And second, to confirm that she had arrived back home from her daughter's home in Minnesota--otherwise, it would be a long trip for nothing.

As he made the call, Rachel sat closely by him on the side of the bed, close enough to hear the phone ringing at the other end as Chenault gazed back at her with a smile. When Marie Koplanski finally picked up he was a bit surprised when after identifying himself she said rather matter-of-factly, "Yes, I've been expecting your call."

"You have?" Chenault said.

"Yes, Martin told me one day that you or Mr.

Valdez might come calling, and I guess since we both know what happened to Mr. Valdez, I assumed I would be hearing from you."

"Yes, it was a terrible tragedy," he said, trying to downplay the murder that could just as well have happened to him.

"You don't really believe his death was just coincidental, do you?" she said.

Realizing Marie Koplanski was probably much sharper than he'd presumed from the image of simple farmer's wife he had imagined, Chenault decided to come clean. "No, actually, I don't. I just didn't want to alarm you."

"Hell's bells, son. After what they did to my husband, do you really think there's that much that alarms me anymore?"

"No, I guess not. Anyway, I'm calling to see if it's alright if I can fly out to meet you and bring a friend of mine along."

There was a brief pause at the other end of the line. "Martin didn't mention anything about you bringing anybody else."

"Well, he couldn't have known then. I've only recently met her."

"And she can be trusted?"

Chenault looked over to Rachel who'd heard the question as well, as a smile spread across her face.

". . .I'd trust her with my life, Mrs. Koplanski."

"Son, no offense, but it's not your life that I'm worried about. After what these people did to my husband, I only trust two people in my life--my daughter and Jesus Christ, and you and your friend aren't either one of them, so you'll understand any misgivings I might have."

"I absolutely do. And if there's anything I can do to help put your mind at ease, like let you speak to my editor, or anything else along those lines, I'd be happy to do it."

". . .No, that won't be necessary," she said after a brief moment of deliberation. "Martin basically vouched for you and Mr. Valdez when he told me I might be hearing from one of you, so you should be alright."

"Well then, if it's okay with you, we should probably arrive in Palmyra sometime around mid to late afternoon your time tomorrow."

"That's fine by me," she said.

CHAPTER 47

Since the recent revelation that Felix Vadez had also been a part of Martin Koplanski's invitation-only scavenger hunt, a number of new questions had been raised. As he sat at the air terminal waiting for their delayed flight to Rochester, Chenault decided to make a couple of calls to hopefully get some answers to a few of them.

The first on his list was NYPD Detective Ronald Wheatly, whose phone number he'd still not taken the time to program into his cell, but whose business card he still had, crammed in with about ten others in the recesses of his overstuffed wallet.

"So how did you really happen to come knocking at my door at three in the morning? And don't tell me it was because you found me in Koplanski's Rolodex--you just used that as an excuse to come knocking."

". . .We had a tip," Wheatly answered after a brief pause.

"Anonymous I'm guessing."

"Are there any other kind?"

"That's what I thought. Did the caller say anything else?"

"Just something about that we should show you pictures of Koplanski from the crime scene to see if it got a reaction out of you."

"Which is why you just happened to have your file with the crime scene photos that day at lunch, so I would be sure to see the bloody character on Koplanski's forehead," Chenault said, more thinking out loud. "And just out of curiosity, did you happen to get a separate tip on Felix Valdez?"

"Yeah, but there was nothing to it. When we called him, checking on his whereabouts, he'd been in frickin' Europe or someplace. But how could you have known about that?"

"Lucky guess. Anyway, thanks. I'll be in touch."

It was now even clearer to Chenault that someone had wanted to make both Valdez and him very aware of Koplanski's death--the first step in reeling them both in. *But again, for what purpose?*

One lingering question Chenault had was from a story he'd covered several months back--the assassination of former Georgia Governor Zeb McCall. Up until this point, it hadn't even occurred to Chenault to make a connection between recent events and McCall being gunned down, largely because the chance they were connected was so remote. However, with Ratchford's recent surge in the polls, along with the fact that McCall, prior to his murder, had been picked by most pundits as the likely nominee, it just seemed to Chenault like it was at least worth a follow-up phone call.

The story of the disturbed young man who had been pegged as the lone gunman in the investigator's final report had never made a lot of sense to Chenault. The fact that twenty-year-old Ricky Gillespie should have probably overdosed from the amount of heroin found in his body was quickly brushed over by local police investigators who had been all too eager to wrap up the case because of their department's embarrassment over the failures of their security detail.

And although he knew it was a longshot that there was any connection between the stories, Chenault figured it couldn't hurt to ring up the Atlanta M.E., a friendly acquaintance of his from their days back in D.C.

"Sam Mitchell. Michael Chenault. How's Hotlanta these days?"

"In the middle of November, not too hot right now. What can I do for you Michael?"

"I meant to follow up with you earlier, but I've been kind of sidetracked lately. Anyway, I just wanted to ask you if you ever fully bought into that story about the Gillespie kid being the only one behind the assassination of Governor McCall?"

"As a matter of fact, no. But that's, of course, off the record, since Atlanta's finest and the State Bureau of Investigation decided to wrap up the case in near record time--but I was never fully convinced. First, as I think I told you before, the level of heroin found in his bloodstream was off the charts and probably should have killed him, as well as their early findings when they did their background on him that he'd never shown any inclination before of having been either political, disturbed, or a drug user, other than maybe a little pot. But the kicker actually came out after the investigation had been closed. I just happened to notice something on the kid's elbow, right on the top at the juncture of his left forearm, which almost looked like a small growth underneath the skin, or a swollen lymph node, but which actually turned out to be this little bulging muscle. Luckily, I recognized it for what it was, which is what a lot tennis of players develop over time from playing a lot of tennis. In fact, a lot of players even call it their 'tennis muscle.'"

"So what, he played a lot of tennis?"

"Yeah, competitively through out high school, before he went off to college and then decided to drop out and smoke a lot of pot."

"So what's significant about that?"

"It's significant," Mitchell said, "Because people, and again, especially tennis players get that overdeveloped muscle from using that arm extensively. The fact that this muscle was on his left arm would indicate that he was most likely left handed. He, however, shot himself in the right side of the head. Kind of hard to do that with your left hand don't you think?"

"Interesting," Chenault said. "And what did the police say when you sent this their way?"

"Take a wild guess."

"Case closed?" Chenault said.

"You got it."

"Thanks, Sam. I'll let you know if I find anything else out."

Next up on the call list was the manager of the Salt Lake City television station that had broken the kidnap/rescue story in their exclusive broadcast.

"So just how did the police and your news crew happen to know that Delmer Lamott was holed up in a flea bag motel on the edge of town?"

"Well, you know we'd been working real hard on that story, following any leads we had to try to break it open, and one of them just happened to pay off?" Myron Sterling, the station manager, answered.

". . .You got an anonymous tip, didn't you?"

"Well yeah, something like that."

It was exactly like that thought Chenault. "Could you tell me who took the call and if I could talk to them?"

Sterling directed him to Kathryn Mayer, the on-air reporter who had fielded the tipster's call, and the first thing Chenault asked her was if she happened to have recorded it.

"No, but by that time we had already fielded about 500 so-called tips, and were assuming as with just about every other call before it that it was either worthless or just another prank caller."

"Well, could you describe the voice?" Chenault asked.

"I remember it was a deep male voice. Also, he spoke rather slowly and very deliberately, almost sort of. . .robotic."

"So it's possible it was an electronic voice maybe, like you hear on a phone answering machine?"

"No, there was definitely a person at the other end. You could tell by the way he paused between words as he thought about what to say next. It wasn't anything prerecorded like on an answering machine."

"So, then possibly he was using an electronic voice altering device?"

"I never really thought about it--I just thought he had a weird voice, but yeah, I suppose."

"Do you know if they were able to run a trace on the call?"

"I think I heard one of the FBI agents say they tracked the number to a 'burn phone' that had been purchased with cash at a Wal-Mart on the south end of town."

"And just one other question. What was it about this particular caller that made you take him seriously?"

"I guess I'd have to say the details. Whoever this person was, as much as he knew and as much as he told me--it was almost like he was in on it."

CHAPTER 48

After several minutes of gazing down through the clouds at the checkerboard of farmland below, and pondering a number of the seemingly disparate facts and leads that had brought him to this point, Chenault turned to Rachel, who was flipping through the in-flight magazine. "I know it's crazy, but the one person who seems to keep popping up in all this, who almost seems to be the behind-the-scenes, shadow puppet master. . .is Koplanski."

"I was thinking that exact same thing," she said. "He sends you the letter telling you to read his book. Probably did the same thing to Valdez. And tells his wife, well ahead of time, that she might be hearing from you or Valdez, and then has his video sent to you from beyond the grave. . .You don't think he might still be alive, do you?"

"Oh, no. He's very dead. I saw the police photos and autopsy report. Not to mention, the police had some harebrained idea that I might somehow be involved in his murder. But possibly working in concert with someone else--a confederate maybe, who Koplanski might have even had drown him to help put him out of his misery, and who then went on to set up the crime scene by slitting his throat. And who could have then followed that up with the anonymous tips to reel Valdez and me in. And I mean one thing for certain, he clearly had someone send me the tape postmortem."

"And maybe then this same person had the Lamott brothers kidnap Ratchford's daughter and kill his wife?"

Pondering that possibility for a moment, Chenault grimaced as he shook his head. ". . .But no, see that's where it stops making sense, where things just don't quite seem to add up--at least where Koplanski is concerned. What would have been his motive?"

"Well, he clearly hated Mormons, and maybe that, along with staging his own murder was like his last act of vengeance or retribution--his way of getting back at them for ruining his life, and in the process, maybe even trying to ruin the one chance of a Mormon actually getting elected President."

"But that would make him like an evil genius, and from the video, all I saw was a very frail old man with a few months to live, whose one pleasure in life was taking a drag on a big nasty cigar. And then there's the matter of sending me on this wild goose chase to find the Plates. Where does that fit into all this? And then finally, the manner of the killings--by Blood Atonement, with 'Apostate' scrawled across their foreheads. With both of them being brought to my attention, there almost clearly had to be some sort of connection. And since it's nearly impossible to connect Koplanski to the Ratchford murder-kidnapping, which took place after he was killed, then logically, it would seem to clear him of what happened to him back in Palmyra."

"Well, I guess. But as it's been shown throughout history, it's always a mistake to underestimate the lengths someone who's committed enough might go to achieve a desired end result."

"Duly noted. Hopefully, the Mrs. can maybe give us a little more insight into the way Koplanski's mind worked."

CHAPTER 49

After arriving in Palmyra in their rented Nissan, the first thing Chenault noticed upon entering the Koplanski's modest, weather-beaten farmhouse was the well-worn furniture throughout, which bespoke of a life that had probably not been very easy over the last twenty years. Despite the fact, though, that they didn't have much, the interior of the house had been kept immaculate, and demonstrated a pride that showed they were still proud of what they did have.

Marie Koplanski, at least in appearance, was close to what Chenault had imagined--a slight woman with a drawn face, dressed in a simple red print dress and dark sweater, with her graying hair pulled back into a bun. Chenault knew, though, through his earlier conversation with her that while she may have had the appearance of a simple farmer's wife, she was still quite sharp, likely well educated, and he needed to remain mindful that under no circumstances should he condescend or be less than forthcoming. Since her cooperation still seemed to be one of the keys to finding her husband's hidden Mormon "artifact," he couldn't risk losing it by saying anything that she might perceive as either disingenuous or patronizing.

After escorting Rachel and Chenault through the kitchen and into the living room, she did her best to make them feel at home before they got down to business by offering a plate of freshly baked oatmeal cookies and coffee or milk to wash them down. After several minutes of pleasantries, Chenault set his coffee cup down on the rickety end table next to him.

"You mentioned that your husband once told you that either Felix Valdez or I would show up one day."

"Well, he said that you might."

"I was just curious, I know Mr. Valdez is, or rather was, a readily identifiable public figure, but how were you going to identify me?"

"Actually, the truth of the matter is, my husband just left me this, and mentioned once, almost in passing, that two men might be visiting after he was gone." She pulled out a large manila envelope, opened it and took out two photos that appeared to have been printed off the internet. The top photo was a posed and grinning headshot of Felix Valdez. The second, an old AP candid photo of a pensive-looking Chenault at what appeared to be an awards ceremony, with the words "Michael Chenault" scrawled in black magic marker under the photo.

"After he was murdered, my first thought was that one of the two men he said might come to see me might be involved with his murder. That's when I took the envelope out of our safe deposit box here in town and opened it."

"Just curious, did you happen to mention either of us--Valdez or me--to the police during their investigation?"

"Well, I was pretty sure that Mr. Valdez didn't take a break from his news show to come up here and murder Martin. You, who I'd never heard of, I wasn't so sure. But I made a few calls and did my own bit of investigating, and found out that you were down in the city when it happened. So no, to answer to your question, I didn't say anything to the police about you. Why? Did they say I did?"

"No, actually, all they would say was that it was an anonymous tipster who gave them my name."

"But why would somebody try to frame you?" she asked.

"I'm still trying to figure that out myself, but I think it had more to do with notifying me than framing me. I mean, the only thing I can come up with is, if this person hadn't given them my name, your husband's murder would have been just another obituary in upstate New York that I never would have known about."

"But what would have been the point of notifying you about my husband's murder?"

"To draw me in. The same reason somebody

anonymously sent me pictures of Senator Ratchford's wife, who incidentally, was killed in the same way as your husband."

"Senator Ratchford's wife was drowned?"

"I'm sorry, you're right. I forgot--your husband had been drowned first. And I think I have a pretty good idea now why."

"Why, please tell me?"

Chenault, with a grim look, shook his head.

". . .If you really know why, Mr. Chenault, I think I have the right to know. Whatever it is, I can handle it. I may look like a frail old woman, but I've led a full life, and I've dealt with a number of highs and lows throughout it. I've lost a husband. I've lost an infant son. In fact, I lost my whole previous life when I was unceremoniously dumped by my Church because of being married to Martin, and then had everyone of my so-called friends in what I thought was my loyal Church family, turn their backs on me and shun me forever. Whatever it is, you can tell me."

Chenault swallowed hard first as he debated whether to reveal his educated guess to Martin Koplanski's resilient widow. ". . .I think he was tortured. I think whoever came to see him applied their version of 'waterboarding' to get whatever information they could about whatever it was they were seeking. They may have even gotten the information, which we won't know until we get to the end of this little scavenger hunt. But apparently, he did give them mine and Felix Valdez's names. I think they then lured us both in and murdered Valdez."

"But if that's the case," Rachel said, "That he gave them your names, then that's probably all they got out of him."

"And why is that?" Chenault said.

"Think about it. Because he knew that you two would be getting his tape sent to you anyway, and that sooner or later you were going to be involved. Plus, hadn't he already written you telling you to read his book? It was information he could safely give them, without ever actually revealing wherever it was he'd hidden his 'artifacts,' since neither of you knew anything. And since you're thinking that they lured you in and killed Valdez, then it sounds to me like they didn't get the information they wanted. It sounds like really, he gave them nothing, since neither of you would know a thing without his string of clues."

"The girl's got a point. Martin always could keep a secret. He obviously kept one from me for over twenty years--one that got him killed."

Despite the horrible and likely truth of her husband's death that had just been revealed, the tears that filled her eyes were not those of horror or sadness, but tears of joy as her face lit up. "God, I loved that man."

CHAPTER 50

To bide some time while waiting for his next instructions, Cloyd Lamott drove aimlessly around the several streets that ran through Palmyra, and then out along the back roads on the outskirts of town. He was even more on edge than usual, as his senses were still heightened by the exhilaration of his first airplane flight that had yet to wear off. Gazing down through the clouds at the miles upon miles of vast deserts and checker-boarded fields, the mighty rivers and mountains, and the great cities and towns rising up out of the ground from nothing, he had the amazing feeling of looking through God's own eyes at the breathtaking and miraculous works created by His own hand.

As he had been instructed in his last communication with The Prophet, Lamott used the false identification he'd been provided to charter a mid-size Cessna turboprop out of West Jordan Municipal airport, just south of Salt Lake City, to fly to Rochester, New York, the regional airport closest to Palmyra. The talkative pilot, Bob, had been quite helpful, pointing out all the sights along the way, but as he was now the subject of a nationwide manhunt, Lamott had no choice but to leave him folded up and stuffed into the fuselage at the rear off the craft. Upon arrival, Lamott had then stolen the first car he'd come across--a dark blue, late model Impala with Vermont plates. Lacking confidence in his ability to hotwire the newer model vehicle with its more complicated electrical system, he'd been forced to take the keys from the owner at knifepoint, and now found himself driving around with the car's owners body in the trunk.

In stark contrast to his awe-inspiring flight, and even the desolate, red chalky streets of his native Hildale, from everything he'd seen so far of Palmyra, Lamott found it almost impossible to believe that the world's one true faith had begun in such an unassuming little town. There appeared to be almost nothing to speak of, but a post office, several stoplights, a canal, and a few scattered stores. Yet despite the modest humbleness of the town, he'd always meant to make a pilgrimage there, to pay homage as a great many of the faithful had done before him to come and see where it had all begun. Joseph Smith's boyhood home and the famed Hill Cumorah were just a few of the sites, along with the grand pageant put on every year in which a thousand actors were brought in to recreate sacred moments and events throughout Mormon history. It occurred to Lamott that after his divinely inspired mission had been accomplished--after the rescue of the sacred artifact and the dispatching of the Gentile reporter--he would take the man's woman as his first wife, and one day return with her and their many children. And here, in the birthplace of his religion, surrounded by all the many sacred sites, he could further lead them on their journey to the righteous path and teach them the many miraculous stories that had been shared with him as he had been brought into the faith.

Upon further reflection, Cloyd Lamott's thoughts turned back to the reporter--the one obstacle keeping him apart from his bride-to-be. He had gone over and over the way he would slay the meddling Gentile, each time refining the plan just a little until he now pictured it the exact same way each time. The only variable was whether or not he would need to shoot the man in order to first disable him. If he could take him by surprise, it wouldn't be necessary, but if he was not able to, he didn't want to engage the man physically. Even though the man was only a mere writer, mostly of slanderous articles against his faith he'd been told, he appeared to be in reasonably good shape and of sufficient build that he could prove to be difficult to subdue. But if he was able to get the drop on him, the first thing he would do would be to slice him across both Achilles tendons to render him "legless" and essentially defenseless. But he definitely wanted the man to stay alive--at least at first. It was important that the man understand not only why he was being punished, but that he be able to fully comprehend his eventual fate. He planned first to stab the man in each of his vital organs, one by one, with the exception of his heart. He would start with his kidneys, then stomach, and finally his lungs. While the man still had his eyes to bear witness to his own slow execution, he would prop him up and then emasculate him. After that, he planned to remove the man's ears, nose, fingers, tongue, and lastly, his eyes, to take away all his senses, leaving him only with consciousness so that he would still be fully aware of his fate when he began the final step of slowly sawing across the side of the man's neck.

Although he couldn't put it into words, Lamott had noticed that the killing of the man was inexorably linked to the first time he would take the man's beautiful woman into his arms, to hold her down and plant his seed into her for the first time. He imagined that perhaps at first she might not be completely willing, but over time, after many, many times of sowing his seed within her, she would eventually know and understand that it was God's will that they be together. With the two acts now so closely intertwined in Lamott's mind, he found himself actually becoming aroused at the mere thought of killing the man. This longing, in turn, only led to him wanting to bring both acts to their speedy completion all the more, as he now literally lusted over the thought of killing this man, whom from everything he had been told, was truly an abomination in the eyes of the Lord.

CHAPTER 51

Chenault had just a few more things to ask Marie Koplanski, but before getting to the million dollar question, he decided to ask the one question that he would have most liked to have asked Martin Koplanski in person.

"Maybe there's something you can tell me, Mrs. Koplanski."

"Please, call me 'Marie.'"

"Marie, I've wondered about how, or why your husband came to, I presume, fall away from the Church. What caused him to start questioning doctrine and the official party line after so many years as a devoted Latter Day Saint?"

"Well, Martin would probably never have admitted this, intellectual that he was, but I think it was more like he felt the Church fell away from him and our family. You see, after I gave birth a second time, there were complications and I lost the child, a beautiful baby boy. I was then also no longer able to conceive. But the way Martin saw it, not only was there very little compassion or understanding expressed by the community, but everybody just seemed to keep asking us and asking us when we were going to have more children. It was almost as if they looked at us with suspicion--like that somehow we were trying to live like Gentiles, having only one child. And after repeatedly explaining I could no longer have children, they finally stopped asking, but then they just started to avoid us all together, like we had some sort of plague they might catch. And then later we heard there were rumors being spread that God was punishing us, and that's why we couldn't have any more children. When Martin heard that, that was it. At that moment, it then seemed to become his personal mission to debunk the entire faith. There, of course, had always been questions floating around, but the proper thing to do, that is if you were an obedient member, was to just let them go unanswered. So when Martin didn't have those constraints anymore, that's what he set out to do, to try to find out the answers, and in the process, he opened my eyes along the way."

"Now it all makes sense. . .I have just one last question. In the video your husband sent me, Martin told me to ask you to bring me a box of his best smokes?"

Despite having never met Martin Koplanski in person, Chenault now almost felt as if he knew him on a first-name basis--from reading his book, to hearing and seeing him in the video, to hearing his loving wife speak glowingly about the cantankerous old professor who had chosen to walk away from the security of academia because he could no longer pretend to be believe in something he no longer knew to be true. Chenault not only felt like he knew him, but admired him more than just about anybody he'd ever met. By writing and publishing the book and by walking away from his tenured position and a church which essentially had been his life, Martin Koplanski had made a choice that very few people Chenault could think of would have had the strength of character to follow in his footsteps and give up what he had given up. In retrospect, it, in fact, appeared to Chenault that the only thing Martin Koplanski had at the time he made those choices were the dim prospects that lay ahead for the last quarter of his life, along with what was very likely a miniscule nest egg. Yet from everything he'd since learned, it seemed as if Martin Koplanski had gone on to live a very full and rewarding life despite the absence of any significant material wealth.

As Marie Koplanski reentered the room with a small, relatively flat wooden box cradled in both hands, the first thing that flashed through Chenault's mind was there was no way that the Gold Plates would fit into what appeared to be Martin Koplanski's humidor. As he recalled from the book, along with several other sources he'd come across, the most common dimensions given for the plates were 6 x 8 inches, approximately 6 inches thick, and weighing anywhere from 30 to 60 pounds. The fact that she was carrying it waist high with what appeared to be relative ease seemed to indicate it was relatively light, which was further confirmed once she handed it over.

As he sat back down on the threadbare camelback sofa, Chenault set the humidor down on a battered coffee table opposite of where he was sitting and slowly lifted the cover. Inside were ten unwrapped cigars along with five in their own gleaming metal cigar tubes and what appeared to be a cheap metal compass.

Chenault was not amused. "Is that it?"

"That's the one and only box of his best cigars," she said.

Chenault looked off in the distance and let out a long breath, as Rachel looked sympathetically over to the frail widow.

"Ma'am, I saw the video your husband sent Michael, and I saw that he clearly had a mischievous sense of humor--which I'm sure is one of the things that you loved about him--but you don't think that all of this is somehow just. . ."

"Of course!" Chenault broke in, snatching a handful of the cigar tubes out of the box. He immediately began to unscrew each tube, one by one, sliding out one cigar after another on to the coffee table. On the fourth tube, another cigar slid out, but bound around it was a discolored piece of paper, stained yellowish brown from having been wrapped around the cigar's tobacco leaf. Chenault slid the paper off, unfurled it, and then read the typed-written note aloud.

Mr. Valdez and Mr. Chenault,
No, not here. Not yet. There are still several steps
that await you. You now need to go to the one
place that they would never look, the one place that
over time they've dug up every square inch of in
search of this treasure--the place where it all
allegedly began. You'll need a compass which I've
thoughtfully provided, and you will need to go to
the southernmost point. Approximately twenty-five
yards up from this spot you will see a small, flat
round stone, roughly eight inches in diameter.
Look beneath that stone.

I wish you the best, and again, always be prepared
to just walk away. Human life is the most precious
treasure we have. It's the one thing I have learned
for sure in this life.

-M. Koplanski

As Chenault looked up from the note, his brow
furrowed with a mildly puzzled look. "'The place
where it all allegedly began'--but wouldn't that just
be here in Palmyra?"

"But didn't he also say, once you get to the
southernmost point to go twenty-five yards up?"
Rachel asked.

Chenault double checked the note. ". . .That's
right."

Almost in unison, Rachel and Marie Koplanski uttered the same three words, "The Hill Cumorah."

CHAPTER 52

Driving the speed limit south down Hwy 21, the six-mile trip to the Hill Cumorah Visitor's Center took less than 15 minutes. Although Chenault and Rachel arrived fairly late in the afternoon, the historical landmark was still crawling with not only a few curious tourists like themselves, but a number of Mormons from around the world. Making what amounted to a religious pilgrimage, these Latter Day Saints had come to witness and touch the sacred mound of earth where they believed Moroni had directed Joseph Smith to find the buried plates -- upon which their entire religion, and ultimately their lives were based.

To kill an hour or so until the crowds and the last tour bus departed, Rachel and Chenault strolled the grounds, stopping off at the Visitor Center, where they picked up a few brochures and watched several of the video displays on the other various historic and religious sites in the area. They then made a pass by the Hill Cumorah to get their bearings before it got too dark, but from their vantage point at the base of the hill, neither was able to spot the round stone Koplanski had described.

By a quarter til six, it was almost dark as the last tour van made its way out the front gate. Besides Rachel and Chenault, the only others who appeared to be left were a couple of staffers and a custodian. A rather plain young woman wearing a dark navy staff jacket and a name tag that had "Darra" imprinted on it, approached them.

"We're just getting ready to close up. Is there anything else I can help you with?"

"My wife appears to have lost her driver's license and the last thing she remembers was fumbling around with her purse and dropping her wallet out near the hill just before it got dark," Chenault said. "If we could just run out there real quickly with our flashlight and double check that would be great."

"Of course, you can. But would you like me to show you the way? I kind of know this place like the back of my hand now."

"I'm sure you do, but we've got a flashlight, and I know you've probably got things to do to get ready to close up."

The young woman opened her mouth to say something, but before she got a word out, Rachel chimed in, "It's probably not even there. I'm such a scatterbrain. It's probably still back in our motel room. But I'd just feel much better if we went back and checked, you know, for peace of mind."

Chenault was impressed, not just by Rachel's

improvisation, but by her proving she could be quick on her feet and play along when needed, a valuable asset to have as his assistant, as well as for the investigative journalist she aspired to be.

"Well, if you don't find it, just let me know if I need to post an alert for it in our 'Lost and Found.'"

"Thanks, Darra. We'll let you know," Chenault said, flashing a friendly smile.

As they made their way back out to the Hill Cumorah, they made sure to keep their eyes open for any staff that might be wandering about. Chenault scanned back and forth with the palm-sized flashlight he'd pulled from his fanny pack, and with the coast seemingly clear, he fished the cheap compass from his pocket. After about half a minute of walking slowly around the base of the hill, they eventually located what appeared to be the southernmost point. Chenault had Rachel stand there as their point of reference as he then proceeded slowly up the gradual hill, counting off the twenty-five paces in his head.

Once he reached the spot, about a third of the way up the hill, he looked directly down at the ground with his flashlight, but saw nothing but patchy, brown grass. He then turned slowly around, carefully shining the light in a five-foot swath to illuminate every square inch of the ground around him. Still nothing. His first thought was that somebody had beat him to it. Maybe someone had even stumbled across it, since hoards of visitors traipsed over the hill on a daily basis. *What could*

Koplanski have possibly been thinking to hide it here?

"You see anything?" Rachel called up to Chenault from her position at the base of the hill.

He turned to call back down to her, but from the sliver of moonlight that shone down, he could just barely make her out. What he did see, though, was that where she was standing, and where he was in relation to her, was that he must have veered slightly off course as he went up the hill. As he recalled from an orienteering lesson he'd had during his short lived Boy Scouting experience, without a distant focal point to walk towards, it was important to take into account which was your dominant step. Otherwise, you could tend to veer off in the opposite direction to the point that if you walked far enough, you could end up walking in circles.

Facing down hill to keep the dimly moonlit image he had of Rachel in view, he took several sidesteps to his left to make up for the obvious veer he'd made while coming up the hill, and on his fourth step, his left foot came down on something solid. Pointing the flashlight down, he lifted his foot to reveal a round, grayish stone, roughly eight inches in diameter that appeared to have no business being embedded in the side of the otherwise grassy hill.

"I think I found something!" he called down to Rachel, as he quickly turned to face back up hill and took a knee. Holding his flashlight with one hand and digging with the other, he managed to get his fingertips along the top edge of the stone, and then very carefully pried it up. After setting the stone aside, Chenault reached in and immediately beneath where it had been, found what felt like a small metal box.

At that exact moment, a large clump of earth exploded two feet to his left, accompanied by a simultaneous gunshot and muzzle flash coming from up the hill above.

"Run!" he bellowed, as he turned tail and sprinted down the hill towards Rachel, who stood frozen for several seconds at the bottom. Her momentary hesitation allowed Chenault to quickly catch up to her as they blindly sprinted across the open field towards their car in the distant lighted parking lot. As two more shots rang out, so loud it sounded as if the shooter was just behind them, they cut sharply left toward the darkened tree line, sensing that the nearby forest might be the only place to evade their attacker.

Gasping for breath as they reached the tree line, they both kept running like they'd never run before as the brittle, low-hanging branches whipped at their faces. As their pursuer's shots seemed to continually hone in on their location, it finally dawned on Chenault that their flashlights were giving them away.

"Cut your light off!" he called over to Rachel in a hushed tone. He then threw his own flashlight as far as he could through the trees as they took off. After going about a hundred more feet, they stopped

and waited silently until they finally heard the
heavy footsteps of their pursuer tramping loudly
through the woods in the direction of the discarded
flashlight, the beam of which they could still see
shining brightly. Taking care to tread as lightly as
they could, and only when they could hear the
shooter moving, they moved as quietly as they
could in the opposite direction.

After about a half a minute had passed, another
gunshot went off, which was immediately followed
by the exploding glass and metallic sound of
Chenault's discarded flashlight being blown to bits.
Instinctively, they both dove to the ground despite
the distance they had managed to put between
themselves and the gunman. Looking back in the
direction from where they'd just come, Chenault
saw that their pursuer had just turned on his own
flashlight about fifty yards away. Several times, the
powerful beam of light passed overhead just a few
feet away, each time seemingly getting closer to
discovering their position plastered to the ground.
After a minute or so of scanning the woods with his
flashlight and listening for any telltale sounds that
might give away their position, their assailant
appeared to give up as he turned and began walking
briskly out of the woods back towards the large
open field.

Chenault and Rachel, however, continued to
remain motionless. Even though the man was over
a hundred yards away, in the stillness of the night
they could still hear the dry leaves and branches

crackle beneath his feet, which likely meant that he'd be able to hear them just as easily if they dared to move.

From their prone position, they watched in silence as the man made his way back across the field and then worked his way back up the hill, shining his light back and forth as he appeared to search for the spot where Chenault had been digging. It dawned on Chenault that what had just seemed like an eternity had probably actually lasted for no more than a couple of minutes, and despite all the gunfire, it would likely still be a while before any law enforcement arrived. He decided in the meantime they would sit tight and wait for their attacker to finally take off.

"I'm guessing that wasn't the night watchman," Chenault said, breaking the silence. By her lack of response, Rachel appeared to be in no mood for levity. *Oh well,* he thought, *we did almost die.* It then occurred to him that what the gunman was looking for was very likely what he still had tightly gripped in his left hand. "Let me see your flashlight."

Wordlessly, Rachel handed it over as she continued to intently watch the man who'd just tried to murder them, excavate the spot Chenault had uncovered just a few minutes earlier. Eerily, the low guttural, almost animalistic sounds that emanated out of their assailant as he furiously dug in vain, carried down across the field and into the woods.

To avoid drawing any attention to their location, Chenault held the flashlight just a few inches off the ground, revealing a mud-speckled Altoids tin in his open palm. As he was about to open it, their would-be killer let out a primal roar of rage so chilling that even though he was several hundred yards away, it still stopped Chenault in his tracks as he waited to see what would happen next. Sure enough, with flashlight in hand, the man started back down the hill, trotting briskly back across the field towards them.

"Jesus Christ, who is this guy?" Chenault muttered. "He's like the Terminator." Cutting the light, Chenault got to his feet and helped Rachel up as they moved back behind a large tree. "Can you make it back to the car without the flashlight?" Chenault asked under his breath.

"I think so."

"I'll try to draw him away and you head back to the car and go for help."

"How are you going to get away?"

"I'll think of something. Here's the keys!"

"I can't just leave you!"

". . .It's the only way," Chenault said.

Through the graveyard of leafless trees, and behind the approaching beam of light, they could see the dark silhouette of the gunman making his way rapidly back towards them. Approaching the tree line, the man slowed cautiously to a halt, while Chenault and Rachel both tried to remain motionless as his flashlight beam panned back and forth through the woods and past their hiding place behind the tree. While shifting her weight from one foot to the other, a twig snapped under Rachel's foot, and even though the sound would have barely registered on a decibel meter, to Chenault and Rachel it sounded like a thunderclap. To their unknown assailant, it was just enough to help him direct his next shot, as he blew a patch of bark off a tree just next to them.

"Just get back to the car and honk once and I'll head for you," Chenault said. He then took off, heading deep into the woods in the opposite direction of the parking lot, running as fast as he could with the flashlight on to draw the shooter's attention.

Rachel waited for several seconds until she saw the gunman was well past her in his pursuit of Chenault, before she moved from her hiding spot along the wood's edge and started back across the field toward the parking lot. While moving quickly, she still tried to avoid any heavy footsteps or noise that would catch the gunman's attention.

As Chenault continued to run with every ounce of energy he had left, his breaths getting shorter and shorter, and his heart now pounding out the front of his chest, he began to sweat like it was the middle of August--a combination of exhaustion and increasing dread. Adding to his torment, a low-hanging branch raked across his face as he tripped over a root. As the footsteps behind him got louder and ever closer, he felt the warm blood from the

scratch across his forehead begin to run down into
his right eye. Wiping at his eye with a quick swipe
of his coat sleeve, he tried to recall what his original
plan had been when he sent Rachel off in the
opposite direction. Then it came to him--when he
felt the shooter was closing in, he'd planned to sling
the flashlight away in the hope of once again
misdirecting the bastard and allowing himself a slim
chance to break away and double back. The part,
however, he hadn't taken into account in his
panicked planning and now realized, was that the
son of a bitch now had a flashlight of his own, and
evading that was going to be next to impossible.
Chenault also sensed by the man's dogged pursuit,
and the fact that he hadn't taken any more wild
potshots at him through the trees, was that his
pursuer had somehow made this personal. The
bastard wasn't just trying to wing him--he was
trying to blow him away.

Figuring now was as good a time as any,
Chenault made a last second decision. Instead of
tossing the flashlight, he pulled up behind a tree and
immediately flashed the narrow beam directly back
into the shooter's face, hoping to temporarily blind,
or at least disorient him. Due to the distance,
darkness, and chaos of the moment, Chenault only
caught a brief glimpse before the gunman quickly
raised his hand up to shield his eyes, but that little
delay was all Chenault needed, as he sprung from
his position and took off even deeper into the
woods. This time, however, his little tactical delay

only slowed his pursuer up for a few seconds, and as soon as the white spots that had burned into Cloyd Lamott's retinas had dissipated, he immediately renewed his pursuit, and within half a minute was back on Chenault's heels.

As the thunderous crashing of Lamott's heavy footsteps got louder and louder as he begin closing in, for the first time in his life the thought crossed Chenault's mind that this might really be the end. Just then, and from out of nowhere, came the rapid, high-pitched twittering of a bird. Chenault then heard it again, but clearer and even more distinctly, and it really did almost sound like the excited chirping of some exotic songbird--only it was electronic and closing in fast. As he continued to run, his lungs burning more and more with each step, he noticed the chirping along with Lamott's footsteps getting fainter and fainter. And then he heard Lamott pull up and come to a stop, and the electronic chirping ended. *The son of a bitch is taking a phone call!*

For good measure, Chenault ran a hundred more yards and pulled up behind the trunk of a massive oak. Heaving his lungs out as he tried to catch his breath, he could feel the rough bark of the tree through his jacket and sweat-drenched shirt as he leaned heavily back against it in his attempt to remain standing. Finally, and he didn't know how many seconds had passed--it might have even been several minutes, but he at last caught his breath and listened carefully, trying to hear something--

anything, but all there was now was silence. *Could the bastard be headed back for Rachel*?

The entire time he and Rachel had been running for their lives, it had never occurred to him to use his cell and dial 9-1-1, and except for the one brief respite earlier, there wouldn't have been any time anyway. But in a moment of clarity, he whipped his phone out to call Rachel, to tell her that whatever she did to not honk the horn and call attention to herself. As he raced down his phone's address book for her number, a car horn began honking in the distance, and not just once, but repeatedly, as if the alarm had been set off.

Chenault never would have made for a very good long distance runner--he didn't have the wind for it, and his occasional smoking probably didn't help. He had, however, run the 200 meter sprint in high school and his first year of college, and with his adrenaline once again surging, he sensed he was now running the fastest he had ever run in his life as he headed back toward the parking lot, back to Rachel.

CHAPTER 53

On her way back to the parking lot, Rachel had decided to take a somewhat calculated risk. Instead of hitting the car horn just once as they'd discussed and banking on the slim chance that Chenault would be able to track her down from half a mile away in the dark, she set off the car alarm and then crawled under the vehicle to wait.

Minutes passed, and despite the blaring car horn going off every second and her being wedged into the cramped, narrow space, she waited silently. Then she heard them--footsteps--growing ever louder as they got ever closer. Then the sounds of heavy breathing and the crunching of gravel with each plodding step as the unknown new arrival slowly made a pass around the car until finally stopping. For her own safety, however, she remained silent, and until whoever it was identified himself, she would continue to do so.

"Rachel!" Chenault finally called out in

desperation.

Soon after they sped out of the parking lot and got back on to the highway, several police cars with lights flashing and their sirens wailing raced by. It then took about ten more minutes for the adrenaline to wear off before they calmed down enough to finally speak.

"I think we ought to find a motel," Chenault said.

"Really? I'm pretty sure Marie's expecting us. . .plus, we left all our stuff there."

"I just don't want to lead whoever that was back there back to her house, out in the middle of nowhere--especially at night. We can pick our things up tomorrow," he said, squinting and turning partially away as the headlights from an oncoming car beamed directly into his eyes.

"Is there something you're not telling me?"

Chenault paused for a moment, but then came out with it. ". . .I didn't recognize him at first--I only saw him for a split second. But I'm ninety-nine percent sure that was Cloyd Lamott back there."

"You're kidding."

Chenault shook his head. "I wish I were. Apparently he's been tracking us since that day we saw him back in Salt Lake."

"Of course, I never actually saw him."

"Well, I did. And I've seen his ugly mug on the news just about every night since then. And since he was almost without a doubt involved in the kidnapping and murder of Ratchford's wife and daughter, and now he's right back here in Palmyra, I'd say that pretty much makes him the prime suspect for taking out Koplanski as well. And since it's looking more and more like these killings were not just connected, but coordinated to bring in my involvement to find the plates. . .well, since Lamott is clearly just the muscle, I'd say that whoever is the brains behind this is still out there. And 'dollars to doughnuts' as my father used to say, somehow Hyrum Lamott and Brockston Ratchford, and or Ratchford's attack dog, Fiske, are involved."

"You're probably right, but I don't even want to think about any of that stuff right now. I'm sorry. . .I'm just so tired."

It occurred to Chenault that it wasn't an unusual reaction--Rachel being almost completely wiped out after all they'd just been through. There were stories he'd heard of soldiers in battle, who after hours of intense fighting, simply passed out or collapsed as soon as they walked off the battlefield from the combination of intense stress and physical exhaustion.

"And I still don't see why we just can't go back and stay at the farm. There's nobody following us now."

"It would just be more dangerous for us and her--we'd all be sitting ducks if Lamott found us."

Rachel let out a little sigh of exasperation. ". . .Okay, you're the boss."

"Rachel, I'm not trying to be the boss. I just

think it would be smarter for us to go check into a motel under some made-up names. It seems like however he's doing it, he's not having too much trouble tracking us, and I'd just like to make it a little harder for him to find us."

"You know you could have said all that without having to say 'it would be smarter.' That just makes me feel stupid."

"Rachel, you're being too sensitive--that's not what I meant. I just don't want anything bad to happen to any of us. . .especially you. You understand that, right?"

Rachel didn't respond, but when he looked over, she nodded as she appeared to wipe away tears from under her left eye.

"I just want to protect you right now--that's all. So please just trust me, okay?"

Rachel again nodded in silent understanding. Even though Chenault knew his next move should be to call 9-1-1 to let local law enforcement know that the subject of a nationwide manhunt was in their own backyard, as he started to make the call, all that he kept thinking back to was Rachel's acting like a petulant child. He'd seen and experienced similar behavior in other women in the past, and had yet to figure out if it was a learned behavior or just encoded in their DNA, but he'd always found it maddening. There had been a few times in the past, before he'd finally caught on, that the tactic had been successful in swaying him, but not this time-- there was too much at stake. And even though there had been a fleeting thought to give in and head back to the Koplanski farmhouse, he stood firm and drove back towards town to find the nearest cheap motel. Along the way, though, it occurred to him that tracking them down in the handful of motels in and around Palmyra might prove to be far too easy, so he headed towards Rochester, about twenty minutes further west, a decent sized city where it would be next to impossible for Lamott to find them.

After they had checked in as the "Browns" at a small, twelve room motor inn just east of Rochester, there was not a lot said between the two. Rachel lay down on her side facing away from him as she pulled the covers tightly down over her. Chenault wasn't sure if she was just giving him the cold shoulder or if she was waiting for an apology or some act of contrition before she would warm back up to him. *And then again,* he thought, *maybe this is yet another reason why I'm still single.* Chenault had never been very good at apologizing, especially when he believed he was in the right, but then again, he'd never recalled feeling this way about anybody else before.

He slid over under the covers until the front of his body aligned with the rear of hers, and then gently slipped his arm around her waist. "I would never intentionally hurt you, and if I did earlier, I'm sorry," he said softly into her ear. "This is the first time I can ever remember where I've hurt someone--and not even on purpose, and it's wound up hurting me even more."

After a few seconds, Rachel took his hand from around her waist in hers and turned partially back towards him with a hint of a smile. ". . .That means that you love me," she said just above a whisper.

And Chenault knew she was right as he leaned in and pressed his lips to hers.

CHAPTER 54

The next morning was one of the most perfect Chenault could recall as the sun beamed down through clear blue skies, making it feel almost like a Spring day in November. The previous evening's near death experience, followed by a night of unbridled passion, had left them both invigorated, and the anticipation of a lifetime of shared moments with Rachel had left Chenault feeling almost rhapsodic, as he couldn't recall ever feeling happier or more alive.

They got up late, around nine-thirty, and after slowly bathing each other in the shower, found themselves once again passionately entwined. After getting dressed, they walked across the street to a small café, where they devoured a huge breakfast before heading southeast back toward Palmyra and the Koplanski farm.

After about a forty minute drive, the lone gray mailbox at the end of the Koplanski's long gravel drive came into view about a third of a mile up ahead. As they passed a grove of leafless trees and began to slow down to turn, the farm came into view a hundred yards off the paved state road. It was then that they saw three large black SUVs, and at least five black and whites parked all around the farm, along with at least fifteen men moving purposefully about.

As he slowly increased his speed and drove on past the driveway turn-in, Chenault prayed that from a distance they looked like just another rubbernecker passing by.

"Shouldn't we go and see what's going on?" Rachel said.

"I've got a bad feeling, and if something's happened to Mrs. Koplanski there's not a lot we can do for her now. I think it's best if we get back on I-90 and head down to the City."

"What about all our stuff? Won't it look more incriminating if something happened to her and we don't come back for it? Not to mention our fingerprints are probably all over the place. And why are we headed to, I'm presuming you're talking about Manhattan?"

"In answer to your first question, I would hope that if they actually suspected us of anything, that they would give us more credit than leaving all our stuff at the scene of the crime. Besides, we can always explain ourselves later. But with all the questions they probably want to ask, and that psycho on our tail, I want to get as far away from here as we can, and New York City is not only a great place to disappear, but according to the instructions I found in the Altoids box, presumably the final resting place of Martin Koplanski's 'artifact.'"

"What, when did you find this out?"

"Just this morning. . .in the bathroom. As I was getting dressed, I was going through my pockets and pulled out the Altoids tin which I'd completely forgotten about, and had kind of assumed was just somebody's bad idea of a joke. But inside was a key and a folded index card that not only has the name of the bank scrawled on it, but the account and box numbers as well."

"So when were you going to tell me?"

"I wanted to surprise you."

Rachel paused for a moment as the news sank in. ". . .So we've got it?"

". . .We've got it," he said with a broad smile.

CHAPTER 55

Under most circumstances, Hal Sikorski would have been described by most friends and colleagues who knew him as "unflappable," but a phone call earlier that day still had him so distracted he was barely able to concentrate on a story he'd just been tasked with editing. To clear his head, he'd been surfing the web for the past half hour under the guise of fact checking when the text message came in.

> **On way back 2 city**
> **C U in couple hours**

Sikorski looked around first. Even though there was absolutely no way for anyone to see he had just received a text from Michael Chenault, he was still paranoid. Just an hour earlier he had been contacted by the FBI, asking if he knew the whereabouts of Chenault. All he had told them was that the last he had heard, Chenault was headed to somewhere in upstate New York.

"We know that much," the investigator, who had identified himself as Special Agent Patterson, replied, "but you don't know where he's staying or where he might be headed after that?"

"I don't," Sikorski had told him, "but could I ask you why you're looking for Michael?"

"Well, you're going to find out soon enough, so I'll go ahead and tell you. He's wanted in connection with the murder of Felix Valdez."

"Yeah, he told me about that, back in Salt Lake, that some anonymous tipster had given his name to the police about a chance encounter he'd had with Valdez the night he was murdered."

"Yeah, but did he also tell you that he left town the day after the police told him to stick around, which at the time didn't seem like that big a deal, but now in retrospect looks really bad."

"And why's that?" Sikorski had asked.

"Because we just got another tip that we followed up on and found the probable murder weapon stashed in the bottom of Chenault's suitcase. We also found his laptop and some bizarre video on the hard drive that was apparently sent to both Valdez and Chenault about some mysterious treasure this Koplanski character supposedly stashed away. So now the motive looks pretty clear. That, along with the murder weapon--it looks to be pretty much open and shut."

For a split second, Sikorski had paused after

hearing the agent's account to consider the possibility. "I can tell you right now you're on the wrong track. That video you saw--I didn't send that to Michael until just the other day, almost a week after Valdez was murdered. And while he might do just about anything for a story, I'm pretty sure he's drawn the line at murdering the competition. And secondly, Michael Chenault is one of the brightest people I know. If he had actually killed Valdez, I can assure you Michael has a lot more on the ball than to stash the murder weapon in his own suitcase. If you can't smell a frame-up. . .and you're saying that all of these leads you keep getting are from anonymous sources. If that doesn't sound like those are from somebody who, at the very least, is heavily involved, then I'm a horse's ass."

"Well, then answer me this," the agent said. "Why would Chenault have skipped town in the first place after being told to stay put, and why, if he didn't have anything to hide, didn't he return to the farmhouse where he was supposed to be staying? My guess is, he either somehow got wind that we were on the way or else he saw us at the farm and took off. Either way it doesn't look good."

"There I would agree with you, that certainly doesn't look good, and I don't have an answer for you, but I can assure you there was probably a perfectly good reason. And I can also once again assure you that you're barking up the wrong tree-- Michael Chenault had absolutely nothing to do with the murder of Felix Valdez."

Patterson let out a short cynical chortle. ". . .I swear, if I had a nickel for every friend or family member who swore there was no way their brother, or uncle, or whoever, could be involved in a murder, who then later turned out to be guilty as hell, I could have retired years ago. . . Let us know if you hear anything," he had said before ending the call.

CHAPTER 56

To clear their heads after several hours of driving, and to refuel both the vehicle and themselves, Chenault pulled off at a mega truck stop halfway between Binghamton and Scranton, just off I-81. Rachel went inside to fill their drink and snack orders as Chenault, after first texting Hal, stood out by the gas pump and watched the digital numbers by the dollar sign race upward far faster than seemed should be legal. After returning the pump handle back to its mount and tearing off his printed receipt, a sequence of three low vibrating hums went off on his cell. Before reading what he assumed was Hal's reply, he happened to glance up to see Rachel talking on her cell as she stood in the checkout line. The text read:

FBI Agent Patterson looking 4 U
think U murdered Valdez
says murder weapon in your suitcase
best not 2 contact me 4 now

You gotta be kidding me, Chenault thought. Just
how far would Ratchford go to not just discredit,
but to destroy him? Or was it Fiske, the man behind
the curtain and the one who seemed to be pulling
most of the strings? And then again, maybe he had
underestimated Ratchford. Chenault's experience
suggested that a man with Ratchford's seemingly
insatiable ambition didn't get to where he was
without doing certain things that most people would
never even dream of or dare. And now there was
also the matter of Patterson, the very agent who had
been sympathetic to Ratchford from the beginning,
and who appeared to have done nothing with any of
the leads Chenault had given him.

Well no matter who was behind it, or who was
possibly working with whom, they clearly seemed
to fear him for some reason--it was the only
explanation. Maybe they had seen him record
Ratchford's cynical admission the day of the news
conference that he had "already moved on" less
than a week after his wife's death. Or maybe they
were somehow on to Chenault's other suspicions
about Ratchford, and simply by his being on the
right track, even without concrete proof, this had

brought out their paranoia to the point that they would do just about anything to stop him--or at the very least discredit him, which in the news world was just as good as destroying someone. By discrediting him, they could spin it in the press, *How can you believe a word that he writes or even what you hear on tape when it's clearly been doctored by a muckraking reporter who will do anything for a story, including possibly even murdering his competition?* It didn't even have to be true. Politicians had learned that long ago. They just had to sling enough mud and usually just enough would stick for some of the less discriminating members of the public to actually believe it.

As Rachel walked up to the car, Chenault looked around to see if there were any security cameras. Not that it really mattered, as he realized that the credit card he'd used moments earlier had just pinpointed their exact location.

"I saw you talking on the phone earlier. You didn't happen to tell whoever it was where we're headed did you?"

"No, I was just checking in with my roommate to see how my cats were doing. Why?"

"Hop in," he said, directing her to get inside. ". . .Because apparently I'm now the subject of a nationwide manhunt."

"What did you do this time?" Rachel said with a smile as she buckled in.

"No, I'm serious. Somebody is apparently doing

a good enough frame-up job on me for the FBI to take it seriously."

"Take what seriously?"

"That I killed Felix Valdez."

"You've got to be kidding me."

He shook his head solemnly. "Of course, this changes our plans considerably. We're probably going to need to go into the city at night to be a little less visible. In fact, I'm thinking I should maybe even hang back and let you go on ahead without me to get whatever it is Koplanski's stashed away."

"Well, if that's what you want to do, I'm game."

With one hand on the steering wheel, Chenault peered down the busy interstate as he mulled over the new plan for a moment until he finally shook his head. ". . .No way. People are getting killed over this. There's no way I'd send you by yourself--especially with that psycho still running around."

"I'll be alright," Rachel lightly protested.

"Absolutely not. I could never forgive myself if anything happened to you."

"Nothing's going to happen to me. I'll just waltz into the bank in the morning and be back here by lunch tomorrow."

He thought about it for less than a second. ". . .I'm sorry, I just can't let you. . .It's too risky." Chenault then glanced in the rear view mirror, not quite sure what he was looking for behind him, but even less certain what lay ahead.

CHAPTER 57

After crossing through the Holland Tunnel and making their way into the city just past twilight, Rachel posed the question Chenault had been trying to come up with an answer to for the past hour, "So where to?"

With the FBI on his trail as the prime suspect in a murder investigation, he knew he'd need to stay away from not only his apartment, but *The Times* offices as well. He also knew that as soon as possible, he would need to eventually face the music to clear his name, but while he was so close to the prize, he didn't want to risk any further delays. From past experience and articles he'd researched, Chenault was well aware that dealing with the bureaucratic black hole that was the FBI could stretch out far longer than he even wanted to imagine, since they could hold him almost indefinitely as they tried to make their case against him. There was also still the matter of Cloyd

Lamott. As of last check, there'd still been no mention of his capture on any of the radio stations they'd tuned to.

With limited options, having spent most of his cash on their motel room the night before, Chenault knew he wouldn't be able to use his credit cards at any ATM or motel in the city with the FBI likely employing some sort of financial trace by now. He was also fairly certain the same held true for Rachel once she'd been identified as his traveling companion. And although he knew that he had plenty of friends who would be more than willing to put him up, not only didn't he want to make anybody aware he was back in town, but for their own safety, he didn't want to involve any of them. That left him with just one place to go.

For the last twenty years, Hal Sikorski had kept what he referred to as his "love nest," a tiny, rent-controlled walk-up in Soho where he first lived as a bachelor and which he still paid next to nothing for in rent. The nickname for the apartment was a bit of joke since he'd been happily married for the past eighteen years, but when it wasn't being used for visiting relatives or guests, or an occasional weekend in the city, it was the site of their regular Friday night poker game, and which was how Chenault knew where to find the hidden key.

Around a quarter 'til eight, they drove up a side street a block and a half from the apartment building, and miraculously found a recently vacated parking spot. Making their way up the sidewalk that ran along the cobble-stoned street, they passed by a number of couples and several groups of friends who appeared to be on their way to one of the various coffee shops or bistros that populated the Soho neighborhood. A number of galleries and boutiques also still appeared to be open, all of which looked to be doing quite well despite the recent downturn in the economy.

One of the things that Chenault normally stopped to admire whenever he was in the neighborhood were the amazing cast-iron building facades that had been put up in the mid-19th century, with their wide sweeping windows, gothic columns, and decorative arches and doorways. Tonight, however, he didn't give them a second glance as he passed by, since his chief concern was to stay out of sight and to get Rachel to a safe place. The guided tour could hopefully wait for another time in the not so distant future--one in which he wasn't still the subject of a nationwide manhunt.

After getting into the apartment, the only thing they could find to eat were a couple of freezer-burned Totino's tightly wedged into an almost solid block of ice in the refrigerator's overhead freezer compartment. Under normal circumstances, Chenault would have considered it a minor sacrilege to even contemplate such an act in the pizza capital of the world, but half-starved and down to his last few dollars in cash, he was just thankful they had something to provide some sustenance. After several minutes of channel surfing and switching back and forth between the several 24 hour cable news networks, Chenault came across the story he was, in fact, hoping not to find. Unlike their television counterparts, who generally seemed to crave the spotlight, print investigative journalists generally liked to retain some degree of anonymity; having his face and name splashed across the country was one of the very last things he wanted. Not only would this newfound notoriety likely complicate his life down the road professionally, but it was going to make it extremely difficult for him to make his way unnoticed down East 34th street the next day to retrieve whatever treasure trove Martin Koplanski had stored in The First Bank of New York.

Thankfully, there was only a brief mention of Rachel as "a female companion," but then what followed next left Chenault at a loss for words. First up was Marie Koplanski, looking her most frail and grandmotherly, standing front and center in front of five or six microphones being thrust towards her, stating for the record that she "Never would have guessed that Michael Chenault was the man who murdered Felix Valdez." She was then followed by Special Agent Ardell Patterson, who relayed how "Chenault came to us with a bunch of crazy theories--none of which either he or we could substantiate." He then went on to say, "We don't know if he's armed at this time, but anybody encountering him should still consider him extremely dangerous." The icing on the cake, however, was Evan Fiske, identified as an aide and campaign advisor to Senator, and Presidential hopeful, Brockston Ratchford.

"The Senator has been both personally harassed and slandered by Michael Chenault, and it really doesn't surprise us one bit to hear that a man of this ilk would be involved in such a heinous crime."

Chenault immediately hit the remote "Off" button as he let out a sigh of utter disbelief. ". . .What can I say? I'm speechless. . .You know, the way this is playing out, it really does almost seem like. . . some crazy, widespread Mormon conspiracy, with Ratchford and his lapdog, Fiske, Hyrum Lamott, the two brothers, possibly even Patterson, and now even Koplanski's widow tied in. I mean, would she have really cooperated with them to the point of getting her husband killed? And looking back, how believable is it that she supposedly had no idea what her husband had really found? Which would also then mean that she probably never really ever left the Church. . .Is any of this even making sense, or am I just getting hyper-paranoid and grasping at straws because I was just accused of murder on national television?"

"I'd say it's a stretch, but I've got to admit, there do seem to be a lot of weird coincidences going on," Rachel said.

"But it almost doesn't make sense, at least for Ratchford and Fiske, that they would go to these lengths to suppress or discredit what they thought I may have had on them, unless. . .they really are tied into all the rest of this and they knew all about Koplanski and the plates from the beginning."

Rachel thought about his conjecture for a moment. ". . .But then why would they try to frame you for murder before you actually got the plates?"

"Now that I don't have a good answer for, but I'm glad to see that you're thinking a little more clearly than I am right now. But all I can think then is, that maybe there are actually two different groups working at cross purposes with each other-- maybe even competing."

"So you're saying that there are possibly two groups involved?" Rachel said.

"Well, let's look at it. Somebody, with the help of the Lamott brothers to do their dirty work, pretty well appears to have lured me in to help them, I'm guessing, find what may or may not be Joseph Smith's actual Gold Plates--that's fact number one. And fact number two is that clearly somebody else is trying to frame me for murder. So you tell me? Or is all this just a bad dream?"

"I hope you're not saying that I'm just part of a bad dream."

Chenault smiled wistfully and shook his head. ". . .You know better than that. In fact, I think you're probably just about the best thing that's ever happened to me."

Rachel beamed as she reached down and took his hand in hers. "Come with me and maybe I can help you forget about all this stuff for just a little while."

Later that night as he lay in bed, it occurred to Chenault that while their lovemaking was just as passionate, if not more so than before, it was now altogether different. What before had consisted of long soulful gazing into each other's eyes while they moved slowly and rhythmically together as one, had now been replaced by a much greater physical element, more along the lines of two finely-tuned athletes wrestling for survival. And while he didn't want to admit it, he had never before experienced anything as intense or exciting, as he found once again that Rachel never ceased to surprise or amaze him.

The next morning, the sun had just started to penetrate through the apartment's thin blue curtains when Chenault awoke and looked over to see the bare back and shoulders of Rachel just a few inches away. When he leaned in and kissed her softly on the shoulder, she immediately rolled back towards him onto her back, smiling, and looking up and over at him, smiling through sexy, half-opened eyes.

"Last night was amazing."

"What can I say? I do my best work when I'm on the run from the law," Chenault said with a sly smile.

"You know what I could really go for about now--some of those famous New York bagels I keep hearing about. You want me to run out?"

"No, why don't you take a shower first and I'll run out and grab a few things. I think I have a couple dollars left. When I get back I'll make us the best breakfast, well, maybe not that you've ever had, but the best that I'm capable of."

"That's all I could ever ask for," she said with a sleepy smile. "But what about being recognized?"

"Check this out," Chenault said, holding up a dark knit toboggan. "I found this in Hal's closet last night." He put the cap on, tucking his hair up underneath, and then slipped on his sunglasses. With the dark stubble of his two-day beard growth, the knit cap and sunglasses, and his light olive complexion, Chenault looked very much like most Americans' conception of a terrorist.

"You're scaring me," Rachel said with a smile.

"Yes, but could you recognize me if you didn't know me?"

"I don't think so. I think you're good."

"Then I'll see you in a little while."

A half an hour later, with bagels in tow, Chenault couldn't help but take in the quintessential New York City street scene before him as he made his way back to the apartment. An old man, bundled against the cold, cleaned up behind his small brown dog by a newsstand, as cottony wisps of steam seeped up from the manhole covers that ran down the center of the street. The seemingly endless string of cars, all parked along the right-hand side, reminded Chenault he might need to double-check where he'd parked, since a ticket or tow would likely pinpoint his location to anyone trying to find him.

Despite the seeming chaos that often went along with living in a major metropolitan city, New Yorkers took their parking very seriously to make way for the trash pickups that occurred on alternating days for one side of the street or the other. So as Chenault rounded the last corner before reaching the apartment, he couldn't help but notice a dark blue sedan, about a half block up, parked on the wrong side of the street.

Probably a city official or a cop he thought, but as he drew closer, he saw the car had Vermont plates. *Typical.* An out-of-town tourist who didn't know any better.

Once inside the building, the first thing Chenault noticed upon reaching the apartment was the partially open front door. Cautiously, he stepped in through the doorway and did a quick scan of the small open living area--it was empty. He set the grocery bag down on the counter and started back toward the rear of the small studio to the bathroom. When he heard the shower still running, he glanced down to his watch to see how long he'd been gone. That's when he noticed a glistening trail of water droplets running along the floor from the bathroom to the front door. His heart skipped a panicked beat.

"Rachel!"

Remembering the dark sedan parked illegally out front, Chenault ran to the front window. The car was gone. Just then, as if on cue, the phone rang. Chenault snatched the cordless receiver off the wall.

"Hello."

"Mr. Chenault?" the deep, gravel-voiced caller asked.

Panic and then terror set in as it dawned on Chenault that not only did this stranger know who he was, but where he was staying. Not even Hal knew that.

". . .Yes."

"We have your lady friend. If you ever want to see her alive again, you will do exactly as we say. Do you understand?"

The voice was much like he'd imagined from the description given to him by the Salt Lake television reporter. It was deep, masculine, very deliberate, and clearly electronically altered.

"Yes."

"Yes, what?" the caller said.

"Yes, I understand."

"You won't see us, but we'll be watching your every move. From the time you leave the apartment, to the time you make your way to the bank to retrieve the safe deposit box for us. And now most importantly, under no circumstance are you to open the box. Do you understand that?"

"Yes, I understand."

"Your eyes are not meant to see what is inside. To ensure that, we will have somebody in the lobby timing how long that it takes for you to make your way into the safe deposit vault and come back out. We know it should take less than thirty seconds from the time you walk in, turn your key, take the box out, and immediately walk back out with it.

Once outside, you will hold it out to display that it has not been opened, and you will then put it into a backpack, which you will then strap to your back. I'll repeat this only once. If you open the box, or we even suspect you opened the box, I personally will not only carve out her throat, but I'll cut off her pretty face and send it to you. Do you understand?"

"Yes, I understand."

"Then repeat back my instructions."

"That I'm not to open the box under any circumstance or you'll hurt Rachel."

"Not 'hurt'--kill. And, of course, if you even think about contacting the police, she's dead. And I promise you, it will not be quick. It will be slow and very painful--and you will be responsible. You will remain where you are until 4:30 this afternoon. At which time, you will then make your way to the bank, and just before closing at five o'clock, you will retrieve the box and start making your way-- walking, towards the Brooklyn Bridge. At approximately 5:30, we will contact you on your cell phone and give you further instructions."

"I presume then you already have my number."

"We know everything about you, Mr. Chenault."

Aside from being vaguely reminiscent of the killer's voice he'd heard in a recent movie trailer that was making the rounds, there was something else odd about it he couldn't quite put his finger on.

"I want to talk to Rachel."

"There'll be plenty of time for that later--if you follow our instructions. If you choose, however,

not to, then you have seen her alive for the last
time."

With that the phone went dead.

<u>CHAPTER 58</u>

As he paced back and forth, the next almost
eight hours were tortuous for Chenault as he
contemplated several desperate courses of action.
Because of everything he had gone through to get to
this point, not to mention a possible ending for his
story, he came up with a half dozen end-run plans,
most of which involved a last minute switching of
backpacks and contacting law enforcement. But in
the end, because Rachel's life was all that really
mattered to him now, he decided to play it safe and
do exactly as he'd been instructed. From the extent
of the planning and the subsequent execution that
had gone in to drawing him in to find Koplanski's
"artifact," and then apparently having his every
move shadowed as he traveled back across the
country, it was clear that he was up against some
very powerful, resolute men who were to be taken
very seriously.

When Chenault reached the bank, what worried

him most was whether or not he would even be able to gain access. From past experience he even doubted it. After his father's death, it had taken over a month and seemingly an act of Congress to finally get his mother access to his father's safe deposit box. And now, despite having the key and box number, unless he could bluff his way in-- which was a long shot--it was unlikely he would be allowed go anywhere near Koplanski's safe deposit box.

After taking several deep breaths to steel himself, Chenault walked into the bank and made his way across the massive, marble-floored lobby. After sizing the employees up the best he could, he came to a stop in front of the desk of an attractive blond bank officer who looked to be just a few years out of college. The nameplate on her desk identified its occupant as "Cynthia Rollins, Customer Relations."

"Miss Rollins, if you have a moment, I'd like to check my safe deposit box," he said, holding out the key as his only proof.

"The number?"

"I'm sorry, number 348."

She pulled a metal clipboard from her desk drawer and flipped the top several pages of the access log back, reading down until she came to the line she was searching for. She then slowly looked back up.

"I see this is Mr. Koplanski's box. Is everything all right? I know he didn't look very well the last time he was in."

Chenault's palms began to sweat. He had counted on the hope that in such a large bank, it would be unlikely anybody would know or even remember Martin Koplanski. He had even gone so far as to practice forging Koplanski's signature all afternoon in the event he needed to bluff his way past. *Great. It could be all over right here.*

"Actually, he did pass away, and I've been sent by the family to retrieve the contents. "

"Well, hopefully you're on the access log, otherwise. . ."

"Miss, I can't tell you how important it is that I retrieve the contents this afternoon," he blurted, as he felt the prickly heat of panic run up his neck.

"Just sit tight. . .What's your name, sir?" she asked, as she casually looked down to the log. It dawned on Chenault that he now also had the not-so-small matter of being a wanted man to deal with, which raised the question, just how widely had his name and picture been distributed? He had only been accused of murdering one of the best known television journalists of the last thirty years, and if she even had a cursory interest in the news, he knew he was finished. But it was also now or never, and if he didn't take the chance, then Rachel was dead.

"Mike Chenault," he said as calmly as he could muster, hoping to throw her off by using his little used nick name, along with the French pronunciation of his last name, rhyming the latter half of it with "snow."

There was a long pause--one that seemed to hang in the air quite a bit longer than Chenault would have liked.

". . .There you are," she said finally. "It looks like it's just you and a Mr. Valdez. Anyway, you want to date and sign here?" she said, pointing at a line halfway down the page. "And could I please see some sort of ID?"

Thank God nobody reads or watches the news anymore.

Just before following her into the vault, Chenault looked around the crowded lobby to make sure that whoever it was who was supposedly watching him saw that he was just about to enter. He then looked down at the second hand on his watch and saw it sweep past the six as he stepped in behind her.

Taking his key and then hers, she inserted them into the locks of one of the larger-sized boxes in the vault, which appeared to be roughly a foot and half square. After unlocking it, she pulled the box out several inches.

"I'll leave you alone now," she said, just before she exited and pulled the large tinted glass door behind her, and just as the second hand swept past the nine. With just fifteen seconds remaining, Chenault jerked the metal drawer out the rest of the way and grabbed the battered, wooden rectangular box from inside with both hands. Despite the fact that the box and its contents easily weighed at least forty pounds, he backed out the vault door with the box clenched tightly to his chest in just under ten seconds.

As Chenault headed south down Broadway, making his way towards the Brooklyn Bridge, it was now even clearer to him from what had just transpired, that he and Valdez had been selected by Koplanski quite some time ago--one apparently the backup if the other failed, or in Valdez's case, was murdered. And then like hungry fish, they'd both been reeled in by a shadowy mastermind who had left a breadcrumb trail of clues and tips for them to follow. This same person, or persons, through the use of planted evidence and a string of anonymous tips to various law enforcement agencies, had also then maneuvered Chenault into a position with few options, where he was now essentially cornered.

And while Koplanski, like a chess master, appeared to have even anticipated some of these moves and subsequent countermoves that had Chenault in the position he now found himself, there was certainly no way he could have foreseen Rachel's involvement and the danger she would be put in. And why had Koplanski even picked him? What was it about him that had Koplanski so convinced he was the right man for the job? Was it because of the accolades he'd received for his investigative work that made him stand out from the crowd? Or was it because he was quick on his feet, which it was unlikely Koplanski could have known? In either case, he'd clearly not anticipated that the life of an innocent bystander would be held in the balance--human currency in exchange for his precious "artifact." So had Koplanski overestimated him as well?

Just then, at 5:25, Chenault's phone rang.

"Hello."

"We see you have followed our instructions so far. Don't disappoint us now, Mr. Chenault," the same deep, electronically-altered voice said.

"I won't."

"Very good. You will now proceed to the pedestrian promenade that goes over the bridge. You, obviously, will approach from the Manhattan side, and will meet our representative at the halfway point. You will transfer the satchel to him and Miss Potter will later be released."

"Absolutely not. She has to be there."

"Mr. Chenault, you're in no position to bargain."

"Actually, I am," Chenault said. "Clearly, you want what's in this box badly enough that you'll go to these lengths. And you won't harm her as long as I have it, because if you do, you'll lose whatever its precious contents are forever with whatever I decide to do with them. So you'll have her there on the bridge, and I'll exchange the box and its contents for her."

The party at the other end let out a short, muffled laugh. ". . .You drive a hard bargain, Mr. Chenault, but that will be acceptable. But that ends your negotiation rights, and since it delays our exchange, you will do everything else exactly as I direct it."

"What happened to 'we'?"

"Do not be mistaken, Mr. Chenault. I represent very powerful people who will do anything within their powers to recover the artifact now in your possession. You're only lucky they've not chosen to have a sniper put a bullet in the back of your head where you stand."

Yes, interesting point, thought Chenault. *Why have I been allowed to live?*

"So again, you will proceed to the midpoint where the exchange will be made--the contents of the box for Miss Potter. And if you try absolutely anything--anything that deviates from what should be a smooth and orderly transfer, our asset will put a bullet in Miss Potter's brain and then yours. Do we understand one another?"

"Crystal clear."

CHAPTER 59

Chenault had always marveled over the Brooklyn Bridge -- not just in its remarkable history, but in the amazing construction of the bridge itself. It was essentially handmade, built before the time of steel cranes and powerful earthmoving equipment, and for years it had even been regarded as one of the manmade wonders of the world. Over time, he had even come to think of the bridge as not just a monument, but a testament to the ingenuity of man, right up there along with the construction of the Pyramids and the Great Wall. Today, however, all he saw was just a mass of steel, concrete, and wire cables--a means of getting from point A to point B, which in this case meant somewhere around the midpoint of the bridge where he was to meet the bastards who had Rachel.

Although foot traffic was rather light over the wooden promenade that ran down the center of the bridge, twelve feet above the busy roadway,

Chenault still found himself having to sidestep a few pedestrians walking in the opposite direction. Due to the crisp November air and the accompanying high winds that could cut through clothing no matter how many layers one wore, only the hardiest of New Yorkers used the bridge this time of year. This meant that most of the rest of the colorfully dressed passersby were tourists, likely from someplace like Iowa or Kansas, and who were only walking the bridge to check off their list of things to do while in New York City. Empire State Building, Statue of Liberty, Staten Island Ferry, Broadway show. Chenault didn't begrudge them. Those were all the places and things he had done upon first arriving fourteen years earlier, but today he just saw the tourists as obstacles, roadblocks in the path of his reaching his destination. And even though he knew he would eventually arrive, he still cursed them under his breath for picking this day of all days to get in his way and slow him down.

As Chenault trudged on across the mile-long bridge, he continued to wonder what possible reason anyone, or any party, could have, that they'd be so willing to kill again and again to secure the contents of the box strapped to his back. If on the slim chance the original Gold Plates were truly contained within the box, was it just a matter of greed that someone wanted the gold from which they were reputedly made? *Surely, that can't be it,* he thought. There had to be a number of far easier ways to get a lot richer with much less trouble. And as far as their religious or historical significance, did somebody really want them so badly, to be able to hold them up and display for all the world to see as the incontrovertible proof that Joseph Smith was a true prophet who had indeed founded the "one true religion?" That would indeed be pretty powerful evidence with the potential to swell the ranks of the religion to unimaginable numbers. Or was it just the opposite? Was somebody actually trying to suppress their discovery and revelation because of their potential to send the whole house of cards tumbling down? And then he looked up.

There, standing twenty-five feet ahead of him was Rachel, and directly behind her with his hand clasped tightly on her right shoulder, the man Chenault immediately recognized as Cloyd Lamott. Keeping his other hand inside his jacket pocket, Lamott's concealed pistol poked into her ribcage as she stood frozen, appearing as helpless as a small child within his powerful grasp. Slowly, Chenault walked up to within six feet of the two, when Lamott, in his very deliberate, low guttural voice said, "That's far enough."

Chenault stopped in his tracks.

By his hate-filled glare, it appeared there was nothing more Lamott would like to have done than to wipe Chenault from the face of the earth, yet inexplicably he held back. "Where is it?" Lamott demanded through gritted teeth.

Chenault slowly turned his upper body part way around to reveal the bulging backpack, as he made a mental note that Lamott, by his question, clearly hadn't been kept in the loop.

"Set it down and walk away," Lamott said.

As Lamott's eyes bore into him, watching his every move, Chenault slipped off the backpack, took a step forward, and then set it down just in front of Rachel before slowly stepping back.

"Pick it up," Lamott said, directing his command to Rachel.

Rachel knelt down to lift the backpack by its straps, and although she was able to lift it with both hands, it appeared to be heavier than she had anticipated as she struggled slightly.

"Now hand it over," Lamott said, extending his free hand and briefly removing his other hand from his pocket.

Chenault, anticipating that Lamott's attention would be momentarily diverted, slipped his hand into his pocket as Lamott took the pack by its straps and effortlessly heaved it back over his left shoulder. Only seconds had passed, but as Lamott directed his attention back to Chenault, he glimpsed a small dark device in Chenault's hand, and a thin wire firing rapidly in his direction.

Piercing his shirt and sinking into the fleshy portion of his chest, the Taser's barbed electrodes sent 50,000 volts coursing through his body, and turned Lamott into a quivering pile of flesh as he dropped like a stone to the wooden promenade. As he went down, the backpack and its contents hit the walkway simultaneously, first with a loud thud, followed by the very distinct sound of metal sheets falling against one another inside the box.

Chenault watched as Lamott twitched uncontrollably for ten seconds, but then couldn't believe his eyes. After first rolling onto his back, Lamott managed to yank the wires from his chest. He then began to crawl onto all fours as he groggily shook his head to clear it. Despite the fact that Lamott still appeared to be quite dazed, Chenault noticed he still had the presence of mind to begin reaching for the pistol in his pocket. Taking a quick step forward, Chenault swung with all his might, and smashed the rock-hard, resin-cased Taser into the left side of Lamott's face, sending him tumbling backwards towards the waist high guard rail.

As he attempted to right himself, the stunned Lamott briefly lost his balance as his upper body pitched a few inches too far back over the edge, and in a split second, he flipped backwards over the railing. Dropping to the busy roadway below, he slammed head-first into the hood of a speeding Mercedes SUV, before sliding back into the windshield and then off onto the road. A city bus, following too closely behind the SUV, then barreled over Cloyd Lamott's flailing body before it came to a screeching halt.

To avert her eyes from the grisly scene of human roadkill that just moments before had been Cloyd Lamott, Rachel turned away as Chenault moved forward to take her in his arms. Although still visibly shaken, she gestured with her upheld palm a step before he reached her that she was alright.

"Are you sure you're okay?"

Rachel nodded. ". . .Thank God. I was so scared."

". . .Were you really?" Chenault asked after a brief pause.

"Of course I was. That psycho was holding me at gunpoint."

Chenault glanced down at her hands and then slowly back up, directing his gaze to her expressionless face. ". . .You're not even trembling. I mean, look at me," he said, as he held out his own unsteady hand.

"So, I'm not trembling. What are you saying?"

". . .I think you know what I'm saying. It's you, isn't it? You're the last piece of the puzzle. All the other pieces were filled in. . .leaving just you. And it didn't completely hit me until just now."

"You. . .you're crazy," Rachel stammered, her eyes filling with tears. "It's me, you know me."

Chenault paused for a moment, still trying to convince himself that it wasn't true. ". . .You're good--I've got to give you that. You never broke character. Not even now."

"I don't understand," Rachel pleaded tearfully. "What do you think is going on?"

The quivering timbre of her voice and the tears seemed all too real, and again for a brief moment, Chenault wondered if this was just his imagination working overtime, trying to give an ending to a story that might otherwise never have an ending.

But the more he thought about it, the more it all made sense. ". . .The police are on the way."

As if by the wave of a magic wand, Rachel's teary eyes transformed into a steely glare. ". . .You're bluffing."

"Am I?"

"Yes, I think you are," she said as she reached around to the small of her back. When she produced her hand again, it was gripped around a small dark pistol Chenault recognized as a 9 millimeter Glock. "Drop it," she said, glancing down at the Taser still in his hand.

"Or what, you're going to shoot me?"

"If I have to."

Chenault had no idea what her next move would be, but with a much clearer understanding of what she was capable of, he tossed the Taser on to the boardwalk. Taking a cautious step forward, and then with a sweep of her foot, Rachel kicked it off the bridge onto the roadway below. She then put her right hand into her jacket pocket to conceal the pistol as she continued to hold it on Chenault.

"So how'd you know?" she asked in a flat emotionless voice.

"Truthfully, I didn't until just a few seconds ago. But I did get to thinking as I was walking over here--for just a few fleeting moments that I wasn't solely focused on saving you--was how in a city of over eight million people could somebody have tracked us down to some random apartment in downtown Manhattan? And then how is it that whoever it was that couldn't find this precious box on their own, all of the sudden knew exactly which bank it was in, which obviously only could have come from you. And I couldn't see you just casually volunteering the information, and there would have been no need to extract it from you if they believed that I, naturally, would give up its location for your life. So that whole thing just didn't quite add up. And then, and I didn't even think anything of it at first--I thought it was just maybe a coincidence--but there was the little matter of your pronunciation that got me to thinking."

"What do you mean?"

"Did you not know that you pronounce your "t's" very distinctly in the middle of certain words?"

"Doesn't everybody?"

"No, they don't. Just you and the alleged kidnapper at the other end of the phone--the one with the electronically altered voice--and oddly enough, Brockston Ratchford. And as much as I would like to believe he was somehow involved, I just couldn't see him getting his hands this dirty. . .I think you need to turn yourself in. From what I hear, they'll probably go easier on you."

"That's brilliant," she replied, her voice dripping with sarcasm. "And I guess if you want me to turn myself in, that probably means your police buddies aren't really coming are they? Now why don't you very slowly, pick up, and hand me the backpack. And don't try anything this time."

On the roadway below, traffic in two of the three Brooklyn bound lanes had come to a standstill, and the drivers still too far back to see Cloyd Lamott's body flattened into the road had already started their chorus of honking horns, which only added to the tension of the moment. Yet despite the noisy chaos below, the pistol pointed at his chest, and the very likelihood that these were to be his last moments on earth, Chenault still wanted to get his story.

"I will. But first, tell me why?"

"You want to know why?" she asked with a look of disbelieving contempt. "Do you even have to ask? Just look around you--this country's going to hell. This horrid city is a perfect example--it's nothing but a cesspool of illegals and degenerates, who would just as soon live off government handouts and fornicate in the streets, multiplying like rabbits. This was once a great nation--maybe the greatest ever--and for years it followed a 'strict moral compass,' but now. . .it's lost its way."

Chenault was fairly certain the irony of Rachel's diatribe was completely lost on her, so he thought it best just to play along, rather than risk asking her how her "strict moral compass' philosophy gibed with the trail of dead bodies that she, and presumably the Lamotts, had left across the country. "I'm still not entirely following. So you and the Lamotts have been working together from the beginning?"

"Actually, they were working for me--they just didn't know it."

"And you've been having them kill various people across the country in order to try to get Brockston Ratchford elected President so he can straighten out this whole mess? Is that really it?" he asked with a look of utter disbelief. "Talk about one of your degenerates."

"Shut your mouth!" she spewed out venomously, as she whipped the Glock out of her pocket and aimed it directly between his eyes. "You have no idea what you're talking about. My father is a great man."

". . .Your father," Chenault repeated almost as if in a daze, and then everything became very clear.

CHAPTER 60

Time at first seemed to stand still as what Chenault had just learned sank in. This woman, whom just moments before, he would have laid his life down for and thought he wanted to spend the rest of his life with, not only wasn't who she said she was, but was very likely going to kill him in the next few moments. And then like a tidal wave, all the events of the past week, and all the little signs he had been completely oblivious to, came at him in a single rush.

Rachel had been the one who had Koplanski and her stepmother murdered and her half-sister kidnapped. She'd also been the one who'd emailed him the photo and had tipped off the police to his connection with Koplanski, knowing with the two events so similarly linked, it would draw him in like a moth to a flame. Then there was their "chance" meeting at the restaurant, which was also where he'd crossed paths with Valdez, whom she'd probably lured there as well. He hesitated to ask his next question, but he had to know.

". . .So how did you decide between me and Valdez?"

"That was easy," she said, as she coolly returned the Glock to her jacket pocket, although still clearly keeping it pointed at his chest. "I couldn't use my 'feminine wiles' on somebody like Valdez--I would have been just another notch on his belt. But you, . .you I could tell had. . .a relatively 'inexperienced heart.'"

"In other words, you thought you could wrap me around your finger?"

"And I did, up 'til now, playing the wide-eyed ingénue."

"That you did," Chenault said with no emotion. "And bravo, that was indeed quite a performance. But how could you have possibly known that about me, meeting me just that once in the restaurant?"

"I didn't leave anything to chance. I'd already had a P.I. work up a dossier on you."

"I presume then you had Valdez knocked off to

only have to worry about one of us finding the plates. But how is it that you knew it was Valdez and me? Koplanski's video didn't get here until just the other day. Did the Lamotts find that out for you when they tortured him to death?"

Rachel gave a little laugh, more as if she was in on a private joke than anything that Chenault said was funny. ". . .The Lamotts didn't kill Koplanski. But it is amazing what a man will tell you when he thinks he's about to die. The traitorous little worm that he was clung on to his miserable life until the very last air bubble. It was actually kind of pathetic. And I didn't have Valdez knocked off--I take care of my own loose ends. . .What are you smiling about?"

"Did you ever stop to think that Koplanski could have just given up the location of the plates to you? But he didn't. Not only did he still try to make it as hard as possible for you, but by giving Valdez and me up, he tricked you in to taking enormous risks in the hope that you'd reveal yourself--and you did."

"Like it really matters at this point."

As cold and emotionless a sociopath as Rachel appeared to be, Chenault still couldn't believe that she was solely behind everything that had gone on. "So what, was this like your father's master plan?"

"Not at all. He just prophesized years ago that one day the day would come when he would need my help, and that I would--by any means necessary--do what needed to be done."

"So then, let me guess--you were the one who

framed up that poor kid down in Georgia for killing the governor--before you shot him in the wrong side of the head not realizing he was left-handed?"

"Yes, I'd say that was my one slip up. But then again, who's going to find out?"

With that statement, Rachel's intentions were now very clear and Chenault knew that his time was running out. Words at this point were his only remaining means of self-preservation.

". . .And Rulen Sparks? Were you responsible for his death too?"

"No, actually you were--though Lamott's the one who actually strung him up. But then again, Sparks should have known better than to run his mouth to an outsider, excommunicated or not."

"So then you were behind it," Chenault said, as he then shook his head in disgust. ". . .I just don't understand why all these people had to die."

"I thought that would be pretty clear to you. You're a man of the world--you know that there are pawns and there are kings--and I don't think I need to tell you which one my father is."

"So let me get this straight, when you're a 'king' or working on behalf of one, you can pretty much justify any of your actions, no matter how reprehensible?"

"When you're working towards accomplishing God's will--to complete his plan--yes, it's alright to lie, to steal, and yes, even to kill."

Chenault let out a short ironic laugh. ". . .Do you even hear what you're saying? So the Ten

Commandments, those were what, pretty much just suggestions as far as you're concerned?"

Rachel shook her head in frustration at trying to get through to Chenault. ". . .Don't you get it? My father's the one they've spoken of in the prophecy. He's the 'Great Restorer' --the one who rides in on the white horse when the country is hanging by a single thread. The one who not only saves it, but then who also unites it under the one true faith."

"'The one true faith?' You mean the one based upon the words of a convicted con man who based his entire religion on what's probably nothing more than a prop in that box?"

"You think it's just a prop? Well, I've seen them--they're very real."

"You've looked in the box and seen the Plates?"

"I don't need to. I've seen them in visions--I know that they're real. And more importantly, my father's seen them. In fact, he's the one who told me where they could be found."

"Which he only could have known about if he knew about Koplanski and the deal he was trying to strike with the church. And how would he have known about that? Some supernatural powers, I'm guessing?"

"If you haven't guessed by now, my father has friends in very high places -- everywhere."

The more Chenault heard, the more convinced he was that Brockston Ratchford had more or less engineered everything though the skillful manipulation of his emotionally fragile daughter.

The only question that remained was how.

"'My father this,' 'my father that'--is everything you do based upon all this delusional horseshit he's fed you over the years?"

"Scoff all you want, but all of this--just about everything that has happened--was prophesized by my father."

"'Prophesized,' or do you mean planned out?"

"He never planned any of this. He just told me years ago that one day, by the grace of God, he would be in a position to become the next President, and that by God's will, his chief opponent would die."

"Well, that certainly worked out conveniently for him--seeing as how you did it. But why have your stepmother killed?"

"That was literally killing two birds with one stone. Not to mention, it got you to come out. I just knew that her death and the whole news drama around it would supercharge my father's campaign, and besides, she was the one who drove my mother to suicide when she came waltzing in to replace her."

"And you don't blame your father for that at all?"

"You still don't get it, do you? My father is the 'The One'--the chosen one--he could have any woman he wanted."

Chenault sensed by the way Rachel was going on and on over her father, especially about his sexual prowess, there was maybe something else going on, something beneath her blind adoration. Maybe this was even the chink in her seemingly impervious armor.

". . .And did he ever want you?"

The pained intensity in her eyes with which she glowered back at him suggested that he couldn't begin to understand.

". . .The things my father did to me he did because he loved me. I was always his special one, and he loved me above all the other children."

"What did your father do to you?" Chenault said with all the empathy he could muster.

"You don't understand," she said. "The special love between a father and his daughter--you could never even begin to understand. You would just twist it up and turn it into something sordid and ugly. I believe that my father's original intention to take me as a sister wife was God's will, but because of his political aspirations, he rejected the idea and thought it best to send me out into the world away from him."

"Take you for a wife?" Chenault said, visibly aghast.

"You Gentiles--you act so outraged and indignant by the whole idea. But when a priest in the service of the Church--like my father--feels attraction to an unattached woman, it's sanctioned by God, and he's rightfully within his divine position in the Church to take her as a wife."

". . .Your mother didn't take her life out of jealousy over your stepmother. She couldn't live with what your Father was doing to you--and there was nothing she could do to stop it. That was the real reason, wasn't it?"

"When my father expressed his love for me and chose me above all the others--including my mother--she couldn't deal with it."

". . .And why wouldn't he want you?" Chenault said. "You're bright, you're beautiful, you're incredibly desirable. . .Except for the fact that good fathers aren't supposed to screw their pretty little daughters. That would make them not only criminals, but degenerate monsters. And you want to know what else I think? For all he did, your father might just as well have locked away you in a closet and brainwashed you. But instead, he fed you this endless drivel from childhood about how what a great man he was, and a prophet, and the savior of the country, and he raped you over and over and over didn't he? And then you couldn't separate the terrible things that he was doing to you from your love for him, and I'm sure he had you believing that you were somehow doing God's will, didn't he? You were his own little 'Manchurian candidate.' Whether you accept it or not, he essentially programmed you to do all this."

"You don't know what you're talking about!" Rachel screamed at him. "Everything I've done I did by choice and out of love for my father. You've probably never heard of him, but there was a man named Porter Rockwell who was Joseph Smith's personal bodyguard, and he too, did literally whatever needed to be done. And they called him 'The Destroying Angel.'. .Well I'm my father's Destroying Angel."

"Don't tell me; let me guess--your father's the one who told you about this so-called Destroying Angel, wasn't he?"

With the realization that what Chenault was saying was probably true, Rachel's eyes begin to well up with tears.

"Wasn't he?" Chenault demanded. "He's the one who put that into your head too."

"No, it's not true," she said as the tears begin to flow, more trying to convince herself than Chenault.

"It is and you know it. Rachel, you've got to let me help you before it's too late."

"The only one it's too late for is you," she said sobbing, as she pulled the Glock from her jacket. "Why couldn't you have just made the switch instead of trying to play the hero?"

"So what, that we could have just gone on and lived happily ever after? Wasn't that what this whole little kidnapping charade was about? But just by the fact it looks like you're getting ready to put several bullets in me. . .I don't think it would have worked. In fact, I had this feeling deep down all along that I kept ignoring because I didn't want it to be true--but it was just too perfect. You were just too perfect to come waltzing into my life like that. So what, I guess you targeted me from pretty much the first time we met? What were you going to do-- stage my suicide and then have me leave a note behind confessing to killing Valdez?"

Rachel started to answer, but then wiped the tears from her eyes with her free hand as it suddenly dawned on her what Chenault's game had been for the last few minutes. ". . .You've been stalling. This whole time you've been talking, you were really just biding time, weren't you?"

"You asked me a question--I was answering. Plus, I guess it's a nervous habit I have when someone has a gun pointed at my chest."

"You were the one asking all the questions. You do have someone coming, don't you?"

". . .You got me," Chenault said, as he casually glanced to his left down the promenade back towards Manhattan. "In fact," he said as he looked back to her, "this is actually the part where my two cop friends finally show up."

Rachel shook her head, semi-amused. ". . .I don't think so," she said as she reflexively glanced to her right to see two men approaching--one, a wiry, well-dressed Latino; the second, a bulky, middle-aged white male in a dark overcoat who appeared to be drawing his pistol.

"Drop the weapon, lady!" Wheatly called out to her as he continued to amble forward, holding her in his sight with both hands gripped tightly around his pistol, while Garcia glided gracefully back around behind her with weapon in hand.

"I thought you guys would never get here," Chenault said, keeping his eyes on Rachel.

"Traffic," Wheatly offered as his only

explanation. "When I got your text you were turning yourself in, we headed straight down."

"That's the only thing I could think of to get you guys down here," Chenault said, as Rachel knelt down and slowly lowered her pistol and dropped it to the wooden walkway. Then very deliberately, she reached over and picked up the backpack and stood back up with it, holding it to her chest.

"Put the bag back down, lady!" Garcia barked from his position behind her.

Rachel turned slightly and looked directly at Chenault. By the glint of sadness in her eyes as she softly bit her lower lip, he took from her forlorn expression that "it didn't have to end this way." With every ounce of emotion that he had ever felt for her, Chenault said under his breath, "Rachel, don't do anything crazy."

". . .It's the only way," she said with the wisp of a smile, as she then looked straight back ahead, and with a surprising burst of speed, took off. Ignoring Wheatly's repeated calls to "Stop!", she quickly reached the outer edge of the bridge after scaling the waist-high guardrail and making her way out over the steel girders that crossed over the roadway below.

"Lady, you've got nowhere to go!" Wheatly bellowed up at her from the platform. "So just climb down and come on back."

Rachel appeared to consider his suggestion for a brief second, but then leapt. As he realized too late what was happening before his eyes, Chenault cried out, "No!" as he reached out in vain for her, while Garcia instinctively fired off a shot as she flew off the edge of the bridge into the dark abyss below.

As she drifted down towards the East River in a one hundred and thirty foot twisting freefall, the seconds seemed to turn into minutes before they finally heard the sickening and solitary splash of her body impacting the water. Had she not been carrying the plates, there was a better than even chance she could have survived the fall if she'd entered the water feet first. But as she clung tightly to the heavy box, the top heaviness of her body upended her, so that as she struck the water head first at an angle, the impact from the surface tension of the water was like diving into concrete. Her body sank below the water's surface for at least half a minute until it floated back to the top, while the plates, or whatever was contained within the box, descended into the briny muck of the East River seventy-five feet below.

EPILOGUE

Only one other item appeared on the front page of *The Times* the next day, below the banner headline that Brockston Ratchford was not only ending his Presidential bid, but stepping down from his Senate seat in order to spend more time with his grieving family. In the lower left-hand corner was a brief mention of Corissa Ratchford, 31, the emotionally troubled eldest daughter of Senator Ratchford, who in her depression over dealing with the traumatic events of the past week, had apparently taken her own life by jumping off the Brooklyn Bridge.

Brockston Ratchford had not gone down without a brief fight. Soon after clearing his name with the police and the FBI, and helping them wrap up a number of their cases with the digital tape recording he'd made up on the bridge the day before, Chenault contacted Evan Fiske. He began by suggesting that the Senator might think about withdrawing from the race and stepping down, and then played the recording he had made of Ratchford talking about how "over" his dead wife he was, and how he had already "moved on."

At the other end of the line, Ratchford's booming voice bellowed, "That's really the best you've got? That's nothing that most these morons will even remember in a week. I'll ruin you. You're through!"

But when Chenault informed them that he'd already given copies of the following recording to various law enforcement agencies, and then began to play excerpts of Rachel detailing her troubled and twisted relationship with her father and the many things that she had done on his behalf, there was nothing but a long silence at the other end of the line.

". . .Senator Ratchford, are you still there?" Chenault had said after cutting the tape off. The stone silence had then been followed by a faint click and a dial tone as someone on Ratchford's end of the line ended the call.

Chenault speculated long and hard as to why Rachel, or Corissa Ratchford, had made the decision to take a death plunge along with the mysterious box that presumably held what Joseph Smith had founded his entire religion upon. The best he could come up with was not that she was trying to shield her father, to give him one last shot at plausible deniability, because in the end, Brockston Ratchford had never broken the first law

or ever given her a single directive. Chenault did,
however, think that perhaps in those final moments,
he had finally opened her eyes to the many ways her
father had both used and manipulated her over the
years. Up until then, she had not just been blinded
by her twisted devotion to her father, but obviously
in denial as well. It was very likely the first time
that she'd ever spoken of their forbidden
relationship and then been confronted with the ugly
truth that her father had not only stolen her
innocence, but had then controlled her through lies
and sexual manipulation for years.

So the only other reason Chenault could come up
with as to why she had jumped, taking the plates
along with her to be lost to the ages, was out of her
even stronger devotion to her religion, which she
clearly still believed in, despite the mounting
evidence to the contrary of it being the "one true
faith." Chenault even partially blamed himself,
because in his attempt to bide more time to allow
Wheatly and Garcia to arrive, he believed he had
probably built up enough doubt in her mind that
what was in the box was probably nothing more
than a cheap prop. And then when the ugly truth
finally came out about her father, and she saw how
he had deceived her all along, she had probably lost
any and all hope that they were real. Believing that
her father was probably lying about the Plates along
with everything else, she then couldn't take the
chance for the survival of her religion that they be
revealed as a mere prop, thus exposing her beloved

faith as a hoax. So she had decided to martyr herself for "the one true faith," doing in the end whatever was necessary.

The ironic part was that for all Chenault knew, the Plates might have even been real. He doubted it, but now there would be no way of ever knowing. As a favor to Chenault for his cooperation, NYPD had sent out two of their best search and rescue divers that morning to scour the riverbed below and downstream from the bridge. No sign of either the box or its contents was found, leading to the only conclusion that they'd been swept out to sea by the powerful undercurrent.

As for his own actions, Chenault guessed he hadn't written the entire story with all its sordid details, out of respect for the memory of the woman he knew and loved as Rachel. He still couldn't help but feel some sympathy, because despite the untold number of acts of evil she had carried out or played a part in, she was after all, not only the first, but last victim in a sad and sorry chain of events set into motion by a twisted megalomaniac many years earlier.

LATTER DAY SAINT'S TIMELINE OF HISTORICAL EVENTS

1805 - Joseph Smith, Jr. is born.

1820 - Smith claims God and Jesus Christ revealed themselves to him.

1823 - The Angel Moroni first appears to Joseph Smith.

1826 - Smith is arrested for "peepstoning," using his magical stones for treasure hunting.

1827 - Smith claims that Moroni revealed the Gold Plates to him.

1830 - After three years of translation, Smith publishes The Book of Mormon (the plates are reportedly recovered by Moroni and are no longer on Earth).

1830 - The Church of Christ, as it is then called, is organized.

1831 - Smith is run out of Palmyra, NY and leads his followers to Kirkland, Ohio.

1834 - The name is changed to "The Church of Latter Day Saints."

1837 - Smith and his followers relocate to LATTER Independence, Missouri, 1000 miles away.

1839 - Smith and his followers are driven out at gunpoint, and relocate to Nauvoo, Illinois.

1843 - Joseph Smith proclaims a revelation, and the Mormon doctrine of plural marriage, or polygamy, is set forth (although may have actually occurred earlier).

1844 - Joseph Smith announces his candidacy for

President of the United States.

1844 - Smith is arrested for inciting a riot. While trying to escape from jail with the assistance of his brother, Smith shoots three men, killing \
two of them, and is in turn gunned down.

1846 - Brigham Young leads the Latter Day Saint followers to Utah.

1890 - A decree goes out from the Church that polygamy is no longer to be practiced

<u>ACKNOWLEDGMENTS</u>

Loads of gratitude to my editors Margaret, Dick, and Barbara for all their hard work, and for the helpful suggestions from John, Gene, and Shannon. Thanks to my family and friends for their encouragement and support along the way, with particular thanks going out to Barbara, Gene, Sam, and John. Thanks for the support and friendship during this sometimes lonely process of Randy, Dave, Rick, Lisa, Trish, Erik, Paul, and John H. And also, a special thanks to Jordan D. for his fantastic cover art, to Ragen, for helping me to keep it in the road, and to my special friend, Elizabeth, who inspires me in more ways than I can count.

And lastly, thank you to the readers who took a chance on an unknown writer. I hope you found the time spent worthwhile and that maybe you even learned a little something along the way.

ABOUT THE AUTHOR

Jack Brody is a writer, entrepreneur, ex-military and an avid traveler. He's had an interesting and varied life, and is fascinated by history, politics, and architecture, all of which play a part in his novels (yes, he has two more in the works featuring Michael Chenault). When not writing, he can often be found hiking with his two faithful dogs, mountain biking, or playing team trivia with friends. He divides his time between his home in the Southern Appalachian Mountains and wherever his passport will take him.

For more information, go to www.themoronideception.com. You can contact him at Jack.L.Brody@gmail.com

29315460R10190

Made in the USA
Lexington, KY
21 January 2014